LAST NIGHT IN TAMPICO

By

Thomas Willis

TIFTON PRESS

First Edition published in 2023 by Tifton Press, West Palm Beach, Fl

For information, contact the publisher at tiftonpress@gmail.com.
West Palm Beach, Fl.

This is a work of fiction. Names, characters, businesses, places, events, and incidents are either the product of the authors imagination or used in a fictious manner. No identification with actual persons (living or deceased), places, buildings, and products is intended or should be inferred.

Library of Congress Control Number: 2023920701

ISBN: 979-8-9893052-2-3 (Paperback)

ISBN: 979-8-9893052-3-0 (E Book)

Book Cover by Stewart Williams

Logo design by Bill Baffa

10 9 8 7 6 5 4 3 2 1

Printed in the United States of America

Contents

Whoever fights monsters should see to it that in the process he does not become a monster. And when you look long into the abyss, the abyss looks into you.

Friedrich Nietzsche, Beyond Good and Evil

CHAPTER 1

The First Crossing

Samuel Orasme was surprised at the letdown he felt as he waded across the Rio Grande and entered the United States. Considering the effort expended over many months to reach this point, somehow, he had expected to feel some sort of euphoria—sounding trumpets or an image of a shining Mother Mary smiling with outstretched arms waiting to welcome them. He and Emelia Rojas had traveled so far and endured so much. Rather, he only felt the cold waist-deep muddy water relentlessly tugging at his legs, encouraging him to simply give in and go wherever it wanted to carry him. But instead, as he felt a growing sense of apprehension, it was concern for Emelia that fueled his anxiety as he thought of the events that had occurred over the last few hours.

They had ridden for at least two hours since leaving the safe house in Ciudad Juárez before reaching the Mexican side of the river around 3:00 AM. Samuel could tell by the glare of headlights that they were being closely followed by another vehicle. During the last thirty minutes of the drive, the headlights had been turned off and the driver used the light of a full moon to find his way. Eight of them had been shoehorned into the van's open cargo space, leaving barely enough room for them to sit side by side on the floor. The rough wooden floor was wet and

reeked of what smelled like a stopped-up toilet that hadn't
been flushed for a long time. If even one of them had not
been able keep their nausea in check, there would have
been a nightmare of a chain reaction. The bouncing van
did nothing to help Samuel's distended bladder. He'd been
so excited when they left the safe house he hadn't taken
time to use the bathroom.

It was obvious early in the trip that the van's shocks
were many miles overdue for repair and with the added
weight of the heavy load, every bump became rougher
until each one felt like a hard kick in the ass. When the
van finally stopped, the rear doors were opened and all the
occupants were quickly pulled out. They were parked in a
clump of scrubby trees filled with thick underbrush. Although the headlights were turned off, there was enough
moonlight for Samuel to realize that the vehicle that had
been following them was parked closely behind the van's
rear doors. It was a beat-up pickup truck with a camper
top covering the bed.

The two occupants of the truck walked toward the
rear of the van. The automatic weapons cradled in their
arms was an ominous sign that was recognized immediately by the entire group. The two polleros from the van were
standing on both sides of the group and each one was now
holding a pistol. Without warning, the previous helpful
attitude of the two guides had made a sudden reversal.
The van driver who was called Roberto ordered harshly,
"Everyone take off your backpacks. Quickly." This was
met with immediate opposition from the entire group,
and everyone started speaking at once. Without saying a
word, the driver had stepped up to the passenger called
Mateo, who was the most outspoken one in the group.
Roberto struck him across his face with his pistol, driving
him to his knees. His face was suddenly spouting blood,

which flowed freely through his fingers as he clutched his face.

"Who's next?" Roberto hissed as he and his companion Felix simultaneously raised their pistols, pointing them menacingly toward the group. Without waiting for anyone to respond, Felix moved forward and ripped off Emelia's backpack, almost knocking her to the ground. Reluctantly, the rest of the group slowly began to take off their backpacks. Roberto and Felix quickly grabbed each pack and threw them into the back of the van.

Before they had left the safe house, they all been instructed to put everything in their backpacks, including cell phones, and were told in no uncertain terms to turn them off. Still, Mateo had the courage to speak.

"What about our cell phones and papers that we'll need?"

"You'll be carrying something a lot more valuable than a cell phone," Felix said as he walked to the back of the truck. He returned carrying a large backpack that appeared to be filled well beyond its intended capacity. One by one, he brought a similar pack from the back of the truck until everyone in the group was holding one.

"Go ahead. Put them on. I'll help everyone with the adjustments."

Samuel was five foot ten and one hundred seventy pounds of solid muscle. The long journey had only increased his strength and endurance, but he staggered under the weight of the backpack. He didn't see how Emelia could carry anything this heavy for any distance. Samuel moved up close to his friend Jonus Atelus, who had traveled with Samuel and Emelia from the very beginning and spoke in a low voice.

"This is wrong. What is happening?"

"Samuel, I think we've been screwed. We were warned."

"Quiet!" Roberto ordered. "I told you no talking. From this point on, silence is absolutely mandatory."

After inspecting each person in the group to be sure their packs were securely adjusted, both Roberto and Felix strapped on a pack on as well. One of the two gunmen from the truck threw Roberto a heavy coil of hemp rope. As he unwound the coil he said, "Everyone find a knot in the rope and hold on tight. This is your lifeline. It's how we stay together in the dark and no one gets lost."

Roberto took the front of the rope and Felix picked up the rear. Somehow Samuel ended up being positioned directly in front of Felix at the back of the line with Emelia directly in front of him. As Roberto started walking, it was clear that he knew the way as they threaded through the heavy underbrush. To his credit, Roberto moved at a steady but slow pace and the group, including Emelia, had no trouble keeping up. Samuel realized how difficult it would have been to navigate without the help of the polleros. He tried to forget the loss of his backpack and cell phone, but he was grateful that his cash and list of US contacts were safely strapped around his thigh in a sealed plastic bag held in place by duct tape. By the time they reached the river's edge, it was close to 4:00 AM. They sat in the underbrush while Roberto and Felix used a pair of night vision binoculars to intently scan the Texas side of the river for several minutes before returning to the group.

"This is it, amigos. Hold tight to the rope and lean against the current. It doesn't look bad tonight, so it should be an easy crossing. Okay, Chivas. Let's go."

As they were led into the cold muddy waters of the Rio Grande, their only thoughts were on getting safely across the river. Roberto was correct though. It was a

LAST NIGHT IN TAMPICO   5

manageable crossing. It was obvious that the Polleros were familiar with the river and knew that it was shallow with a slower current at this point. But still, they were relieved as they climbed up a muddy bank and followed a path lined with underbrush on the US side. Struggling by now, Emelia had to be helped up the slippery bank. Samuel could only hope she was okay.

After leaving the river, they went a short distance through a clump of short scraggly trees and up a small incline that descended down into a small open area. It wasn't visible at first because of the darkness and because it was partially covered by underbrush, but as they came down the slope, they could see a vehicle. In the dim light it appeared to be similar to the one that had brought them from Juárez. An obvious track led out of the open clearing and disappeared into the bosque thicket beyond. Felix dropped his end of the rope and moved quickly into the clearing behind Roberto, who was muttering obscenities to himself. The rest of the group remained still, holding onto the rope, unsure of what to do next.

Samuel immediately took advantage of the confusion. "Emelia, I've got to pee. I can't wait any longer," he said as he dropped the rope he was still holding. Unnoticed by anyone, he disappeared into the thick surrounding foliage. As Samuel pushed himself into the dense underbrush on the crest of the riverbank, he had to move several yards into the tangle before he found enough room to unzip his pants and pee. He felt a flood of relief as he finished and started to zip his pants back up. The sudden explosion of a single gunshot caused him to flinch and nearly circumcise himself with his zipper. His next move was to follow the instructions his parents back in Haiti had ingrained in him starting when he was barely able to walk. He fell flat on the ground and remained motionless. He found himself wedged tightly between trunks of thick bushes as the scraggly grass that grew up underneath tried to push into his nose. Suddenly. Emelia and Samuel's dreams of a new life in America became a nightmare instead.

CHAPTER 2
Survival

When Samuel finally gathered enough courage to lift his head slightly, he had a narrow line of sight—under the branches and through the grass—of the clearing below. He could see Roberto sprawled out flat and motionless on the ground and Felix standing behind him with his hands held high in the air. There were several men dressed in various types of camouflage or military clothing standing in a semicircle facing Felix and the rest of the group who were still holding onto the rope as if it were some sort of lifeline. All the men were carrying short-barreled weapons with long clips. The apparent leader stepped forward and motioned for Felix to step forward and at the same time barked, "Take off your backpacks and leave them on the ground. Then move slowly toward me." Another man used a lantern-type flashlight to shine on the group, one by one, as they struggled to remove their backpacks.

When the light from the lantern reached the last person in the line, the beam stopped on Emelia. The light continued to shine on her, partially blinding her, and one of the gunmen walked over to where she was standing and pulled her away from the others. He half-led, half-dragged her back to the group of gunmen and shoved her to the ground as if she were a bag of trash.

Samuel had been watching in shock and confusion, but when Maria was shoved to the ground so violently, he instinctively started to stand up and scream out in protest. At that same moment, the entire group of gunmen facing the group now directly in front of them who were still clutching the rope, opened fire. Felix and Emelia, now behind the gunmen, were spared, but the poor men in the group, including Jonas, were slaughtered within a few seconds. As the bullets tore through the brush around him, Samuel tried to melt into the ground. He was protected by being on the riverside crest of the high bank, but the shock and noise left him in a state of shock, and he was completely immobilized.

When the ringing in his ears had subsided enough, he could hear the leader of the gunmen saying to Felix. "Okay, amigo, now you have a story to tell. Lleva un mensaje a tu jefe. This part of the border belongs to Señor Mendez. This is what will happen to anyone crossing this river without his permission. Comprende? The next time you'll join the ones lying in front of you. Now go and take this message with you. You should remember my name, too. I am known as El Carnicero."

One of the gunmen was holding a bloody machete in one hand and Roberto's head in his other. Another man dumped the contents of one of the backpacks on the ground and then held it open so the one holding Roberto's head by its hair could drop it into the empty pack. The now bloody backpack was roughly shoved onto Felix's back and tightened before he was pushed back up the path leading to the river.

As Felix was pushed back toward the river, two of the men, one on each side, unceremoniously picked Emelia up by her arms, carried her to the rear of the van, and shoved her in. She screamed, and this time Samuel shouted, "No! Stop!"

As he tried to stand up in the dense underbrush a light flashed over his head, and he could hear curses coming from the gunmen. At the same moment, the ground under his feet seemed to crumble. In the dark underbrush, Samuel didn't realize that he'd been standing so close to the edge of the riverbank where it had been washed out, leaving a hollowed-out area underneath. Falling backward, he tried to grab something solid, but he only tore his hands on a thin thorny bush before he landed flat on his back in the water. By now there were a couple of men at the crest of the bank using their lights trying to find him. The river in the area along the bank where he'd fallen was much deeper than the spot where they'd crossed, and he found himself underwater for a moment. Just as he managed to get his head above water, he was briefly blinded by the beam of one of the lights. There was more shouting and cursing coming from the bank above him as the men tried to find him again with their lights. Fortunately for Samuel, the thick underbrush lining the riverbank made it difficult for him to be seen from edge of the bank above. The next time he was in the light's beam there were multiple gunshots, and he felt a sharp stinging sensation in his thigh. By now he had no control over his movements as the river carried him in its current, which seemed to grow stronger with each moment that passed.

He was soon well beyond the gunmen, and as he tried to keep his head above water, he started to look toward river's edge, hoping for a clear area. The banks on either side were either thick undergrowth or high banks. He was getting weaker by the minute, and he wasn't able to get the backpack off. Just as he was about to give up, he came around a bend in the river and was pushed toward the bank where a small muddy area was visible at the water's edge. He could feel the ground under his feet as he struggled to reach the bank. He realized that he couldn't move his right leg, but he managed to crawl out of the water and onto the flat muddy area. After lying motionless for several minutes while he regained his breath, he looked down at his leg. His pants were bloody, and he could see a torn hole in his jeans. Struggling to sit up, he finally managed to get the backpack off. As he did, he saw two bullet holes in the back of the pack. There was a white milky-looking substance leaking out. Recognizing what it must be, disgusted, Samuel used both arms and pushed the pack back into the water and watched it sink as the river took it away.

After Samuel took off his belt and tightened it around his leg, he tried to think about what had happened. He could only imagine what might be happening to Emelia, and he was filled with dread. But he was overcome from the loss of blood and exhaustion from fighting the river. As the dawn approached, he slowly sank into a black hole.

CHAPTER 3
Emelia

Emelia Rojas tried to sit up after she was thrown into the back of the van. One of the men had gotten into the van behind her and was holding her down with a smelly arm wrapped around her neck and his hand firmly over her breast.

"Muy bonita," he said as his other hand searched for her other breast. The rest of the men were now in the van, which was moving rapidly away from the river. Two men sat in the driver's and passenger seats. Two other men in the rear of the van were watching and laughing at Emelia, who was still struggling. The smell of so many sweaty bodies in the confinement of the vehicle was making her gag. Someone in one of the two front seats yelled back, "Leave her alone! We'll check her out later and see if she's worth anything before we share her."

The man holding her finally released his strong pressure around her neck, but his hand stayed on her breast. Emelia, finally realizing that her struggles were useless, went limp in a state of resignation—or was it shock? —beginning to set in. She'd seen the men being shot, and she had heard Samuel shouting with more gunfire following. If Samuel was dead, what was left? Memories flooded her mind as the van continued to bounce and sway in its acceleration.

Emelia had known Samuel since they were ten years old. They were an example of contrast. She was white with almost blonde hair inherited from her German ancestors. He was a light brown from his mixed ancestry of Spanish conquistadors and African slaves. Her wealthy family owned apartment complexes and office buildings in Santiago, Chile. Samuel's parents had fled Haiti during the reign of Francois "Papa Doc" Duvalier. Both of Samuel's parents had been educated in the US but had returned to Haiti with the expectations of helping the Haitian people. Unfortunately, "Papa Doc" was intolerant of most educated professionals. Even the slightest and unintentional mistake could put anyone on Duvalier's blacklist. Samuel's father was a surgeon who had operated on a political enemy of Duvalier, and that was all it took for "Papa Doc" to retaliate. Fortunately for Samuel's parents, one of their trusted housekeepers had a relative in Doc's inner circle and was able to warn them. They'd fled in the dark of night with only the clothing they wore, a small amount of cash, and jewelry.

After a long and torturous route, they'd finally settled in Santiago, Chile. With a lot of determination and hard work, his parents had built a reputation for managing properties and over time became the primary manager for Emelia's family's properties. Although the families were not on the same social level, Samuel's parents were able to send him to the same schools Emelia attended. Although the ruling class of people in Chile were predominantly of European descent, Samuel was such a minority that he was accepted by other children and skin color was not a factor. By the time Samuel and Emelia were completing secondary school, Samuel's dad had died, but before he did, he'd sold the business knowing Samuel's mom would need the resources to live well. Now his future educational prospects were not looking good. Emelia, however, had family with resources to continue school. With every year that passed, their relationship had become more and more intense. When Samuel started to talk about going north to the US because his prospects in Chile were looking bleak, Emelia was emphatic in saying she would come with him. Emelia's parents sensed that their relationship had passed the simple boyfriend-girlfriend stage and tried to do everything they could to discourage it. But everything they'd done only pushed the two lovers even closer together.

The only other Haitian friend that Samuel had was Jonus Atelus, who was the same age as Samuel. He'd been born in Chile to Haitian immigrants who had come to Chile before Samuel's parents. When he told Samuel that he had family in the US who would sponsor them if they could reach the US, Samuel and Emelia made the decision to go. They were also encouraged by all of the news reports that seemed to indicate that crossing into the US through the southern border had never been easier. If they were ever going to do it, now was the time.

As all of these thoughts flashed through her mind, Emelia couldn't help but wonder how it had come to this. Jonus was dead and probably Samuel as well. Her future, which had seemed so bright only a couple of days ago, was now filled with uncertainty and despair. The three men with her in the rear of the van couldn't take their eyes of her and grinned in anticipation of things to come.

CHAPTER 4
Samuel

Samuel was confused. He was being carried by his father, who was saying "Go! Go!" There were loud bangs and his mother's voice, urging, "Faster! Faster!" He could see a running torch as he realized that it was actually a person on fire. Then he was in a rocking boat with the sound of rushing water, which was slowly replaced by unfamiliar voices.

"Think he'll make it?"

"Depends on how much blood he's lost."

"I called ahead. There should be medics waiting when we dock."

"A little late for those others. That was one of the worst I've seen."

"That's the world these guys live in."

Samuel tried to open his eyes. He wanted to ask about Emelia. But he didn't have enough strength to even do that, and the steady drone of outboard engines pulled him back into the blackness.

When Samuel came out of the darkness, he was no longer a child in Haiti fleeing for his life with his parents but was instead lying alone in a bed. At first, he thought he was in a single room, but instead his bed was separated from a much larger room by white curtains hanging from long cords attached to thin columns at the corners. It took him a couple of minutes to remember what had happened, and as a vision of Emelia being shoved into the back of a van filled his mind, he tried to sit up. That's when he realized that he had absolutely no strength and he fell back down. He could hear voices, but nothing made sense. He tried to call out, but only a faint and hoarse whisper came out of his mouth. Someone must have noticed his attempt at movement, as the curtain was parted and a portly lady dressed in scrubs approached his bed speaking in Spanish.

"You're a miracle man, I'm hearing."

Realizing the confusion showing on Emanuel's face, she continued. "You seem to be the only survivor of a massacre on the border. And a lucky survivor as well. You'd lost a lot of blood when they brought you in. A bullet went through your leg and nicked a large artery, but it missed any major nerves. The papers and wad of money taped to your thigh apparently partially deflected the bullet. If you hadn't tied your belt around your leg before you passed out, you wouldn't be here now. I'm going to get you something to drink. Some people are very anxious to talk to you. They've been waiting for you to wake up."

Speaking in English, Samuel managed to whisper, "How long have I been here?"

"Since early this morning," she answered as she left him.

When she returned with water and ice, two men were following her into his cubicle. They were both wearing Border Patrol uniforms. The nurse used pillows to prop Samuel up in a sitting position against the head of the bed before leaving him alone with the agents. One agent held a pen and notepad while the other one had what appeared to be a recorder of some type.

Even though he had a pounding headache, Samuel's head had cleared enough for him to realize he was in trouble.

He had to make a quick decision. Should he cooperate or just plead ignorance? If he chose the latter, he'd probably be sent back to either Haiti or Chile as soon as he could walk. If that happened, he knew he'd never have a chance of seeing Emelia again. The only way he might have a chance would be if he could be of some use to the US authorities by telling them everything he knew. He decided to cooperate.

The two agents were a contrast in appearance. One was thin with white skin who hadn't seen much sun, while the other was heavyset and very brown. The thin one spoke first.

"How are you feeling?" he asked in Spanish.

Samuel responded in English, "Okay, I guess. I'm alive."

"And lucky to be so," the brown man replied. "Can you answer some questions for us?" he asked as he changed to English.

Samuel hesitated a minute before replying, also in English, "Will you find Emelia?"

"Amigo, we can't promise you anything until we know more. You've got to start at the beginning, starting with your name and how you ended up on the US side of the river with a gunshot wound. We're going to record this and take some notes."

Samuel drank some water, which made talking much easier, before he started at the beginning. Starting with how he, Emelia, and Jonas left Santiago, Chile together up to being washed up onto the riverbank. He left nothing out. The two agents let him talk without interruption.

When he was finished, the pair looked at each other and nodded.

The brown man spoke, "Samuel, we're going to detain you for the present. I'm sure there are some people who will have a lot more questions. We can't promise you anything at the moment, but you may be able to help us. You don't know how lucky you are to be alive. As far as Emelia is concerned, anything you can do to help us will help Emelia. For now, rest, regain your strength, and we'll be back later."

CHAPTER 5

Two Days Later

Breathing a sigh of relief, Roe Estes turned off the Arlington expressway in Jacksonville onto University Boulevard and eventually into a side street leading toward the St. Johns River. From the street, the house was barely visible, but as she turned into the driveway and passed through a tall hedge, the huge structure of native Florida lime rock and massive cypress beams seemed to rise up and greet her like an old friend. A large garage appeared on her left, and one of the three large doors was open. Before she was able to get out of her car, a big man dressed in jeans and a Jacksonville Jaguar sweatshirt appeared in the open doorway of the garage. As his nose was set a little bit off center and a scar ran across his forehead, a person might have been apprehensive as he approached. But his smile was warm and welcoming as he held out his arms to hug her. "Welcome home, Roe."

A casual observer would have had a difficult time judging the relationship between the two. Actually, the bond between Roe and Mark was that of a parent and child, coupled with a deep friendship. Although Roe was not Mark's biological daughter, she was the only family he had. At one time in the past, Roe had been Mark's daughter Kim's best friend. Roe's past had been a rocky one that had led her from being a college student to a walk on the wild side in a world involving drugs and other criminal activity.

After Kim's murder, followed by the death of his wife, Mark and Roe had experienced a convoluted and sometimes violent series of events. Afterword, the spacious one-bedroom apartment over the garage had become Roe's permanent home. Even after turning her life around, finishing college, law school, and her subsequent employment with a major state agency, the garage apartment continued to be Roe's primary home and permanent place of refuge.

"Mark, you don't know how good it is to be home. I know you're dying to hear what I've learned about Andre Mendez. We both have been so sure that the slimeball was dead. Let me change out of my lawyer clothes. Get some wine ready and I'll see you in a minute."

"Is my curiosity that obvious?"

"Anymore and you'd trip over it," Roe smiled as she headed up the stairs to her apartment.

The river side of Mark's home was accented by a flagstone patio that stretched across the entire length of the house facing the St. Johns River. The view looking across the river was breathtaking. During the period when Mark was a university professor, there was constant speculation by other faculty on how he was able to afford such an expensive home, especially knowing what meager pay even a full professor received from the state. It was for certain that it was not a subject that Mark wanted to discuss, even though a large portion of his wealth resulted from a perfectly legal and fortunate inheritance. The rest of his wealth came from actions that only he and Roe knew, and they both planned to keep it that way.

Roe had changed into sweatpants and a light sweater when she walked out onto the patio. Mark had a bottle of ice-cold Pinot Grigio waiting for her and a glass of Tanqueray over ice with lime for himself. As he poured her wine and they each settled into a deck chair, Mark had a flashback to the time they sat in the same chairs while Roe poured out her soul to Mark, as she tearfully blamed herself for the murder of his daughter. Mark was continually amazed at the transformation that Roe had undergone from being a scourged victim to the strong confident woman she was today.

"Okay. Start at the beginning. You told me you think Andre Mendez may still be alive. Why?"

"Not maybe. I'm sure of it. You never met Angel Ruiz. He has an interesting background. His father escaped from Cuba after Castro took over. His mother was an undercover Israeli agent working in South Florida. She was part of a team looking for a Nazi war criminal that had come to the US through Cuba. She met Angel's dad while she was in Miami, and after becoming pregnant with Angel, she chose to stay in the States. Angel grew up in Miami and absorbed the best of all three cultures—Cuban, American, and Israeli. After graduating from the University of Florida, he started working for the state and progressed on a fast track through the bureaucracy. He was in charge of the district office I first worked in. He was a great boss, and I learned a lot from him. I always thought that he wanted to ask me out, but since he was my boss he never did. He developed such a good reputation he was recently moved to the federal level working for the DEA. Since he's no longer my boss, he finally asked me out and we've met several times. I've been planning to tell you about him, but I haven't had the chance. I'll admit that I've been a little nervous about mentioning him. It should be my parent's opinions that I'm worried about, but I'm more concerned about your opinion than theirs."

Mark smiled as he spoke. "Roe, there was a time when I might have questioned your ability to make good decisions. Not anymore. I'll never question your judgment. If something feels right to you, I'm sure I'll feel the same. Speaking of your parents, they must be pleased."

Roe let out a deep breath of relief after Mark's response. "Wow, I don't know why I was so nervous getting that out."

"Roe, I'm pleased that you feel that way. Now tell me what you've learned from Angel."

"For years now, the feds have been working closely with local law enforcement at both state and local levels to enforce drug laws. Now, with the huge increase in human smuggling for both labor and sex, it's become hard to separate drug smuggling from human smuggling. Without going down rabbit holes of policy, I spent the last couple of weeks at a conference on human trafficking in Dallas. Angel was one of the presenters, and I was having dinner one evening with him and a couple of other people who worked out of the Del Rio district. They kept talking about the impact of the Colombians on the border crossings. I'd always assumed that the border was totally controlled by the Mexican cartels. That's only partially true. It seems that actually, a Colombian family runs one of the largest cartels in Mexico. The family patriarch was a wealthy Mexican whose children migrated to Colombia and ultimately became entrenched in the Colombian drug trade, bringing drugs mainly into Florida and then later into the US through Mexico. I heard them mention Mendez, but that's such a common name and I didn't pay much attention until one of the agents asked Angel if he knew why Mendez had suddenly left his operations in Florida several years ago. I almost choked on my food when Angel told him that Mendez had left because a rival cartel had basically destroyed his business and Mendez was lucky to have survived. Apparently, Mendez's family never blamed him for the Florida fiasco and just moved him into the Mexican operation."

"Did the Colombians ever find out who was responsible for what happened in Florida?"

"Thank God, no. Otherwise you and I wouldn't be sitting here now."

"Roe, I don't know how you feel, but I'll never be at peace knowing that the main person responsible for Kim's death and for what they did to you is still breathing."

"Mark, I'm with you all the way. I've been able to achieve some peace of mind thinking that somehow I'd made up for the part I played in Kim's death. Yes, we punished all the people directly responsible, but we missed the main target, which was Mendez. We were so sure that Mendez had been killed, but we were wrong. So, what should we do next?"

"Why did you tell your friend Angel that you were interested in Andre Mendez?"

"I told him that a friend of our family had died from an overdose of drugs that had been supplied by his distributors. He promised he'd let me know if he heard anything else. I didn't want to raise any red flags. I wouldn't want our names to be connected to Mendez in any way, at least not yet."

"Roe, that's smart. I still have a couple contacts from the time I was in the Army. One of them is a college professor in El Paso. I'll start with him. For now, I have two rib eyes thawed out. Why don't you enjoy being home right now. Until we learn more there's nothing we can do tonight anyway.

After eating on the patio and watching sun set over the river, Roe stood up. "Mark, it's been a long day and

I'm beat. I hope you don't mind me checking out early. We'll put our heads together tomorrow and decide how we want to start."

"Not at all, Roe. I need to sit out here a little longer and think about what you've told me."

Before she went back into the house and up to her apartment, Roe turned to Mark, who was still sitting in a deck chair.

"I don't think I'll ever say it often enough but thank you for everything you've done for me. You've never blamed me for Kim's death. You could have but you didn't, and I'll always be grateful. Kim would thank you, too."

As Roe disappeared into the house, Mark sat motionless as he was flooded with memories of his wife Marge and his daughter Kim before their tragic deaths. Kim had been killed only because she'd tried to help her friend Roe, who was desperately attempting to run from her past. Kim's mother, Marge, had died soon after from alcohol and sleeping pills, having never been able to cope with the death of her only daughter. What followed was a brutal path of vengeance inflicted on the individuals responsible for Kim's death. Mark never blamed Roe in any way for her death, and Roe was a willing and helpful participant in all the ensuing events. Roe never tried to take the place of Kim, but there was a bond that had developed between Mark and Roe. It was as strong as any father-daughter relationship could ever be.

Mark wiped his eyes with the sleeve of his sweatshirt and tried to refocus on the next step of his search for closure which he thought he'd found. As he lay his head back on the cushioned chair, his mind went back in time, and he relived a part of his past that he'd kept suppressed for so many years. He couldn't help but wonder, as he often did when he let his defenses down, if losing his wife and daughter was karma for the things he'd done. Memories he'd never shared with any other living soul, like a massive tsunami, flooded his mind.

CHAPTER 6

Mark Price

1972

Mark Price disappeared the day he was called into his commander's office. He'd been lecturing a group of new recruits on the basics of the M16 rifle before they were allowed to actually hold one. The level of ignorance and misconceptions of most of the young kids toward firearms was scary. He knew that many of them were going to eventually be on the receiving end of a bullet once they deployed to Vietnam. But for now, besides teaching them how to survive in Vietnam, he had to keep them from accidently shooting themselves before they even left the base.

After he'd graduated magna cum laude from college, he could have qualified for admission to most graduate programs. Not wanting to put his mom under any possible financial stress and not wanting to incur any long-term debt, he'd opted to volunteer for the US Army. The United States was mired in the conflict in Southeast Asia and the Army welcomed volunteers with open arms. Upon entering the military, Mark fully expected to be deployed to Vietnam. It didn't work out as he'd expected.

Every part of his basic training came easily and naturally to him. He'd grown up in a rural part of the Florida Panhandle, where familiarity with firearms as well as stalking game in the woods and swamps were ingrained in him. He was in peak physical condition from his four years as a starting quarterback in college. His skills plus his leadership abilities were soon apparent to his instructors and officers. He rose quickly in the enlisted ranks. He was offered the option of going to Officer Candidate School, but Mark turned it down largely because he had no intention of making a career of the military. Even after volunteering for and training with the special forces, he was not deployed overseas. Instead, the ranking officers at his base decided to keep him on the base as an instructor, believing that he was most valuable as a teacher.

The staff sergeant simply told Mark to come with him. When Mark asked the sergeant where he was taking him, he only told him they were going to headquarters. He had no idea why they were asking Mark to report on such short notice. It was an unusual request. As he drove through the base toward the offices, Mark was not worried, but he was curious. He'd seen the camp commander from a distance, but had never even been up close to him, much less met him. There was a huge gulf separating a sergeant like himself from a one star general. During his four college years, he'd been so focused on football and academics that he had no time for ROTC, which would have allowed him to enter the Army as an officer. He followed Army protocol by showing the customary respect to officers, but he was never intimidated by rank.

When he walked into the general's office, he was met by a black lady dressed in civilian clothes who must have been the general's secretary. Seeing the concerned look on her face, Mark experienced a moment of apprehension himself until she leaned up close to him and whispered in a low voice, "Sergeant Price, the general isn't here, but he wanted me to let you know that you don't have to worry.

You're not in any trouble. Follow me." Mark followed her down a short hallway. She knocked on the door at the end.

"Come in."

Mark walked into a large office that stretched across the width of the barrack. Seeing the general with two stars caused Mark to instinctively stand at attention and salute. The general gave a quick return salute, saying, "At ease, sergeant."

Mark immediately became aware of two other men in the room. One was an African American and the other was a blond, white guy. They both were dressed in black suits and ties that were almost identical. With the dark sunglasses, they were poster boys for the Mafia or CIA. If not for the color of their skin, you'd never be able to tell them apart. The general was clearly in charge, as he motioned for Mark to sit at a conference table on one side of the room. The general sat on the opposite side, flanked by the two agents, who'd finally taken off the dark sunglasses, as if they'd established the proper image without having uttered a word.

"Mark, I'm General Hinson. I work in the Division of Military Intelligence. This is Agent Tucker on my right and Agent Weiss on the left. I know you must be wondering what you're doing here, and I'll explain in due time. First, I want to verify a few things about your background. Correct me if I misspeak. You grew up in Shirleyville, near the Alabama border. You were a star athlete and an A student. You attended a small college in Mississippi on a football scholarship and again you graduated with high honors with a minor in Spanish in which you are fluent. You immediately enrolled in the Army as a basic recruit. Your service records indicate your skill and aptitude with firearms, physical ability, and endurance, as well as an instinctive ability to lead, has been outstanding. Your superiors, from sergeants up to company captain, went to great lengths to keep you here on base permanently as an instructor. We also know that you are not married and have no dependents who rely on you. How did you manage to stay here in the US instead of shipping out to Vietnam?

"General, my records should show the number of times I've requested to be sent to Vietnam. That was one of the reasons I volunteered instead of going to grad school."

"So, Mark, are you saying that you'd prefer an assignment that would include combat duty?"

Mark thought for a second before replying.

"General Hinson, I'd be a better instructor if I'd actually experienced what I'm teaching."

Agent Weiss finally spoke.

"Sergeant Price, would you be willing to go on a mission that would take you off the radar for at least a year?"

"Agent Weiss, please explain what you mean by *off the radar*."

"It would mean that you'd be part of a small group that would not be acting as an agent of the US government. You'd be totally on your own, and if anything went south, you couldn't be guaranteed support from the government. You'd be working undercover on an operation that would be extremely dangerous. You would be given tactical support in an indirect way that couldn't be traced back to any US agency. I know you want to know more details, but before we get into that, we need to know whether you'd even consider doing something like this."

Mark took a deep breath and looked directly at General Hinson. "General, I'm not worried about the danger part or even the risk. If this mission is not recognized by the Army, can it come back to bite me at a later date?"

"Mark, as you'll understand if you accept this mission, the US government will want this to be buried so deep it will never come to light. This period in your record will be listed only as a 'Special Assignment.' You will receive back pay for hazardous duty and you will have the option of an immediate honorable discharge on completion. You'll be guaranteed a full ride in any graduate school if you choose to do so, and you'll be qualified for full veteran benefits." Looking intently at Mark as if to bore into his mind, Agent Tucker spoke.

"Sergeant Price, we need an answer now. If you need more time to think about it, you're not our man. Also, one last small detail that hasn't been mentioned, and I have to ask. Are you willing to kill? I don't mean hogs or deer. I mean other people that are enemies of our country. They may not be wearing military uniforms, but they are a threat just as much as the Viet Cong. If you have any reservations, we need to know it now."

Mark looked directly at General Hinson again as he replied, "Our country is sending troops to Southeast Asia to kill people who have been designated to be our enemies. I want to believe that our leadership knows far more than I do. Every day I'm teaching young boys how to kill. If I can tell them it's the right thing to do for their country, I have to be willing to do the same."

Over the years that followed Mark would replay this conversation over and over in his mind like an endless reel. If he had not been so young and naive, would he still give the same answers?

The three men across the table from Mark looked at each other and nodded. General Hinson said, "Go pack your gear. Our plane is waiting."

Without saying a word to anyone, within thirty minutes, Mark was lifting off the ground, accompanied by the general and the two agents, blissfully unaware of what lay ahead.

CHAPTER 7

Angel

Mark had returned from an early morning run along the St. Johns River and had taken a cup of coffee out onto his patio. A thick bank of fog still hung over the river. As the morning sun was beginning to burn off the fog, Roe joined Mark on the patio holding a cup of coffee as well.

"I can't tell you how great it was to sleep in my own bed last night. The novelty of travel wore off a long time ago."

"Roe, I couldn't agree more. There are few places in the world that I haven't visited in the last few years. Every time I come back home; I wonder why I ever wanted to go anywhere else."

"Mark, did you come up with any thoughts about Mendez?"

"Other than the thoughts of what I'd do to him if I could find him, I'm really not sure where to start. My only thought would be to go to the area where he's supposed to be operating and start asking questions. Maybe Angel will learn more."

Roe realized her cell phone was buzzing. She dug it out of the pocket of her jeans and answered, "Yes, Angel, you're getting an early start today."

"Good morning, Roe. I'm assuming you're up and about by now. I've been chasing illegals along the river all night. I'm on my way back to the office and I wanted to pass some information on to you. You expressed interest in that Mendez character. Well, we had a literal massacre on the US side of the river and one survivor was found. The story he told was fascinating. What you might be interested in was his mention of Mendez in his tale. We're going to do an in-depth interrogation later today. If you want, I'll send you a transcript of it."

Roe was looking at Mark, who had a questioning look on his face as she pumped her fist and grinned.

"Thanks, Angel. That would be great. I hope you'll be able to get some rest after such a long night. I'll look forward to getting the transcript. Are you going to hold the individual?"

"Yes, for now. He has a gunshot wound and won't be going anywhere soon. Then there's something about his girlfriend being taken. He wants help in finding her, so that should keep him close for now as well."

"Thanks again, Angel. We'll stay in touch. Later."

"Mark, our question about where to start has just been answered. I have a lot of vacation time built up with the state. I think now is the time to take some of it. Let's go to Texas."

After considering all options, Roe and Mark thought it would be best for Roe to fly out to Texas immediately. Roe was worried that the man who survived the massacre might be released with notice to appear as so many aliens were. He could possibly go anywhere in the country and disappear. His information regarding Andre Mendez was the only tangible lead they had at the moment. Mark would start driving west immediately. This way they would have their own car and whatever other items they might want to bring.

Since Roe served directly under the state attorney
general as liaison to the counsel on human trafficking, she
was considered a member of state law enforcement and
thereby entitled to carry a firearm ether openly or concealed. With the close cooperation shared by Florida and
Texas, she could carry her sidearm, even on a commercial
flight, with no problem.

Part of Roe's job was to coordinate efforts to combat human trafficking with state law enforcement agencies as well as to conduct training sessions with different
departments. She had also developed a good working relationship with federal agencies, especially the DEA and
the US Department of Immigration. Since Florida and
Texas were two of the states most affected by drugs, illegal
immigration, and human trafficking, she was able to work
with the mirror agency in Texas. Roe had climbed the bu-
reaucratic ladder rapidly and was considered to be a rising
star. Both Roe and Mark realized that they'd have to be
very careful not to let their obsession with finding Andre
Mendez do anything that might damage her career. Mark
himself couldn't give a rat's ass about his own reputation,
but Roe was a different story. Only Roe and Mark knew
the anguish and heartbreak that Mendez had caused. The
drive for revenge could never be understood by anyone
other than the two of them. They each knew that as long as
Andre remained alive, neither of them would ever achieve
closure from the past.

Roe repacked a suitcase and left immediately for the
airport. It took Mark a little longer to put together the
things he thought he might need. But he soon left Jacksonville and was on I-10 headed west with a full tank of gas
and a large thermos of hot coffee at his side. Mark had no
fear of what might lay ahead. Since the time years ago when
he'd lost his wife and daughter, he had lost all concern for

his own mortality. He felt that every day of his life was only borrowed time. Roe, however, was a different story, and he'd sacrifice his own life in a New York minute to protect her.

CHAPTER 8

1972

The plane was a small military transport with a large empty cargo area. Mark was told to make himself comfortable because it would be a long flight. The plane landed once at what was a commercial airport but didn't approach any of the public terminals, instead stopping at a large hangar on the airports fringe. Someone brought food onboard and another solder in fatigues came onboard as well. No one made any effort to introduce the new person, so Mark, after eating, found an open spot on the cargo floor and went to sleep.

He awoke as the plane was descending again. He was told to get his gear and follow. They were at the landing strip of a military base. An unmarked gray van was waiting, and without any conversation the general and two agents along with Mark and the new arrival climbed in.

General Hinson said, "I know you're both wondering where we are. This is Fort Bliss in El Paso; we're going to a private airfield outside the city. Save your questions. You'll be briefed shortly."

There was no further conversation as the van ride lasted for forty-five minutes. There was the sound of metal doors clanging open and the van finally stopped. When its doors opened, Mark could see that they were inside a cavernous metal building that looked like an airplane hangar. As he looked around, his thoughts were confirmed by a small, fixed wing aircraft and a large helicopter.

"This way," General Hinson said as he started walking toward the side of the hangar. A set of double doors led into a long cinder block hallway with closed doors lining both sides. The end of the hallway opened into a large room that resembled a lobby-bar area of a luxury hotel. There was a small bar, but there were sitting areas with comfortable-looking upholstered chairs as well as several small tables. A door led into a dining area off from a kitchen. There were two men and one woman in the room who immediately stood up as the general walked in.

General Hinson waved his arm. "At ease, everyone. Let's all pull up a chair." After everyone was seated, except for Agents Tucker and Weiss, who remained standing sphinxlike with arms crossed on either side, he spoke again.

"You all were given a rather vague description of why you're here. First, I want to introduce everyone. Each one of you has gone through the same exhaustive evaluation. Failure to meet any of the required criteria would have disqualified you. I will tell you that in all my years in this man's army, I've never seen a more talented group than what I'm looking at right now. Each one of you has excelled in everything you've done. You each have some unique qualities different from the rest. One of two common denominators though is the ability to work well with others. Also, each one of you has shown a strong sense of patriotism. You love this country and you're willing to fight for it. I want to emphasize one last time the importance of secrecy. As you will come to realize, it's not only to protect the government, but also to protect each one of you. As you were told, if this project goes south, if one of you becomes compromised, then this facility and me as well will disappear in a millisecond. There is no paper trail, bank accounts, or records that will show that we existed. In taking this assignment with the accompanying risk, you will all be well compensated as you were promised. Now, let's make some introductions.

"Since I grew up in the south and still believe in 'ladies first,' I'll start by introducing Rosa Gomez. Rosa is on loan from the secret service. She grew up in Mexico City before moving to the US when she was fourteen. Her previous assignments involved gang and drug infiltration at our southern borders. She also participates in triathlons and handgun competitions. She is a tough lady. Because of her familiarity with the smuggling operations, she will be given the assignments from an undisclosed source.

"To her right is Rich Holtz. Rich comes from the Army Corps of Engineers. Don't be fooled by his baby face. He is an expert with all forms of explosives and is proficient with rifles and handguns.

"Next, the skinny guy behind Rosa is Lou Croft. He's an Army sniper who's won every long range shooting competition he ever participated in. He's also a gourmet chef and loves to cook. Whatever you all want to eat, you'll get.

"The big black guy sitting next to Lou is Marcus Jefferson. Marcus is a Marine. He also is a karate black belt and a cage fighter. Although he is qualified as expert in pistol and rifle, he is probably more lethal when he gets his hands on you. Incidentally, Marcus holds a master's degree in religion.

"And lastly, the other big man sitting there is Mark Price. Mark comes from the Army and Special Forces. He's an expert with just about every weapon the military uses, including knives. When he was in high school, he hunted wild boar in southern swamps alone, with only a handgun and knife. He, like all of you, is proficient in Spanish."

At that moment, another man entered the room. General Hinson pointed to him and said, "Last and certainly not least is your pilot, Ron Lassiter. Ron is Air Force with combat experience and is uniquely qualified to fly both fixed wing planes and helicopters. He's the one who will get you there and, most importantly, get you back. Ron will also be responsible for ordering weapons, and whatever other equipment you need.

"Now, I'm going to let Agent Tucker explain why you're here."

CHAPTER 9

1972

As Agent Tucker begin, to speak everyone in the room seemed to draw closer to listen.

"For some time now, all branches of the military have had a problem with illegal drugs. A lot of different things have been tried, but the problem continues, and it is getting worse. The Mexican government has refused to work with US authorities and has basically turned a blind eye to all of our efforts. We have even offered to cross the border and eliminate some staging spots. There is no way they will allow us to do anything inside Mexico. Apparently, it's hit home at all levels. Some people at the top have decided no more. The decision was made to use extreme measures to stop it. Even though diplomatic efforts have met with no success, there is still some concern about alienating other countries. That's why nothing can be traced back to our government. You will be perceived as either a group of vigilantes or possibly another drug cartel. Most likely as another cartel, because only a cartel could afford the hardware that you'll have access to. You will be able to pick and choose your targets. As you know, the Texas-Mexico border covers a lot of territory. There is illegal activity along the entire border. We believe that by interceding at different areas, the word will spread. We want to instill the fear of God in everyone involved in the drug trade. Any questions so far?"

Mark asked, "How do we get the information we'll need in order to know where and when the traffickers are operating?"

General Hinson answered, "Both the FBI and Secret Service, as well as local authorities, compile information on a weekly basis. For some time now the DEA has had informants within the cartels as well. Unfortunately, informants have a notoriously short life expectancy. There will be a government site that condenses this information, and you'll have access to the site. Someone who knows and understands more about the drug trade than anyone is sitting right here. Agent Rosa Gomez will be invaluable in using the information from the site to make those decisions. Once you've picked your targets, Sergeant Price will plan the details of the missions. You have a plane, a helicopter, and a van at your disposal to take you to any area on the border. Everything is unmarked with vague origins. It will be critical that you all will be wearing clothing with no insignias or labels, and of course, no dog tags. Any contact with friends or family is going to be almost nonexistent. You are all well trained and each of you are in peak physical condition. There won't be any training involved. You're own your own. And I will remind you all that you are to use extreme prejudice. No warning shots or messages are warranted. You are being sent to kill an enemy of your country. It's no different than if a Viet Cong soldier was coming at you holding a claymore mine. Do not hesitate to do so.

"Now, I'm going to disappear along with Agents Tucker and Weiss. We never existed. Your communication for supplies will be through your pilot Ron Lassiter. He will have a one-way means of relaying your needs to the right place. Before I leave, I want to say this one more time with utmost emphasis: As far as the US government is concerned, you do not exist. Any one of you who can't live with this can leave with us now."

Agent Weiss had left the room but returned with an easel and a whiteboard, which he set up so all could see. He left the room with Agents Tucker and General Hinson. No one left with them. Mark would only see General Hinson once more.

CHAPTER 10

Emelia

The van ride seemed to last forever, and the men were finally tired of staring at her. At some point Emelia realized that they were in a town or city because of the sounds and the van's stops and starts. When they finally stopped and the engine shut off, the driver opened the back door of the van, and everyone climbed out. Emelia was pulled out last.

It was El Carnicero who ordered, "Get her inside and locked up. No one is to touch her unless I say so."

They were inside a compound surrounded by concrete walls that were at least eight feet in height. The tops of the walls were covered in large pieces of broken glass which were imbedded in the concrete. The compound must have covered most of the block, and the house seemed to be several different structures that had been haphazardly connected together. One of the men took Emelia roughly by the arm and led her into the closest building and down a series of hallways before opening a door to a small room and shoving her in. The door was closed behind her, and she could hear some sort of lock or latch being closed. As she looked around the room, she saw there was a single cot, and in one corner was a large ceramic pot that she immediately realized from the odor must be her toilet. The only light in the dim room came from a small narrow window at the top of one wall. Even if she could have reached it, it was far too small for even a child to get through. Feeling trapped like an animal in a small cage, Emelia collapsed on the cot—which smelled of sweat and urine—and sobbed in total despair.

She cried until she'd used up all her tears before dropping off into a fitful sleep. When she was woken up by the sound of the door being unlocked and opened, she'd lost track of time and had no idea how long she'd been sleeping. The same man who'd brought her to the room told her to get up and come with him. She was groggy and her head was splitting as he shoved her down a hallway. He guided her down another series of hallways by pushing and pointing until they entered a large room with a high arched ceiling. Her first impression was that it was a small church sanctuary before she realized the men from the van were in the room, which was filled with tobacco or some sort of plant smoke. As she panicked, she tried to turn and run, but she ran right into the man who'd brought her from her room. As he forced her to turn around, it was El Carnicero who spoke. He was sitting in a large, upholstered chair with his feet propped up on an ottoman. He had a bottle of beer in his hand.

"Whoa, whoa, slow down, chica. No one is going to hurt you. Don't worry, we will take good care of you. Carmila, bring her a drink. She must need one by now."

A young woman who was wearing only panties and bra was sitting on the floor next to the ottoman. She quickly stood up and poured some liquor from a bottle into a small glass and brought it to Emelia as El Carnicero spoke again. "Drink up, chica, before you show us what you're worth."

Carmila handed the glass to Emelia, who took it with both hands. Fearing she would spill it if she didn't drink it quickly, Emelia brought the glass to her lips and took a large swallow. It was straight tequila and it burned as it went down her throat. The men all clapped and shouted as she downed the rest of the contents.

"Okay, chica, I promised the men they could at least see what they'd found. Now take your clothes off."

Emelia stood still, as if in a trance, as El Carnicero told the woman who'd brought Emelia the drink, "Carmila, will you help the poor girl take her clothes off?"

Carmila, who had been standing at the side of the room, walked over to Emelia and started to undress her. Emelia stood frozen in fear as Carmila unbuttoned and removed her dress. When Carmila unhooked her bra, she tried to cover her breast with her arms, but when Carmila pulled her panties down, she no longer had enough arms to cover herself. She could only stand in utter embarrassment and humiliation as the men all cheered loudly.

El Carnicero only shook his head and whispered, "Muy hermosa," before he told Carmila to pick up Emelia's clothes and take her back to her room. Turning to the men in the room, he said, "This girl is a treasure. Her beauty will be worth a lot, but we'll give Señor Mendez the first chance to test her. He will be grateful to us for saving her for him. All of you listen carefully to what I say. The man who touches a hair on her head will get his member cut off and stuffed down his throat. Comprende? We'll keep her here as a maid and cook for the time being."

Carmila had already draped Emelia's dress over her while she led her back to the same room. As she watched a shaken Emelia sit down on the cot, Carmila told her that some food would be brought to her later.

"You're lucky. They think you're worth a lot of money to someone. I wasn't so lucky. By this time every one of the bastards had used me. You're okay for now, but eventually they'll find a use for you too." She closed the door and the latch closed again.

Emelia thought things couldn't get any worse. If only she knew.

CHAPTER 11

1972

Rosa Gomez stood up and walked over to the whiteboard. Rosa was roughly five foot eight and one hundred fifteen pounds. Her skin was a light bronze, but the contrast with her jet-black hair and expressive dark brown eyes made it appear even lighter. Her facial features were a mixture of classic Spanish and Aztec aristocracy. She wore no makeup and was dressed in jeans, sweater, and light windbreaker. As Mark watched her pick up a marker and begin to speak, he thought she should be on a movie marquee. He tried to overlook her beauty, but it was hard to do. She was the most beautiful woman he'd ever seen. She gave the impression of being someone who was confident and secure in their skin. She wasn't trying to impress the group, but as she spoke in a matter-of-fact conversational tone, it became obvious to everyone in the group that she knew what she was doing.

"I wish we had more time to get to know each other. I know I'm impressed with each one of you. For me, this mission is a dream come true. For three years, I've had to watch this border become more and more porous. I know what effects the drugs are having on not only our troops but on the American people as well. That's not mentioning the human smuggling and its toll. Our Border Patrol is stretched so thin they are almost useless. When we have known in advance that a crossing is imminent, our hands have been tied by conventional rules and regulations. I think we're going to shake the tree. This is where we start."

She drew an outline of the Rio Grande and indicated the location of El Paso and then a small town southeast on the Mexican side of the river.

"Just south of this point, there is an area that's become almost like a smuggling highway. Our informants have indicated that the cartel in this area is using this one spot on a regular basis. It's ideal for them because once they're across the river, they have so many roads available to move inland or back toward El Paso. The area on the US side is mainly farmland but is still well isolated with minimal habitation.

"We believe that they've stockpiled a large stash of drugs on the Mexican side and are planning to make a movement any time now. We'll get an approximate time within the next twenty-four hours. In the meantime, we'll look at detailed maps, and with Sergeant Price's help, we'll decide on a plan and what weapons we'll need. This will be a test run to see just how serious the general is in getting us what we need. Although when you consider what they've spent in providing our aircraft, I don't think there'll be a problem."

After looking at the satellite images and maps, Mark made a few suggestions that met with everyone's approval. They all had preferences in weapons and Mark made up a list which he gave to the pilot, Ron Lassiter. Ron immediately used the phone line he'd been given and made the request to the person who answered. He was told to open the hangar door where the van was parked at exactly 3:00 AM the next morning.

Ron then directed them to a small room off the long hallway. The room was lined with shelves on three sides.

The shelves on the right were stacked with green camo fatigues of all sizes. The wall to the left was identical except the fatigues were a brown camo. The rear wall contained boots and a top shelf with a collection of hats of different variations in green and brown camo.

Ron told the group, "I think we'll all want to all wear the same shade of fatigues just to make it easier for us to identify each other. There are no markings on any of the clothing items. Even the 'Made in Sri Lanka' labels have been removed."

Rosa spoke, "Guys, there's nothing else we can do today. Let's go to our private bar, have a drink, and then see what kind of food they left us."

Lou Croft spoke up, "I'm ahead of you there. My three favorite things in life are fighting, food, and sex, in no particular order. Since we can't fight yet and it looks like sex will be off the table for a while, that only leaves food. I've already looked in the kitchen, and if you'll trust me, I'll work up a meal. I hope there aren't any poor hunters in the group." Smiling, he continued, "I mean vegetarians." When no one responded, he headed for the kitchen. Everyone else headed for the bar.

The rest of the evening was basically spent with everyone getting to know one another. The general was correct when he'd said that compatibility was a prerequisite for the group. The dinner Lou prepared was amazing, and by the end of the evening, Mark felt good about his teammates.

Ron volunteered to stay up and open the hangar door for the early morning delivery. Everyone was up by 6:00 AM and in the hangar to see what was delivered. Ron said, "At exactly 3:00 AM, I rolled open the door and within two or three minutes an old beat-up van similar to the one left for our use rolled into the hangar. Two men dressed in civilian clothes jumped out, unloaded the contents, and left in less than two minutes."

It was almost like Christmas morning as everyone rummaged through the contents looking for their own particular item they'd asked for.

Mark had asked for a World War 11 BAR "Browning Automatic Rifle" in 30-06 caliber with five extra magazines. He'd asked for this particular weapon because it was perfect for what they planned to do. It was a compromise between a semiautomatic rifle and a light machine gun. He also asked for a Smith & Wesson Model 39 semiautomatic pistol with extra magazines. He watched with curiosity at the other's choices.

Rosa was checking to be sure her M16 was capable of being switched to fully automatic, which was how the early M16s had been built. The military soon stopped issuing those to the men because it was found that in combat situations a soldier would panic and empty their magazines too quickly when the gun was set on automatic fire. That left them more vulnerable holding an empty rifle with an enemy charging at them. Rosa had also selected a Browning Hi Power 9mm pistol.

Rich Holtz was also partial to the Browning Hi Power for a handgun as well as an M14 rifle in 7.62 cal. Marcus Jefferson had selected an M14 and an Army issue 1911 pistol. The pilot Ron Lassiter only asked for a 357 cal. Colt Python with a three-inch barrel.

The choice that intrigued Mark the most though was what the sniper Lou Croft had chosen. It was a modified Model 700 Remington with an adjustable cheek rest and a bull barrel. It was in 7.62 by 51mm NATO caliber. Mounted on it was a Schmidt & Bender 3-12 by 50 scope.

When he saw Mark's interest in the rifle, he told Mark, "I'm assuming that there won't be any need for a silenced weapon because we'll all be shooting at the same time. Later, if we need to shoot quietly, I'll ask for the rifle that's being tested right now. It's a modified Winchester Model 70 that fires a 458 by 1.5 Barns cartridge. It's a subsonic bullet that's muted with a suppressor. Even the shooter can barely hear it. It might take more than a few hours to get one of those. With the rifle I have here, I can get off several accurate shots within a few seconds."

"That's good to know. You're right in assuming that we'll make a lot of noise this first time. I noticed that you didn't ask for a handgun."

Lou smiled when he replied, "No, I've found that when I'm rolling around on the ground trying to get into a perfect firing position, a pistol gets in the way."

There were also stacks of boxes of ammunition and multiple pairs of binoculars, some with night vision as well as several flare guns.

Later, Mark watched Rosa from a distance as she spent the rest of the morning working at the computer desk that had been set up in the lounge. Around noon, she called for everyone's attention. "We're on for tonight. I want everyone to understand we may sometimes pick the wrong spots or times. There's always the risk of faulty information. Let's hope that tonight pays off."

By late afternoon, the group was packed into the old beat-up van with a faded El *PLOMERO* written on the side and driving south along the Rio Grande. They had all agreed to euphemistically call themselves Los Plomeros— "The Plumbers"—because of the name on the van. They followed the winding road along the Rio Grande and approached the suspected crossing site in the late afternoon. The state highway was less than one mile from the river at that point. Both sides of the river were lined with stunted trees and thick underbrush. The thick growth stretched out to the paved state road on the US side. They turned off the paved road and onto a narrow-rutted path that led straight toward the river. In less than half a mile, the path abruptly ended at a canal that continued straight on and connected at a right angle with the river. It was an anomaly that had been created many years ago when the river was a vital part of transporting agricultural products toward the Gulf of Mexico. It provided access into the river because the riverbanks on the US side were too high for easy access, and it created a perfect site for smugglers to cross the river and enter the canal. Following it to its shallow end, they could easily transfer their loads into a waiting truck or van with no worry about the strong river currents and high banks. They then would have options for leaving the area on several state roads.

Ron Lassiter dropped them all off where the path ended at the canal. He went back out to the road and drove several hundred yards until he found a spot to drive the van off the road and into the brush so that it wouldn't be seen. His job was to wait until Mark signaled him to return and pick them up.

As they had planned, Mark and Rich Holtz started up the right side of the canal toward the river while Marcus Jefferson and Lou Croft headed up the left side. Rosa Gomez remained at the canal's head. There was no conversation. Everyone knew exactly what was expected of them. Their watches were carefully calibrated, and before dark they were all placing themselves in positions that gave them good coverage of the target area.

Mark found a small tree that allowed him to rest the BAR between two branches that provided stability and ideal coverage of the entire area where the canal opened into the river. Rich found a similar position a few feet away. Across the canal, Marcus Jefferson and Lou Croft found comparable locations. Lou used a range finder to calibrate his point of aim to a spot across the river where a clear path led down to the water. Back toward the main road, Rosa Gomez had concealed herself in a clump of small mesquite. Her position gave her a clear coverage of the end of the canal where the pickup vehicle would have to park. Soon they had nothing to do but hurry up and wait.

CHAPTER 12

Roe Meets Samuel

Samuel had repeated his story so many times for so many people he was becoming discouraged. As hard as he'd tried to get some information about Emelia, the more evasive his questioners became. He soon realized that he wasn't going to get much help from them. His biggest concern was that they would send him either back to Chile or even more likely back to Haiti. In either case he knew he'd never have a chance of seeing Emelia again. He'd been removed from the medical clinic and into a type of barrack within a fenced compound. The occupants all seemed to be comprised of men who'd been attempting to cross the border illegally. A few were distraught at having been apprehended, but most were nonchalant and were simply saying they'd just keep trying until they got in. Some were expecting to be released into the interior with notices to appear some at some future date. There were a lot of jokes made about the likelihood of ever reporting to anyone if they were fortunate enough to be released.

When Samuel heard his name being called, he almost had a panic attack as he approached the officer, who simply said, "Come with me." He followed the officer into a mobile office and was directed to have a seat in a small room. He could hear people speaking outside the room, and soon the door opened and a man wearing a Border

Patrol uniform and a young woman dressed in a pantsuit entered the room.

The officer spoke first, "Agent Estes, this is Samuel Orasme. You've read the circumstances of his border crossing. We have questioned him extensively, and I don't think there's anything else he can tell us. At the moment, his immigration status is pending. Samuel, meet Agent Estes. She's come all the way from Florida to ask you a few questions. Roe, I'll leave you with him. I'll be around the office all day today. Let someone know when you're done. Oh, he's fluent in English and Spanish."

"Thanks, Angel. I think Samuel and I'll get along just fine."

The woman's demeanor allowed Samuel to relax slightly. He wasn't looking forward to another interview, but at least the woman didn't seem threatening and accusatory like some of the Border Patrol agents had been.

"Samuel, I know you're tired of repeating your experience so many times, but it would be a big help to me if you'd do it one more time. But let's start at the beginning. Tell me how you ended up crossing the Rio Grande in the first place. What was your starting point?"

If Roe's intent was to help Samuel relax and open up, it worked like a charm. Samuel started with Emelia as his main interest from beginning to end. Samuel felt like someone was really listening to his plight as he talked on. It didn't bother him that she wrote down exactly what he said as he repeated the words that El Carnicero uttered during the assault. She also seemed keenly interested in the polleros who brought the group across the river. After Samuel had told her everything he could think of, he asked her if she had any idea how he could find Emelia.

"Samuel, the people who took Emelia are really bad people. I wish I could offer you some assurances, but I can't. I can tell you that I will be looking for this El Carnicero. He may have information I need to find his boss, Andre Mendez. These people are also your best chance of finding Emelia. At the moment, most individuals in your position are being sent back to Haiti. Since you do have contacts in Florida through your friend that was killed, we might be able to have you released into the US. You'd be given a future notice to appear and have your status examined more closely. If this could be done, would you agree to help me?"

Samuel was overwhelmed with gratitude as tears poured down his face. "Yes, ma'am. I'll do anything you need."

CHAPTER 13

1972

The crossing occurred sometime after 2:00 AM. Headlights on the Mexican side first appeared in the distance well before the sound of engines could be heard. It was hard to tell because the trees lining the other side of the river blocked the view of most of the vehicles. Mark was surprised how open the operation seemed to be. Three large inflatable rafts were dragged down the path to the river before being loaded with large, wrapped packages brought from the trucks. The leading raft had an outboard engine that started up as soon as the rafts were loaded. The leading raft was connected to the two trailing ones by ropes, creating a raft train. Just before the train left the shore, multiple individuals climbed aboard all three rafts and sat on top of the loaded packages. The outboard engine on the first raft had to work at its max to pull the train across the rapid current of the river and toward the open mouth of the canal. When the leading raft was maybe thirty yards from the entrance to the canal, several things happened at once.

The night suddenly became day as a flare from both sides of the canal exploded in the night sky. Mark had set the BAR on full auto, and he emptied the entire twenty-round clip into the last raft in the train. Quickly ramming in another clip, he did the same thing with the second raft and finally focused on the leading raft with the third clip. In the meantime, on the other side of the canal, Lou Croft was focusing on the vehicles that were visible across the river before targeting the three men still standing on the opposite bank. All three rafts had been devastated by the fire from Mark's BAR. The individuals who had been crowded on the rafts had either already been hit or the ones who were alive were struggling to hold onto the disintegrating rafts. Meanwhile, both Marcus and Rich were using their M14s to target the many men who were desperately trying to stay afloat.

Everything happened within sixty seconds. At that point the flares had died out and bodies, drugs, and most of those left alive had been carried down the river and out of sight by the current. One of the men on the last raft had managed to get back to the Mexican side of the river and was clinging to a large branch that hung out over the river. He was the last vestige of life left in the river. Lou fired one round and the man released his grip on the branch and dropped backwards into the river. Between the fast-moving current and the strong breeze, within a minute there was no indication that anything unusual had ever happened. A solitary vehicle in the woods beyond the river started up and its lights rapidly disappeared into the night.

Wasting no time, the four Plomeros headed back up the banks of the canal back toward the road. Rosa was standing there waiting with her M16 resting on her arm. Parked at the end of the canal was a large truck from a well-known line of rental trucks. However, the windshield and the driver's side window had been blown out with shards of broken glass hanging down. There was some movement on the passenger side as Rosa walked over to the truck. The man in the driver's seat was obviously dead since the top half his head had been blown off. The passenger who was trying to speak was still alive but was only able to make a rattling sound. With no hesitation, Rosa took her pistol from its holster and fired one shot point-blank into the woman's head. As the woman slumped down into her seat, she made no further attempts at conversation.

Rosa looked straight at Mark saying, "She was going to die anyway."

By this time Ron was arriving with the van and all five secured their weapons and climbed in. The van carried them up to the main road and back toward their safe house.

CHAPTER 14

The Team

When Mark arrived in El Paso, he went straight to the hotel where Roe had reserved a room for him and checked in. He called Roe, who had just returned to her room after interviewing Samuel. They met at the large hotel bar where there were quiet nooks where they could sit and talk. Roe went through her interview with Samuel leaving nothing out.

"Roe, that was smart of you to offer to help him if he'd cooperate with us."

"You know how I feel about illegal immigration, Mark. We either have laws or we don't. No pun intended, but it's a Mexican standoff. Even so, I'll have to admit, my heart goes out to this Samuel kid. I don't think he had a clue about the risk he and his girlfriend were undertaking when they left Chile. At this point he's not the least bit concerned about whether he stays here permanently or not. He is really torn up over what happened to her and his friend. I think he'd be willing to walk over hot coals to find her."

"I'm looking forward to meeting him and listening to his story. On the long drive out here, I've thought of several possibilities. When can we talk to him together?"

"Angel told me he could facilitate his release immediately. He said he would be released with a date to appear in court and then he could go anywhere he wanted. He also reminded me that if the kid decided to run, there was nothing we could do to stop him."

"If he's sincere about finding his friend, hopefully we can convince him that his best chance will be to stick with the two of us."

"Agreed. Samuel is supposed to have a final check from the doctor tomorrow, so I'll see if we can pick him up immediately afterward."

Around 10:00 AM the next morning, Mark and Roe drove to the detention area. Mark waited in his car while Roe disappeared inside. Thirty minutes later, Roe emerged with a young man who was dressed in an oversized T-shirt and a pair of baggy trousers held up with a piece of nylon rope tied tightly around his waist. Mark estimated that he was maybe five foot ten and around one hundred seventy pounds. He had had handsome features, light brown skin, and close-cropped dark hair. He walked with a slight limp as he approached. Roe opened a back door of Mark's Land Cruiser, and as Samuel got in the back seat, Roe introduced him to Mark. "Mark, I want you to meet Samuel Orasme. Samuel, this is the gentleman, Mark Price, that I spoke to you about."

Mark turned in his seat and said, "Samuel, it's good to finally meet you. Roe here has told me most of what you've been through. You're lucky to be alive. I'm looking forward to hearing all the details myself. I can tell from looking at you that Homeland Security didn't bust their budget with your clothes. Roe, let's find a big box store and get Samuel something decent to wear."

Speaking in flawless English, Samuel replied, "I'm sorry Mr. Price. The money I had is gone and I can't afford to buy anything."

Roe responded, "Let's just say that you're being paid to help us, and this is a part of your pay."

Mark remembered passing a shopping district close to his hotel. There was indeed a big box store where they were able to buy several changes of clothes and a few toiletries for Samuel. Samuel in turn was overwhelmed by the kindness that Mark and Roe showed him and was profusely thankful. They went from the shopping area back to their hotel, where Mark was able to get a room for Samuel on the same floor as theirs.

By now it was early afternoon and after Samuel had a chance to shower off the taint of the detention center and change into decent clothing, they all went down to the hotel restaurant. After finding a table off to one side of the room that offered some privacy, Mark began the conversation.

"First I want to tell you why we think you can help us, Samuel." Without going into any details that could incriminate either himself or Roe with anything they'd done in the past, he gave Samuel some of the reasons why they wanted to find Andre Mendez. Mark explained to Samuel that going up the chain of smugglers toward Mendez would also be the only chance of finding out what happened to Emelia. Mark was also brutally honest about the possibility that what they found might not be the result that Samuel was hoping for. These were bad people. Their brutality and total lack of compassion were well-known. The fact that the individual leading the group that took Emelia enjoyed his nickname, El Carnicero, was a perfect example.

Mark was somewhat surprised at the way Samuel responded. Samuel's level of understanding and maturity were more than what he was expecting as he spoke after Mark had finished.

"I'm not the same person I was when we left Chile. What we've been through, what we've witnessed, has changed my view of humanity. I hate to say it, but I don't have much love in my heart at the moment. I know that if or when I find Emelia, it might not be good. At this moment, I only want to hurt someone really badly. If you have to do the same in order to find this Mendez, count me in."

Mark and Roe looked at each other and nodded as Roe spoke, "Then let's go hurt someone."

CHAPTER 15

1972

There was no conversation at all during the long ride back to their quarters in the hanger. Each one remained in silent contemplation of what they'd just done. Mark was surprised that he felt almost no emotion. Yes, his heart rate must have gone up, but otherwise he felt nothing. It was as if he had responded to the situation like a well-programed robot. For a moment he wondered if he would become dehumanized by his actions. Shrugging off the thought, he instead mused over the boys he'd been training to do the same things that he'd just done. If they were told to do it, he had to practice what he'd been preaching to them. He watched Rosa as she nodded off to sleep with a big smile on her face. She was obviously not affected by what she'd just done.

As soon as they'd reached the safety of the hangar, they all agreed to get a few hours' sleep before meeting in the lounge for a debriefing. After stowing all the weapons, they went to their individual rooms and crashed. At noon, they were all gathered in the lounge with mugs of tea and coffee. Rosa started the dialogue by first asking if anyone in the group had a problem with what they'd done earlier. It seemed that everyone had taken the action in stride. She next asked if anyone had any suggestions about the plan and the way it was set up. The only one to speak was Ron Lassiter, who had driven the van.

"I was sitting in the van about a mile south. I was well-concealed off the road. The gunfire was loud, but there's no way to avoid that. What did concern me were the flares. The Border Patrol makes random night flights up and down the river, always picking a different location. A plane in the sky wouldn't hear gunfire, but they might see a flare from a long distance. It might even be picked up on satellite imagery."

Mark replied, "He has a good point. If we can avoid flares it might be a good idea. We could find a way to use a powerful spotlight and keep the beams low. We might sacrifice one shooter to operate a light."

After they had reviewed and agreed on any changes, Rosa laid out the next target.

"American authorities have known all about this place for as long as I've been working for the government. It's a major indoor marijuana production facility that is considered to be the largest single supplier to the US. The reason it's an indoor facility is not to avoid detection but to enhance production. They're able to create conditions that will give maximum output and quality. If you look at these images, these huge outbuildings house the generators. They make their own power. The operation is located on the edge of a small village on one of the major routes leading to El Paso. The livelihood of the entire town is dependent on marijuana production. Security is lax because the cartel owns it and no other cartels have made any successful efforts to compete with it. Our only tool so far has been to use informers to let us know when a large shipment is set to cross the border. Unfortunately, informers disappear as fast as they appear, and they're good at sending us on wild goose chases. It's just barely within the range of the helicopter from this point. I'm going to get satellite images and detailed maps this afternoon. I'll also get the latest information on the operation from the web site we have access to. Let's meet together again, say around four o'clock."

Everyone was back in the lounge at four where Rosa had maps and images spread out on a long table.

"The location is both good and bad. It's good because it's set well outside the town, so it will be easy to find and also for the copter to land. We don't have to worry about civilians being harmed. It's bad because we'll be open and visible to anyone from the town who decides to take any shots at us."

Mark asked, "How many people can we expect to be at the site at 3:00 AM?"

"Good question. From what has been reported, most of the collection, drying, curing, and packaging occurs during the day. The nighttime crew is mainly the agricultural crew. They do the planting, fertilizing, watering, and whatever is needed to keep plants growing. They are good at what they do. They even have a brand name that's supposedly well-known in the world of users.

"It's called Montezuma Green," Mark said, "because the final product has a greenish tint. The kids who come through basic talk about it openly. They must have pretty good distribution networks. But going back to the plan, what about guards?"

Rosa answered, "There doesn't seem to be a heavy presence of designated guards. The operation is so engrained in the community that there's no chance of anyone stealing or doing anything to hinder the production. I'm sure the workers have small arms close by, but how likely they are to use them, I don't know."

Mark spoke again, "The key for us is to get in and out so fast, that even if they have an army of cartel soldiers close by, we'll be gone before they can seriously react. They'll obviously not be expecting us. If we come in low and land on the side of the buildings away from the town, we'll have a short window of surprise. We'll need to cover the entire area with incendiary and explosive devices as fast as possible. I'd suggest that we land, spread out, and go through the buildings toward the town clearing out any opposition. We then move back toward the helicopter, setting off the devices as we retreat. The idea being that the explosions and smoke from the fires will help give us cover. The chopper will be running and waiting for us to haul ass."

Rosa spoke once more, "Because most of the people who work there are civilians from the town, we can extend some degree of mercy to any of them we encounter. That's assuming they don't offer any resistance. At the first sign of a weapon, we take them out. Any cartel people present will be armed and easily identified. Some individuals may live to relate what happened, so it will be important that we all wear masks and speak only Spanish during the operation. Having the cartels suspect another cartel is part of our goal. Okay, let's make out our wish lists again. So far, we're batting a thousand with our requests."

Mark already knew what they'd need in terms of arms, and he seriously doubted they'd get everything they wanted this time.

CHAPTER 16
Emelia

Emelia had passed out again out of stress and the exhaustion it brought. She was startled awake when the door was opened, and a short dark man wearing a chef's hat entered the room and told her to follow him. Eventually they ended up in a large kitchen where the man walked her over to a sink and pointed to a counter with stacks dirty dishes.

"Start by washing those. You can eat after you're finished." There were two women in the kitchen doing other things. Both were older and they seemed to move like robots.

After Emelia had finished with the dishes, the man pointed toward a table where the two women were now seated. "There's food on the table. Eat what you want."

The sight and smell of the food suddenly made Emelia realize how long it had been since she'd eaten. In spite of her plight, she was ravenous. She sat across from the two women who ignored her as she sat down. It was not a gourmet selection of food, but what was there tasted great to her as she wolfed it down. As she ate, she watched the two women finish eating, get up, and clean their plates before shuffling out the door.

The man with the chef's hat watched Emelia finish eating before asking, "Can you cook?"

"Some," Emelia replied.

"Okay, you've been assigned to me. Tomorrow morning you will help me cook. I'll wake you up when it's time to start."

As Emelia was washing her plate, Carmila came into the kitchen. "Okay, princess. Time for bed."

That's when Emelia noticed the bruise on Carmila's cheekbone and her blood-red eyes as she followed Carmila out of the kitchen and down the series of hallways toward her room. When they reached her room, Emelia couldn't help but ask, "Why did they hurt you?"

"Not they. *He*. Diego."

"Diego?"

"Diego Cano. That's El Carnicero's real name. He's tried to fuck me many times, but he can't keep it up long enough. I don't know what his problem is. It's not me. I was stupid and reminded him that none of the other guys here had a problem getting it up for me. That's when he beat up on me and told me that if I mentioned it to any of the men, he'd gut me. He's a pig."

"Are you the only other girl here besides me?"

"No, there are at least two others here."

"You mean the two women I saw in the kitchen?"

"No. Those two women are being held for ransom. They were caught crossing the border like you were. They both had the identity of relatives here in the US and Diego expects the relatives will pay for him to let them go."

"What if they don't pay?"

"He'll kill them."

"Who are the other girls here?"

"They are both very young. The men here pass them around. They'll keep them locked in their rooms until they get tired of them, and then they'll get rid of them and bring in some new unlucky border crossers. If another man doesn't grab them then they'll be sent to the houses in Mexico."

"Houses?"

"Whorehouses. They'll be lucky to survive any length of time."

"Why are you still here?"

"I'm being held because they like to screw me, and they know I have a rich uncle in Mexico. I keep telling them he'll pay a lot for me."

"Have you tried to escape?"

"No, I haven't, but I had to watch what happened to a girl who did try. They hung her up by her arms in that big room, put a big washtub under her, and gutted her like a deer. They made everyone in the compound watch. I'll never forget it as long as I live. It took her a long time to die, and we had to watch until she did. The men even took bets on how long the poor girl would remain alive. Even if you tried to get out, it would be hard to do. The outside walls are eight feet tall with broken glass and barbed wire. The only entry is the front gate and it's always locked. The walls are not to keep people out. No one in their right mind would try to break into this place. The walls are to keep people in. Diego doesn't just keep girls here. Sometimes a young boy or, once, an entire family, will be kept here. Diego has a way of smelling money, and he'll squeeze it out of a turnip if he thinks he can. The cook told me that there is a single door somewhere in the back that opens up into another house outside the wall. That's where the men and the cook sleep. But even it is controlled by a lock that only a couple of people have a key for. My advice is just don't try it. Just try to stay as invisible as possible."

With that, Carmila closed the door, leaving Emelia feeling more alone and helpless than ever.

CHAPTER 17
The Plan

As Mark started to outline what he had in mind, he watched Samuel carefully to gauge his reaction. If they were going to use his approach, it would require a huge commitment plus a lot of trust from Samuel. Samuel didn't blink though. He was focused on only one thing and that was to find Emelia. He didn't know exactly why, but he trusted both Mark and Roe. There was an aura of strength and confidence that emanated from them both.

On its surface, the plan seemed crazy. It would require him to return to Mexico and go through the same dangerous process that had brought him here in the first place. There were so many things that could go wrong, but at this point he knew he had very few options acting alone.

Both Roe and Mark felt a degree of responsibility toward Samuel. They knew what a risk he would be taking, and although they were going to do everything in their power to protect him, they were concerned for his safety. He would be carrying the most advanced version of a tracking device. It was used by both the DEA and the Border Patrol. Roe had no problem in getting the device from her friend Angel Ruiz.

Mark and Roe left Samuel at the hotel, drove to an economically deprived area of El Paso, and stopped at a neighborhood convenience store. Mark went in and bought a couple of local newspapers and a sort of local swap shop paper. After they both looked in the auto sale sections, they wrote down three or four likely options. Using the payphone outside the store, Mark started making phone calls. He finally appeared to get what he was looking for and went back to where Roe was waiting in his car. He told Roe, "I don't want you or my car seen with me. Park at that gas station across the street and watch. If you see me get in a car and drive it away, you'll know I made a good transaction. Head back to the hotel and I'll meet you there."

Moving into the driver's seat, Roe took Mark's SUV across the street and parked so that she had a view of the convenience store. Mark went back into the store and bought a bottle of water, then came back outside to wait. It was not long before a beat-up gray older model Toyota sedan drove into the store's parking lot. A lady wearing hospital scrubs got out of the car and looked around until her eyes settled on Mark, who walked toward her. He estimated her to be in her early forties and her light brown skin and jet-black hair indicated a Hispanic background. She spoke first, "You must be Mr. Smith?"

"Yes, and you must be Mariane. Tell me, Mariane, why are you selling your car? It's an older model, but these cars are good for a lot of miles."

"Mr. Smith, I do hate to sell it. I've taken good care of it. My problem is that I need an SUV so I can easily carry my son's wheelchair. He has spina bifida. It's a special chair that can't be collapsed and it just won't fit in this car's trunk. The lid won't go all the way down. I've tried to trade it in with several dealers, but they won't give me what it's worth for scrap. Mark knew exactly what she meant. It might be sexist to say it, but most single women were sitting ducks when they walked into a car dealership.

"What's the best offer you've gotten?"

When she told him, Mark could only shake his head.

"Do you have the title?"

"Yes, It's in the car."

Mark walked around the car looking at the tires before asking her to start the car and open the hood. Mark listened to the engine as he looked carefully into the engine compartment. He then kneeled down and looked under the car. Standing back up, he told her to turn off the engine. "What if I gave you four times what your best offer was? Would that help you out? It would be cash of course."

Mariane had a sudden look of shock on her face as she computed Mark's offer in her mind. "Are you serious?"

Mark reached into a front pocket of his pants and took out a flat stack of hundred-dollar bills and counted out the amount.

"If you'll get the title out and sign it, it's a done deal."

Mariane wasted no time in taking the title out of the glove box and signing the part authorizing a transfer of title.

When she handed the title to Mark, her hands were shaking, and there were tears in her eyes. Mark smiled and said, "Why don't you sit down in the car, count this out, and put it somewhere safe. It's probably not a good idea to be standing in the front of this place counting money. Do I need to drive you home?"

"No. My sister planned to come pick me up if I sold the car."

Mariane sat in the car with Mark until her sister arrived to pick her up. "Mr. Smith, I don't why you're doing this, but God bless you. You have no idea what this means to me."

Mark watched her leave before cranking up the car and driving back to the hotel. He laughed at himself. He'd either just done a good deed or he'd just been conned. Either way, he had an anonymous disposable car that couldn't be traced back to him. He made one stop at a Walmart before he left the area and bought a couple changes of work clothes. He managed to find cargo pants with huge pockets that were big enough to be loose on him. He also found work boots that had thinner soles so he wouldn't look any taller than necessary.

By the time Mark returned to the hotel, Roe had already made arrangements with her friend Angel Ruiz to provide a temporary visa for Samuel to enter Mexico from the US. Angel was curious but didn't question Roe's intentions. Mark had brought a 357 Charter Arms target bulldog among other guns, which were in the rear of his SUV. The gun was one that had been traded for something out his dad's hardware store many years ago and there was no record that connected him to the firearm. Rather than trying to hide it in the car, Mark just put it in one of the large pockets of his cargo pants. He put a leather sap in another pocket. The odds of actually being searched when traveling into Mexico were slim.

By late afternoon, Mark and Samuel were appropriately dressed and waiting at the border in a long line of cars carrying people returning to Mexico after a hard day's work in the US of A.

CHAPTER 18

1972

The Plomeros were loaded in the Huey, following the river until they were out of any area of habitation before swinging south. Soon after entering Mexico, the chopper swung back toward the main highway. Once they identified the road, they ran without lights with the moonlight and the lights of vehicles on the road guiding the way. When they approached within several miles of the target, the chopper swung away from the small town and approached it from the south and behind the facility. Ron eased the power back as much as he could before gently setting down a couple hundred yards from the plant. Ron stayed with the Huey, leaving it running.

Just like the first mission, everyone knew their part as they headed toward the buildings. Each one of them had a large heavy tennis bag hanging from their shoulders. From their other shoulder, hanging by a sling, was a 9mm Heckler & Koch MP5SD suppressed machine gun. The guns had collapsible stocks and were set to fire a three-round burst each time the trigger was pulled. Each gun was loaded with a thirty-round magazine, and everyone carried two extra ones on a utility belt.

All of the buildings were well lit, especially the grow area that was housed under acres of glass. As they got closer to the buildings, they split up. Mark and Rosa went off to

the right toward what was assumed to be the processing
and shipping area. Lou and Marcus went straight ahead
toward the growing area. Rich went to the left toward
the generator plant, which was separated from the main
buildings. Next to the generating plant were the huge
propane tanks that were mounted on concrete supports.

As Mark and Rosa approached the processing plant,
they could see a large loading dock. They were almost to
the dock itself when a door opened, and a woman walked
out onto the dock with a quizzical look on her face. She
was holding an AK-47 casually by her side. Before the
woman was even aware of their presence, Rosa had fired
one three-round burst and the woman dropped like a rock.
Quickly climbing up on the dock, they stood one on each
side of the open door, expecting someone to follow the
woman out. The suppressor on the MP5 had done a good
job of silencing the shots. When they looked into the
room, the sheer size was impressive. There were literally
hundreds of pallets stacked with bundles of what must be
Montezuma Green waiting to be shipped.

When they slipped through the door, Mark went to
the right and Rosa went left. Two workers immediately
stepped out of a side door and instinctively Mark shot
them both. As he approached the door, he could hear
noises like chairs scraping the floor and raised voices. He
took a fragmentation grenade from a section of the tennis
bag and threw it into the room while firing several bursts
through the door at the same time. He moved to the side
of the door before the grenade went off. The second after
the grenade exploded, he stepped back into the room.

It must have been break time, because there were at
least twenty people in varying stages of distress lying or
trying to stand. It was a mess. He saw only one weapon
as a man tried to raise it toward Mark. With no hesitation

Mark methodically put one three-round burst into him. Looking around the room, he didn't see any other threats, only dead or dying people. Leaving the room, he could see Rosa fire at something but couldn't see her target. After the grenade had exploded, he knew their presence was no longer a secret. He'd reached the end of the room before he met up with Rosa. The end of the warehouse was lined with ovens for drying the plants.

"Rosa, we need to start with the incendiaries."

"Roger that, Mark. Let's hope everyone else is on the same schedule."

Lou and Marcus were indeed setting off several chemical grenades as they retreated back across the growing area. At the center of the huge greenhouse was a room where they kept all the chemicals and fertilizers. They watched as two workers ran into the room, probably planning to hide there.

"Bad choice," said Lou.

Marcus told Lou, "When we throw the incendiaries in this area, we need to run like scalded dogs, or we'll be ones ourselves."

"Got it," Lou replied as he reached into his tennis bag for an incendiary grenade.

Meanwhile, Rich Holtz, the demolition specialist, was in his element. The decision to have him go alone to the generators was based on the theory that at this time of the night, it would be unlikely anyone would be there. It was reasonable to make that assumption, but, in this case, they hadn't counted on Juan and Gloria using their break time to sneak into the generator building for a little fun time. The steady hum of the generators hid the sound Rich made as he hurried toward the rear of the building. As he rounded one of the huge machines, he tripped over something and fell, sliding across the floor. As he stood up and turned around, he saw Juan trying to step into his pants while Gloria was covering herself with a handful of her clothes. Rich didn't see any weapons, so he waved his arm and said "Vamos" as the frightened couple ran into the night trying to put on clothes as they ran.

He continued on toward the back of the building where he started throwing incendiary grenades as far as he could while retreating rapidly from the ensuing firestorm. An incendiary grenade will burn at 4300 degrees and was developed specifically for burning things up. He threw a grenade under each generator, and as he came to the last one where he'd tripped over Juan and Gloria, he realized that he'd made a tactical error in letting the couple go when he saw Juan coming back toward him carrying an AK-47.

When he saw Rich, he raised his gun and fired. Rich instinctively dropped to one knee, firing at the same time. The rounds from Juan's Kalashnikov knocked Rich's hat off his head. Juan wasn't so lucky, as two 9mm rounds hit him in his stomach. When Rich approached where Juan lay clutching his stomach and staring expectantly, Rich looked at him and said, "Sorry, buddy, but I'm doing you a favor. This is easier than burning up." He fired two bursts into Juan. When he came back outside, the entire building was starting to glow red. He ran to the area where the propane tanks were mounted, and from a distance, he threw several incendiaries toward the tanks. With his knowledge of explosives, Rich knew that some huge explosions were imminent, and it was time to run.

By now everyone had worked their way back through each building, leaving incendiaries in their paths. They all exited the buildings within a few seconds of each other and headed back toward the Huey. Suddenly, seemingly out of nowhere, a truck with a fifty-caliber machine gun mounted over the cab came around the burning buildings from the direction of the town. Fortunately, the driver was so focused on the buildings, he didn't see the idling helicopter in the distance. As the truck roared toward the retreating Plomeros, the machine gun opened fire. The distance between the retreating group was still too great for the MP5s to be effective and the fifty-caliber was zeroing in on the group. They were saved by the pilot Ron Lassiter, who had retained the Browning BAR from the earlier mission. He fired the entire magazine toward the cab of the truck. It was well within the range of the BAR and the result caused the truck to veer off course and straight toward the burning buildings. The men in the rear of the truck who were manning the machine gun bailed out as the truck continued down the sloped loading dock and into the concrete wall.

Mark yelled, "Everybody keep going! I'll make sure they're not trying to follow us. While the group ran to the helicopter, Mark lay down in a clump of grass and waited. Just as he'd suspected, three men were running toward the Huey. Two of them carried AK-47s and the third one a handgun. Mark waited until they were within twenty yards before he fired his MP5 ten times, sending out thirty rounds of hot 9mm rounds. The three men were caught by surprise and not one of them had time to react and fire back. By the time Mark reached the copter, everyone was onboard, and as Mark threw himself inside, it lifted off. When the Huey had enough height, they could see the result of their action. The only disappointment was the lack of fire from the growing areas. Not seeing any other approaching vehicles, Mark asked Ron to hold up before leaving. He had everyone put all of their remaining grenades in his tennis bag.

The Huey picked up speed and swooped down as low as Ron could safely go. As the chopper passed over the grow area, Mark threw out the bag now loaded with fragmentation and incendiary grenades over the glass enclosure. There could be no doubt now as the entire grow area lit up like the Fourth of July. There was going to be a severe shortage of Montezuma Green for some time to come.

Chapter 19
Emelia

Emelia lost all track of time. The cook would come get her every morning. She'd spend the day in the kitchen doing whatever the cook directed her to do. The cook, whose name was Arturo, turned out to be an okay guy. He soon learned to appreciate her help in the kitchen. When she had to venture out into the large eating and meeting area, she was pretty much left alone. She did get a few leers and covetous glances, but never when El Carnicero was present. She knew she was fortunate at the present as she watched the way Carmila and some of the other girls that passed through were treated. There wasn't a single one of the men in the group who had any vestige of decency. It was as if they had to outdo each other in terms of crudeness and cruelty. Next to Diego, the one called Bruno was the worst. The things he made Carmila and any of the other girls do in front of the others was so degrading that Emelia thought she'd kill herself if she were subjected to the same treatment.

One morning when she came into the kitchen, one of the two older women was sitting at the table with her head cradled in her arms and sobbing like a baby. Emelia put her hand on the woman's shoulder and asked, "Are you okay? Is there anything I can do?"

The woman only answered, "She's gone. They gave up on getting any ransom from her relatives. They came for her this morning. She won't be coming back."

Emelia didn't know what to say. When she looked at Arturo, he only shrugged and shook his head.

They came for Emelia when she was least expecting it. Sometime late at night, the door to her room was thrown open and she was blinded by a bright flashlight. El Carnicero himself pulled her off her cot and told her to stand up.

Just as he'd done before, he said, "Take off that shirt." Emelia was sleeping in a huge old T-shirt that reached to her knees like a nightshirt. When she hesitated, he grabbed the T-shirt with both hands and jerked it over her head.

"Don't make the Señor wait, chica."

Still in a state of shock, Emelia felt the light from the flashlight roam over her body.

Again, Diego told her, "Turn around, chica, so he can get a good look."

Emelia couldn't see much of the other man, because she was still partially blinded by the bright light. She could only tell that it was another man, and that he was wearing a heavy gold necklace, but she couldn't see his face. When he spoke, he only said, "You were right, Diego. I thank you for saving her for me. Get her ready."

CHAPTER 20

Second Crossing

Crossing the border and entering Mexico was a non-event. Mark and Samuel were waved through with hardly a glance from agents on either side of the border. The car Mark had bought seemed to drive okay. The only thing Mark had done was to put four new tires on the car plus a new spare in the trunk. He'd also bought a large gas can, which he filled up and placed in the trunk. They drove through the city to the major highway that led south. Mark wanted to retrace the route far enough south before Samuel joined a group of migrants headed north. It was important that he establish some credibility by blending in with a group of travelers who had come a long way. Mark thought that if he appeared out of nowhere in the city, there might be some question of his background.

Samuel had told Mark and Roe that as he, Emelia, and Jonas Atelus approached the city of Juárez, there was a point where two northbound routs converged. It was at this point that different alliances were formed for the purpose of crossing the border. Samuel was confident that he would be able to hook up with a group with no questions asked. The trick would be to associate himself with the right group.

It was only a three- or four-hour walk into the city from this point. As he explained to Mark, during the journey from Santiago, Chile to the US border he'd learned how to survive on the road, and he felt comfortable blending in. There were different areas covered with makeshift tents. Multiple campfires created a smoky atmosphere. In some places, small children ran and played in the dirt. Further on, there was a commercial district with small grocery stores and shops selling cheap clothing. Having arrived so close to the US border, there was an almost euphoric and carnival atmosphere among the various groups.

Mark drove off the main road and into a section of dilapidated houses. He went down a dead-end street that ended at the edge of the desert.

"Samuel, let's make sure you've got everything. Money is strapped to your leg, and you're going to buy yourself a cell phone. You know my number as well as Roe's."

"I'm ready to go, Mark. Don't think I'm crazy when I get out of the car and roll in the dirt. I was almost always dirty before. I know how I'm supposed to look."

When he got out of the car, Samuel did indeed roll on the ground and drag his hat through the dirt a few times before shaking it out and crumpling it up. He looked at Mark once more and smiled before walking back toward the main road. Mark was impressed. Samuel was voluntarily going back into the lion's den. Knowing Samuel's previous border crossing experience, Mark realized the courage required for him to do it again.

Mark started the car and headed back the way they'd come. He headed back toward Juárez and started looking for a motel on the main route into the city.

Meanwhile, Samuel walked back toward the area with the shops. He saw a shop that had used backpacks hanging on an outside wall. He selected a well-worn one and went inside the store and picked out a few other worn pieces of clothing plus a cheap cell phone good for ninety days' service. He traded his new cap for a worn cap with the logo of a famous Mexican soccer team. He now felt like he could reenter the migrant world as a weary traveler. As he got closer to where most of the migrants were camped out, he stopped at a sad looking restaurant covered with a rusted tin roof and an outdoor bar area in the front. A makeshift awning, held up by thin wooden poles, covered three plastic tables and chairs, extended out from one end of the main structure. The bar consisted of several long boards held up by two stacks of concrete blocks. There were several coolers with ice sitting behind it. He sat up close to the bar on a stool that rocked when he moved. He paid for the beer—which the seedy-looking man behind the bar picked out of one of the ice chests—with an American twenty dollar bill, making sure the bartender saw the roll of bills in his hand.

"Are you planning to cross into the US, my friend?"

"Yes. I was traveling with a group that had it already set up, but we got separated when a group of Mexican police raided our camp. I'm afraid some of them were arrested and now I've got to start over to find a guide."

"Do you know who you were supposed to meet?"

"No. All I know is that they said it was the group that controlled this section of the border, and they were the safest and most reliable."

"Where are you going once you cross?"

"I have an uncle who is a US citizen. He lives in Jacksonville, Florida. I know he has a big house, and he has two new cars. He's promised me a job if I can get there."

"You know, my friend, that it takes a lot of money to make it safely across the border?"

Samuel knew that he was setting himself up as he spoke. "I've been saving for this for a long time. If I need more money, I'm sure my uncle Martin will help me."

"You are fortunate indeed. Most people passing through have little money and no prospects in the US even if they can make it over. I'm trying to think of the name of the people who might help someone like yourself. What is your name?"

Samuel quietly took five of the twenties out his pocket and laid them on the bar with one hand covering them.

Leaving his hand firmly on the bills, he told the bartender, "My name is Samuel Orasme. Maybe you can think of a name while I'm finishing my beer."

"Just a moment," replied the man as he disappeared behind the coolers. When he stepped back out, he was holding a card in his hand, which he slid across the bare planks toward Samuel's hand that was covering the money. Samuel looked at the card. It had printed on one side, *Travel Associates*, and on the back was a handwritten phone number and the name Raul.

"I think these are the people who may be able to help you, Samuel."

Samuel looked at the bartender before lifting his hand off the money. "Señor, if you are playing me for a fool, you will see me again."

His money swiftly disappeared behind the bar as the man replied, "Do not worry. I cannot afford to cheat my customers. I have done business at this place for a long time."

Samuel took his time slowly nursing his beer while watching the different groups of migrants. He didn't see the bartender disappear again behind the coolers and make a call on his cell phone because he was intently watching the different groups as they passed the bar. He soon saw what he was looking for. A group of maybe forty to fifty people were starting to move northward up the road. Leaving the bar, he joined them as if he'd been with them all along. No one paid any attention to him, because as he remembered from his previous journey, this was a mixing point. Some had stayed to rest longer, and some had merged with others to continue northward. The important rule was to stay with a group. The larger the group, the less chance of rape or robbery. The downside was the larger the group, the more attention you got from the Mexican authorities.

As he walked, he looked around at the people in the caravan. It didn't take him long to realize the group was almost completely made up of younger males very similar to himself. There were also cliques within the group. Most of the travelers had cell phones and there was always someone talking on their phone at any given time. When he used his phone to call Mark's number, no one paid any attention. Mark answered almost immediately. Samuel simply said, "I have a name and number."

Mark replied, "Stay on the main road coming into the city. I'm in the Motel La Sinca. If you stay on the main road, you'll reach a large roundabout where five main arteries into the city converge. It's along the side of the overpass. You might have to ask someone because it's off the main roads. Call me when you get here, and I'll meet you out toward the front."

Samuel stayed with the group, which was beginning to thin out as they entered the city. As they approached the roundabout, the group had shrunk down to only a few who seemed confused about where to go next. The area was mostly commercial, and everything nearby seemed to be low rent. Samuel had no problem dropping out of the group and heading toward the only group of shops and restaurants he could see. He saw the name of the hotel on a sign with an arrow pointing around a corner. He called Mark again, and after couple of minutes, Mark came out of the front of the motel to meet Samuel. As instructed, Samuel ignored Mark but followed him around to the side of the motel and out of sight of the street before Mark spoke to him.

"I need to let you know what to ask for when you register. This is a low rent, but it fits our needs perfectly. Because of where it's located it has to have some security. The entire motel is within a walled-off area, and car parking for occupants is inside the compound. But first you need to register for a room on your own. Tell the clerk that you want a room in the new section that was just remodeled. That should put your room close to mine. They are catering to migrants, but it won't hurt to flash your roll of American dollars. Once you get your room, casually walk to my room, make sure no one is paying attention, and come inside. I'm anxious to see if the phone number you got from the bartender will pay off."

Samuel had no problem getting a room and having US dollars helped speed it up. There were several people in the registration area, which was connected to a small dining area. There were what were probably migrant children playing cards at one of the tables. The parents were busy with their cell phones. No one paid any attention to Samuel. He didn't have to work hard in order to blend into a role he was intimately familiar with.

After he'd paid for his room, he located it in the newer section just as Mark had described. He washed the grime of the road from his face before walking down to Mark's room. The rooms were all located on a walkway around a courtyard. Mark's room was only two doors down from his. There were more kids splashing in a small pool in the center of the courtyard. The pool was filled with questionable light green water. Once he was inside Mark's room,

Samuel gave Mark a detailed summary of his interaction with the bartender.

"Samuel, I'm beginning to think you were some sort of secret agent in your past. You handled yourself well. Now let's see what happens when we make the phone call."

Samuel took out the card he'd been given and dialed the number. A voice answered, "Yes?"

Samuel asked to speak to Raul.

CHAPTER 21

1972

Everyone was wired and wide awake on the ride back to their hangar home. Instead of immediately going to bed after securing all their armament in a safe room, they all met in the lounge. Mark proposed a toast to the pilot Ron Lassiter for his support. "If Ron hadn't had the presence of mind to bring the BAR and the ability to use it, we may not be here now."

Eventually fatigue set in for everyone. Before they separated, Rosa said, "Let's meet tomorrow afternoon at four. I should have our next assignment by then."

Everyone drifted off to bed, but Mark was still wide awake and remained in the lounge deep in thought. He eventually realized that he wasn't alone. Rosa was still sitting in a chair behind him. She asked, "Nightcap?"

"Sure," Mark replied. "What can I get you?"

"I'll just have a cup of that coffee you're drinking."

Mark stood up and got another cup of coffee for himself and one for her. He sat in a chair opposite her and propped his feet up on another chair before speaking. "Somehow, I think I should be feeling some sort of remorse for what we've done, but I don't."

"Mark, believe me. If you only knew the misery these people have created, you wouldn't even be asking yourself that question."

"How did you end up doing this?"

"Both my parents were lawyers who worked for the Mexican government. We lived in Mexico City. They were associated with the part of the government that really wanted to prosecute the cartels, and my parents wouldn't accept any bribes. They were both horribly tortured and killed, along with my twin brother who just happened to be there. I was away on a school trip out of town, or I'd have been killed as well. The American ambassador was good friends with my family, and he took it upon himself to bring me back to the States as a part of his family. Since both my parents had come to Mexico from Colombia, I had no other relatives in Mexico. I was only twelve at the time, but my English was perfect, and I was able to adapt quickly. But I never forgot why my family was killed and who did it. Everything I've done from that point on was to put myself in position to hurt the cartels any way I could. I don't mean it as a boast, but I don't think anyone alive knows more about the Mexican drug trade than me. Being picked for this mission, was a dream come true. So, no, I have no remorse and I don't want you or any of the others to feel any either."

"Do you have any idea which cartel was responsible for your family's death?"

"Yes. We're working our way toward the family that runs the cartel. I know where they are most of the time and I'm waiting until the time is right. They've got to be in the right place at the right time for us to be able to hit them. And don't worry, Mark, my desire for revenge is not clouding my commitment to this mission, nor will I put any of us at increased risks just to satisfy my personal vendetta. Anything we can do to hurt the drug trade is good. Avenging my family would only be icing on the cake."

"What you've told me explains what I've wondered about. I've watched how you act without hesitation or emotion. I understand now. It helps me understand something about my father that I never understood. He never talked much about his experience in World War II. I only know that he was sent into Europe well before Normandy and was involved in a mission that involved Dachau. I don't think he ever recovered from what he experienced. Just promise me that you'll let me know when our mission targets the ones responsible for your family's deaths. It will give additional meaning to the mission."

"I promise I will, Mark. And please keep this conversation private. I feel good working with you. You have something special. I can see why you were picked for this team."

Mark stood up to say good night. "And if I don't get some sleep, I won't be good for anybody."

The next morning, Rosa was up before anyone else, and by four o'clock she was outlining their next outing.

"There's a border bridge six hundred miles south of us that's in an area of really rough terrain. It's out in nowhere land. The bridge was built by Osterfeldt Chemical Company. I'm sure you've all heard the name. They have mines in Mexico, but their processing plant is on the US side. They built the bridge at their own expense just to haul the ore from the mine to the plant.

"Part of the agreement they made with the government was that they would provide personnel to monitor noncompany bridge crossings. It's been a disaster. It's being used time and time again by the cartel to haul everything from pot, cocaine, and gang members into the US. It's just too easy to bribe an employee to be asleep at night when their vehicles cross. It's so secluded that our government won't put out the funds to operate a border station at the bridge. There is a small settlement growing on the Mexican side. It's become a prolific crossing point for them. We've not been allowed to officially intervene because the chemical company has so much political clout in DC. I think that now is the time to intervene. The site is well out of the helicopter's range, but there's a small landing strip near the plant on the US side that's within two miles of the bridge. We'll land there and hike to the bridge crossing point. Same as before, let's look at the maps and aerials and make a plan. I'm waiting for more information about the times they'll be sending shipments. By the time it's a go, we'll be ready to leave at a moment's notice."

CHAPTER 22
Ciudad Juárez

"Raul, my name is Samuel Orasme, and I'm looking for a way to cross into the US. The person who gave me this card said you might help me."

"Did the person tell you how much it would cost?"

"No."

"Just to get you across the river will cost five thousand American dollars. To get you further into the US will cost a lot more. Do you have the money?"

Samuel answered carefully, knowing full well that he was continuing to set himself up as a vulnerable target. "I can pay to cross the river. I can get more money from my uncle in Jacksonville to get me there. He is a rich man."

"Where are you now?"

"I'm spending the night in a motel on the edge of the city."

"Do you have a pen and paper?"

"Just a minute. Let me get my backpack." Samuel made some noise as if searching before replying, "Okay."

The voice on the phone gave Samuel an address which he wrote down.

"Come to this address within the next twenty-four hours. A crossing is scheduled soon. This might be a way for you to make some additional money if you're interested."

"Yes, I am!"

"Good. Tell them Raul sent you," was the last Samuel heard before the line clicked dead.

The phone had been set on speakerphone and Mark had heard the entire conversation.

"This may be what we're looking for," Mark said as he was looking up the address on a map. "They won't be expecting you before tomorrow, so let's go to the restaurant next door and eat. We'll get you set up tonight so you can start out early. I'll drive you part of the way and you can walk the remainder of the way, so you'll look authentic."

There was a small restaurant just around the corner from the motel. They found an empty table near the rear and ordered. The menu was limited but the food was good. While they ate, Mark explained to Samuel how the transmitter worked. "You don't realize it, but you've been wearing it ever since we left Texas. Remember when I brought you the belt you're wearing and told you to wear it because it might help identify you from a distance in a group if your face wasn't visible? See the brass objects imbedded in the belt? One of them is what the satellites can see. The beauty of this one is that the receiver, which Roe is operating in Texas, can track you almost anywhere on the planet. If you're out in the open it will show your location within three meters. Unless you go into a tunnel or a basement in a large building, it won't lose you. Roe told me they often put them in cell phones, but because they took your cell phones before, we can't trust that you'll be keeping yours. Even if they scan you for a wire, nothing will be picked up because it's not emitting a signal. But, the satellites are able to track it. Our biggest question is going to be when to intercede. Do we do something at the address you're going to, or before? If this group is the Mendez Cartel, then you should be okay. I'm thinking they will see value in you as a potential source of more money from your uncle once you've crossed into the US.

"I think that is true. Every time I mention my uncle and more money, I can almost hear them salivating."

"Samuel, it is a pleasure to be your Uncle Martin. My cell number has a Jacksonville area code, so they shouldn't question it. As long as I don't have to show up in person, we'll be okay. They might question the difference in our skin color."

Samuel smiled at Mark's comment. "I can't imagine why."

"It might be a good idea if you'd call my number now just to have it visible in your phone in case anyone looks at your recent calls."

The next morning, Mark drove Samuel toward the address he'd been given. They followed one of the main roads leading from their motel toward the eastern part of the city. Juárez was a poor city even in its better parts and most all neighborhoods were an accumulation of small concrete cells packed tightly together along narrow streets badly in need of repair. Most houses were surrounded by high cinder block walls with either solid gates or fences made from every type of fencing material from iron bars to corrugated steel and razor wire. Yards or lawns were nonexistent and consisted of just enough room to park a couple of vehicles inside the wall. There would be an attractive-looking house behind a fence only to be sitting between two houses that could be derelict junkyards complete with barking Pit Bulls.

Mark discreetly dropped Samuel off well before they reached the area of the house. Mark continued driving on toward the address. The actual location was slightly more upscale than most of the neighborhoods they'd driven through. The neighborhood wouldn't have been considered upscale in the US, but there were many homes that were very individualized, and the front courtyards were larger and well cared for. The house was at the end of a street with a tall block wall separating it from a vacant lot on the corner. The lot had several cars parked randomly as well as a tired old school bus. The house was an anomaly because there was no wall, gate, or fence closing off the courtyard. Two sets of bare concrete strips provided parking for two vehicles, but there were none present at the moment. Several houses down from the address and across the street next to a small grocery store was the Hotel Gloria. A two-story structure, it sported a single door set back off the street as well as two large wooden garage-type doors with no windows. There was a balcony with decorative iron rails extending across the entire second floor. Several iron tables and chairs were visible on the balcony.

Acting on pure impulse, Mark parked on the street and entered the hotel through the single entrance door leading into a tiny room with a counter. There was no one there, but there was a bell hanging over the counter which he rang. Almost immediately, an older woman appeared out of the door behind the counter.

"May I help you?" she asked in Spanish.

"Do you have a room available?" Mark replied, speaking in Spanish as well.

"Yes, for how long will you need it?"

"I'm not sure. Do you have a safe place for me to park my car?"

"Yes, but it will cost more."

"That's okay. What is the balcony for?"

"Upstairs we have a small bar, and we serve breakfast and dinner for those that want it."

"Can I get a room close to the front then?"

The lady might have been old, but she was shrewd as well. She sensed money when she replied, "Yes, but it will cost more."

Mark had to smile. "That's okay."

After paying the lady for two days in advance, Mark hurried back out to his car, and by the time he'd backed his car back up to the hotel, one of the wooden garage doors was opened. The young boy who opened the door closed it behind Mark as he drove into a surprisingly large courtyard that extended all the way to the back of the building. There was an iron gate across the rear, and the boy explained to Mark that when was ready to leave, he'd just drive out the gate into an alley which led to the street. Mark thought to himself that he couldn't have planned it any better if he'd tried.

Mark had just sat down on the hotel patio when Samuel came around the street corner looking for the right house. When he'd found it, he walked up to the door and knocked. Mark watched as the door opened and Samuel disappeared inside.

CHAPTER 23

Emelia

Diego ordered Emelia to get dressed. He stood leering and holding the light on her as she dressed as quickly as she could.

"Follow me," he said after she was dressed. She followed him until they came out in the large courtyard. There was a newer model passenger van with windows on the sides.

"Get in," Diego ordered. When Emelia climbed into a back row seat, she realized she was not alone. There were at least two other women sitting in the van. No one said a word as a man got into the driver's seat and a female sat down in the front passenger seat. The gate was opened, and the van drove out of the compound. The van was soon out of the city and was traveling at speed on a major highway. Unable to sleep, Emelia watched the barren countryside slip past until a faint light of dawn begin to appear in the direction they were traveling. By now she desperately needed to pee. Almost as if the driver were reading her mind, the van slowed and pulled into a rest stop. The driver turned in his seat and addressed the three women in the rear.

"Good morning, ladies. My name is Miguel. This is Belinda sitting here with me. We are going to set up some rules of the road. Rule number one: You only speak to

Belinda or me. Never speak to anyone other than us. Rule number two: Never wander away from us. This is going to be a long drive, and if you do as we say it will be a pleasant drive. If you break our rules, it will become a very unpleasant drive. Does everyone understand? Nod your head if you do. Good. Now you can all follow Belinda into the women's restrooms. If you need to pee as badly as I do, it will make you all happy."

Everyone left the van and headed toward the restrooms, with the men's room on the left and women to the right. Belinda simply said, "Stay close to me."

In the early morning light, Emelia could clearly see the other two women for the first time. One had very light skin and the other had a decidedly dark skin with high cheekbones. Both would be considered to be beautiful except for the looks of despair that was evident on their faces. Emelia realized they were very similar to herself. They were definitely not here of their own choosing. Belinda watched closely as they all used separate stalls. When they came out, each one of them took advantage of the sinks to wash faces and hands. They followed Belinda back to the van where Miguel was waiting. After the three women were seated again, Belinda said, "My turn," and went back to the restroom.

After leaving the rest stop, Miguel turned off the freeway at the next exit and went through a fast food drive through. Not bothering to ask anyone, he ordered burgers, fries, and soft drinks for everyone. Eating as he drove, Miguel reentered the turnpike and continued east. Belinda took food out of a bag before passing it back to the three women in the rear, saying with a smile, "Eat up."

The van trip seemed to go on forever. The only stops were for gas, restroom breaks, and drives through fast food restaurants. Miguel and Belinda shared driving. One would drive and the other would sleep. Emelia recognized the road as I-10. During times when she was awake, she recognized the names of San Antonio, Baton Rouge, Pensacola, and Tallahassee. After Tallahassee the road changed to I-75 and then to Florida's Turnpike.

During the trip, the three women in the rear were allowed to talk among themselves. Emelia learned that the dark-skinned woman was from Somalia. The other was from Argentina. All three were of similar age and each one shared the same experience of having been separated from their traveling companions while crossing into the US, although neither of the other two women had experienced a massacre as Emelia had done. None of them had any idea of where they were headed or why. When they passed West Palm Beach, all three knew enough about US geography to realize there were not many destinations left in the direction they were heading.

All three girls were awake and alert at this point, because they knew they had to be nearing their destination. Suddenly, after passing West Palm Beach, the van turned off the interstate and traveled east toward the coast. Eventually the road ended when it reached the coastline, and the van turned toward the north. The ocean side of the road was lined with thick heavy foliage that hid the enormous houses overlooking the beach. They had occasional glimpses of towering rooftops or vast walls of marble. The ocean was hidden behind the curving driveways that led from the opulent iron gates and into the green mansions beyond. It was as if the wealthy owners of the opulent oceanfront homes were entitled to ownership of any view of the ocean as well.

The van turned off the road and stopped in front of a huge, black gate supported by tall columns on either side. Miguel drove up to a small stone column with a built-in speaker and pushed a button. After a couple of minutes, a garbled voice replied, "Okay."

By the time Miguel had rolled his window back up, the two large sections of the gate were already slowly separating and sliding open to the right and left, leaving the driveway open for passage. The brick road passed through a veritable tunnel of green before emerging into a huge courtyard. Emelia glimpsed a tennis court and a large building off toward one side. As the van followed the circular brick driveway curving around the front of the house, Emelia's breath was taken away by the scope and grandeur of the main building. The van continued to follow a driveway around one end of the main house, leading to the side of a two-story extension of the main building. At the end it opened into a huge parking area with several large garage doors on the sides. One of the doors was open and Miguel drove through the open door before stopping inside.

Belinda opened the rear van door and said, "Okay, ladies. Out you go. Follow me." Zombie-like, they followed her through a door at the back of the garage and into a hallway where a set of stairs on either end led up toward a second floor. A large, closed door in the center of the wall looked as if it might lead toward the main building.

Belinda led them up the stairs to the second floor and into a hallway covered with a plush carpet. There were multiple doors fronting onto the hallway. Standing in the hallway waiting for them was a tall slim woman, maybe in her fifties. She was dressed in a black, expensive, silk pantsuit. Her hair was pulled back tightly in a bun. She was holding a large ring with keys in one hand. Belinda said, "Girls, this is Ava. She's in charge now. Take my advice and do as she says. Life will be so much easier for you," was the last thing she said as she turned and disappeared back down the stairs.

Ava stood for a moment looking at the three confused and frightened girls before she used a key on the ring she was holding to open one of the doors. She pointed at Selma and Mariana and said, "This will be your room for now." Pointing at Emelia, she said, "You take the next room."

Not knowing what to expect, Emelia went through the open door into a room that was worlds apart from the one she'd been shoved into back in Texas. This room could have been a luxury room in a Hilton or a Hyatt. She was immediately aware that there was another person in the room. The room contained two twin beds and there was a girl propped up on pillows on the bed reading a magazine.

"Meet your roommate Katrina. There are clothes in the closet. Something should fit you. Someone will come get you later and take you to eat." With that last statement, she closed the door and Emelia could hear the lock click.

Looking around the room, Emelia walked to a window that did not open and was probably unbreakable hurricane glass.

Katrina smiled and asked, "What is your name?" She had a pronounced accent that Emelia didn't recognize.

"Emelia."

"Where did you come from?"

Not really sure how to answer, Emelia simply said, "South America."

In despair, she sat on the empty bed. "I don't understand what I'm doing here or why."

Katrina said, "I was the same. I didn't understand either. I came from Russia to America thinking I was going to be married to a rich bachelor. This was not what I expected."

"What do you mean?"

"You really don't have any idea why you're here, do you?"

"No."

"Well, you'll find out soon enough. The only good part is that they'll let you keep any tips you might get."

"Tips?"

"For doing a good job and making them happy."

"Making who happy?"

"Whoever Andre wants to reward."

"I still don't understand."

Exasperated by Emelia's lack of understanding, Katrina finally said, "You fuck them and whatever else they want."

Everything hit Emelia at once. How could she have not recognized why they'd looked at her the way they had? Everything Carmila told her suddenly made sense. She was just like Carmila except on a more sophisticated level. Gulping air, she walked to the window and looked out.

Katrina said, "You won't get away from here. They watch you all the time. If you try to fight or resist, they'll hurt you. My last roommate tried to run but never made it out of this compound. She just disappeared. We were told that she was having to work in a far worse place now. At least here you are safe, and the food is good."

Emelia sat back down on the bed in despair. So much for coming to America, the land of the free.

CHAPTER 24

Samuel

As Mark watched Samuel disappear through the door of the house, he had to acknowledge his growing admiration of the young man. Mark was again impressed at the strength and courage that Samuel was showing. But then it was not hard to remember his own sense of determination when his daughter had been killed. The drive that had pushed him to find her killers had been reawakened after learning that one of those responsible was still living and thriving. Roe, who was also a victim of Andre Mendez's cruelty, was having the same reaction. Just as he thought of Roe, she called him on his cell phone.

"Mark, I'm tracking both Samuel and your car. It looks as if you're next door to each other."

"Good to know the trackers are working so well." He went on to explain to Roe about the opportunity to observe from the hotel balcony.

"Mark, you are amazing. I'll never understand how you make things happen like you do. What do you think we should do next?"

"Roe, since I've gotten this observation point, let's just sit and watch for the moment. We know we can always come back to this point if all else fails. I'm curious to see who comes and goes from the house. Why don't you take a break and rest? I'll let you know if Samuel leaves the house so you can track him again."

"Be careful, Mark."

Mark had been sitting on the end of the patio bar far enough from the two occupied tables so that his conversation with Roe couldn't be overheard, but as the bar began to fill up, he realized he'd have to text instead of speaking next time he used his phone. Realizing that he might be in this spot for a while, Mark signaled to a waiter and ordered Tanqueray over ice with a lime wedge and made himself comfortable.

After a few minutes, a white, beat-up van parked in one of the two spaces in front of the house he was watching. The driver, a small wiry dark man, got out of the driver's seat and opened the van's rear door. Two young males who were in their twenties climbed out of the van. They were both carrying backpacks and were dressed in worn-out jeans and dirty frayed sweatshirts. They followed the small man to the door of the house where he knocked several times. The door opened and the two young men went inside. The man got back into the van and drove away.

Mark ordered food and another drink as he continued to sit and watch. As dusk began to settle over the neighborhood, the door opened, and Samuel came out with the two men he'd seen enter earlier. They were having a casual conversation as if they'd been lifelong friends. The trio looked up toward the lit-up balcony bar that now had music being played from a boombox set behind the bar. Mark quickly turned his head, hoping Samuel didn't recognize him. He didn't want to do anything that might distract Samuel.

The trio crossed the street, and as they started to go inside, Samuel said to the other two, "Hey, I've got a good signal. I'm calling my uncle while I can."

Mark's phone rang. He answered quickly and held the phone tight against his ear as he heard Samuel say, "Uncle Martin, I'm getting close. We will be crossing the border tomorrow night. I'll call as soon as I can after I'm in the US. I am really excited. I'm sure I've chosen the right group to get me across. Sorry, but I can't talk more right now. I'll see you soon," and the call was ended.

When Samuel came out of the grocery store, he was carrying a paper bag filled with sodas and junk food. The other two young men carried similar bags of food. As they reentered the safe house, Mark was already struggling with a dilemma. Should he let Samuel continue with his border crossing or should he intervene while he still could? Realizing that if they aborted now, they might not get such a good chance again. By setting himself up as a potential victim, Samuel had probably guaranteed a safe crossing. What happened after he was safely across would depend on Roe and himself.

CHAPTER 25

1972

With Ron Lassiter sitting in the pilot's seat and Rich Holtz, who also had a pilot's license for small craft, in the copilot's seat, the Beechcraft King Air twin turbo left the ground in the late afternoon. The Plomeros were wearing desert tan fatigues in anticipation of a barren desert terrain. They planned to make a pass over the landing strip at an altitude high enough to not attract attention so that Ron could get a clear view of the landing strip while there was still daylight. Once he had a clear vision of the layout in his mind, he'd wait until just before total darkness set in before landing. The strip was set well away from the processing plant as well as the settlement on the south side of the river where most of the employees lived. Because there were so few areas flat enough for a runway, the strip was actually on the other side of a small ridge. That was good, because it offered some concealment, but that advantage was offset by the shortness of the runway as well as the surrounding ridge. There were no landing lights on the strip it because was designed for daytime use only. Landing with minimum light would be difficult, but after flying over the site, Ron was confident he could land safely. Taking off was another question entirely. *One step at a time,* he thought to himself.

Ron brought the plane in without any problem and all the group except Ron left the plane and set out across the ridge toward the bridge. It was a good hike, especially with the weapons and gear they were carrying. As they carefully approached the bridge, they stayed hidden behind mesquite and cactus plants. The only traffic crossing the bridge by now was foot traffic. The plant was a daytime operation only and the workers were heading to their homes across the border. By the time they reached the small building that served as a gatehouse, the area was deserted.

Mark and Rosa approached the small building, which was little more than a large shed, from the rear. After pulling their balaclavas over their faces, they quietly entered the unlocked rear door of the shed. The only occupant was a man wearing what was supposed to be some sort of uniform made of a wrinkled, faded green fabric. An aviator hat that didn't match the rest of his uniform sat on his head tilted to the side and looking as if it would fall off any minute. The moment he became aware of the two figures standing behind him, he jerked his body around, causing it to finally fall off, revealing a huge bald spot in the center of his head. He was wearing a holstered revolver, but before he could even think of drawing it, Mark had already taken it out of its holster. It was an ancient Webley 38 with several spots of rust visible.

Speaking in Spanish, Mark said, "Amigo, you could hurt yourself with this weapon. Are you sure it's safe to fire it?"

Stuttering, the man replied, "Who are you? What are you doing here?"

"We'd like to watch you work. We've heard what a good job you're doing protecting the border. I can see that you've already dropped the crossing arms down across the bridge to close it off for the night. Are you expecting anyone to cross this late? I suppose that since the factory is closed for the night, you'll get a lot of sleep."

"This is private property. You are not allowed to be here."

Rosa walked around and leaned in close to the man. "What is your name?"

"Mateo."

"Okay, Mateo, we're not here to argue with you. I don't have the patience or the time," Rosa said as she took Mateo's revolver from Mark's hand. She broke the gun open and while holding it directly in front of Mateo's face she ejected all the shells. Holding it so that Mateo could clearly see, she placed one shell in a chamber and closed the cylinder back in place. She then rotated the cylinder several times. Without any hesitation, she placed the muzzle of the Webley under Mateo's chin and pulled the trigger. There was a loud click and Mateo jumped. A large wet stain began to spread across his pants and down his leg.

"Only five to go, Mateo. Are you ready for the next one?"

Mateo could only mumble, "What do you want?"

"We only want your cooperation, Mateo. What time do you expect the trucks to cross tonight?"

"I will be a dead man if I tell you."

Again, Rosa placed the muzzle of the gun under Mateo's chin. "Mateo, you'll be dead before they get here." She cocked the hammer again.

"Okay! Okay! They usually come around eleven. They're probably in the village eating dinner right now."

Mark asked, "How many trucks?"

"Two or three and sometimes a car with some important people."

"What do the trucks carry?"

"They never tell me anything. I just know they bring whatever they please. Many people cross here. They bring different things. No one tells me what they bring, and I never ask."

"Okay, Mateo, you just sit tight. My friend will stay with you and keep you company for now. Do as we say, and you may get to see the sunrise tomorrow."

With that, Mark went back out the back door and motioned for the others to join him. They had already laid out a plan based on photographs of the bridge. After they'd gone over their individual assignments, they immediately split up and headed toward their positions.

Marcus went down the road a short distance away from the bridge while Rich crossed the road with Lou. Mark stayed on the same side behind the building. By now they were accustomed to waiting and each one of them had a place in their mind they could retreat into as they patiently waited. Mark could replay a football game from start to finish with every play etched in his mind. Rosa retreated back to her early years and relived a better time spent with her twin brother. They had been inseparable. Rosa had been the dominant one and had on many occasions saved her brother from actions resulting from his impetuousness. Over time, without realizing it was occurring, her brother became dependent on Rosa's opinion for so many things.

The sounds of engines brought them all out of their reveries. The sounds were soon followed by bouncing headlights as the trucks began moving across the bridge. There were three vehicles in the caravan. They crossed the bridge and continued for another fifty yards to the checkpoint where the crossing bars were still down and blocking the road. The truck that was leading the convoy rolled up to the cross bars and stopped. It was a large panel truck resembling a small moving truck. Behind it was a larger semitruck, and a Mercedes limousine brought up the rear. They were all three positioned to the right side of the gatehouse.

The driver of the first truck got out and walked toward the gatehouse where he could see Mateo through the large plate glass window.

"Mateo, you dumb shit. Are you asleep again? Open the goddamn gate. You're holding up Señor Torres and his family."

What happened next was a bloodbath. Each one of the Plomeros were armed with the Heckler & Koch MP5s that they'd used on the previous mission. But even more lethal were the M72 LAWs they each carried on their backs. The LAW—lightweight tank weapon—only weighed five and a half pounds and was only twenty-four inches in length. It was the US Army's replacement for the World War II bazooka that was designed for tanks. Accurate out to a hundred fifty yards, it took only a moment for an operator to flip a latch and pull on the tube, causing it to telescope out another twelve inches. This also activated the sights and armed the missile inside. Now all the operators had to do was to pull out the safety, and with the tube balanced on a shoulder, aim and fire. In this instance they were firing them point-blank into the three vehicles without any armor.

Rosa stepped out of the gate where she'd been hidden behind the door and fired two three-round bursts from her MP5 into the truck driver who was still walking up toward where Mateo was sitting. That was the signal for the carnage to begin. The first one to fire his LAW was Marcus, who stepped out of the shadows into the road directly in front of the first truck and fired right through the windshield, causing it to erupt in a fireball. From the other side of the road, Rich fired an LAW into the engine compartment of the semi and Lou fired into the center of the trailer behind the cab, creating two more fireballs. Mark was the last one to fire, because as he later told Rosa, he'd heard the man from the truck mention the word *family* and that caused him to pause for a second before he fired. His LAW struck the limousine dead center, causing it to rise up off the ground when the 66mm missile detonated. When it settled to the ground, it was a solid ball of fire.

There was no movement around the first truck or the limousine, but there were men coming out of the rear of the semi. Some were only fireballs, but a couple of men were still intact. When Rosa fired her LAW into the rear half of the semi, no one else came out. She then systematically shot the two who had made it out.

Throughout this, Mateo sat watching with wide eyes, not believing what he was witnessing.

Everything seemed to stand still for a few moments. Once it was apparent to the team that the trucks and car were totally destroyed and there were no survivors, they all regrouped at the gatehouse. Continuing to speak only in Spanish, Rosa said to the gatekeeper, who was in abject fear for his own life at this point, "Mateo, you should tell them what you saw here tonight. Tell them that if they continue to use this bridge to cross the border, we will be back."

With that statement, the group merely disappeared into the dark they had come from. The pace going back to the runway was much faster because there was no concern about secrecy. They were aware that lights were approaching the bridge on the Mexican side, but so far none were seen coming from the plant area on the US side. The plane was backed up as far as possible at the end of the runway, and while he was waiting for them, Ron had placed two battery-powered lights at the far end of the runway. After everyone had climbed onboard, he revived the engines to their max, released the brakes, and aimed for the lights in the distance. They were soon safely in the air and heading home. Only Ron and a wide-eyed Rich sitting in the copilot's seat gripping the side of his seat in a death grip knew how close to death they'd been. After they were safe back in their hangar in El Paso, they could all see the pieces of cactus and mesquite embedded in some of the rivets on the belly of the plane.

CHAPTER 26

Emelia

Emelia had little time for self-pity. Their doors were unlocked by someone knocking on the door. She followed Katrina down the hallway past the stairwell to the end of the hall where it opened up into a room containing two tables lined with chairs. Along one wall was a long table with buffet-style food. Selma and Mariana joined them, and they followed Katrina's lead by picking up plates and shoveling food onto their plates. Emelia realized how long it had been since she'd eaten a real meal. The food looked great, and for a brief time she forgot where she was and enjoyed her meal. The four girls sat together at one of the tables, and Ava, who had ushered them down the hallway, sat at the other table. Soon two men entered the room and went straight to the buffet. They sat at the table with Ava and paid little attention to the girls. One of the men was wearing a dark suit and the other man was much larger and looked as if he spent a lot of time in a gym. He was dressed in a uniform resembling a mall cop, except he carried a real gun on a gun belt. As Emelia would learn in time, the man in the suit was a limo driver and the other man was one of three full-time guards who guarded the house around the clock.

The four girls ate without conversation and Ava walked them back to their respective rooms after finishing.

She told them, "You all have tonight off. We'll have company tomorrow evening, so rest up."

By now Emelia realized what was happening and knew what was going to be expected of her. She thought she now knew what a condemned man felt as his execution approached. Katrina was watching Emelia and tried to calm her down.

"Look, the key to surviving is to make all this work in your favor. There's no point in trying to fight them. I've finally accepted the fact that I'm still better off than I was back home in Russia. I was destined to work on a farm married to a drunken oaf and being his breed mare."

The mere thought of home caused Emelia to burst out in tears as she thought of hers, and most of all, of Samuel. Knowing that he was probably dead accelerated the flow of tears. Katrina only shrugged and picked up another magazine. Emelia eventually cried herself to sleep.

Breakfast was served the same as the previous day. Afterward as they were returning to their rooms, Ava took Emelia's arm and led her back to the room they'd just eaten in.

"Sit down. What is your name?"

"Emelia."

"Emelia, do you know why you were brought here?"

"Katrina told me a little. I can't do the things she said she did."

"Emelia, I want you to listen very carefully to what I'm going to tell you. First of all, outside this house you are an illegal alien. Do you know what happens to girls like yourself? You'll be lucky if you just end up being sent back to Mexico. Most likely you'll end up working all day in a sugarcane field with the snakes and spiders. At night you'll be entertainment for the male workers. You are a beautiful girl. You could do well helping us here to entertain some wealthy men, and a few women. If you get tips, which you can certainly do, I'll help you keep the money safe so that one day you may be able to do something different. I will warn you now that the people I work for are not people you ever want to cross. If you can't do your job, you will be useless to them. I understand that you spent some time in Diego Cano's compound in Texas. That should give you some idea of the type of people I'm talking about. Now, go back to your room and let Katrina help you pick out something attractive to wear tonight.

When she was back in her room with Katrina, she looked at the clothes in the closet. She immediately realized what kind of outfits Ava was referring to. They were all the kind of things you'd find in an adult entertainment store. They were all different versions of see-through provocative clothing, or as Emelia thought, no clothing at all. Even after she'd chosen the most modest one she could find, she still felt humiliated just by wearing it.

When Ava came to get the girls, she looked at Emelia carefully. "You look very nice, Emelia. I suspect you'll be very popular."

As Emelia and Katrina came out into the hallway, Selma and Mariana were coming out into the hallway. Selma was hysterical and kept crying. "No, I will not go like this." Not only did she feel violated personally, but she also felt all of her religious beliefs were being trampled.

Two men had come with Ava in anticipation of resistance. Without saying a word, Ava nodded to the two men. They were a Mutt and Jeff pair. The short one was dark, heavyset, and completely bald. The taller one had a pockmarked face with a large, hooked nose. He had a small goatee and a long black ponytail hanging halfway down his back. Without saying a word, they stepped forward, and with one on either side of Selma, they lifted her up and carried her down the hallway and through a door which was closed behind them.

Ava stared at the three girls who were watching. Her face was set in stone and her eyes were cold as ice. "Anyone else have a problem?" No one said a word. "Then let's go."

They followed Ava down the hallway to an open door. Passing through, they entered another long hallway. They reached a stairwell that took them down to the first floor of the main house. If Emelia was impressed with her room, then the opulence she saw now was beyond anything she'd ever seen. The walls of the marble stairway were lined with what had to be priceless artwork. And it was only one of several stairways. When they reached the main floor, a huge room opened up in front of her. On one end she could see a really massive stairway leading up to a landing. On the other end was a fireplace of native limestone that reached to a ceiling that must have been at least forty feet in height. The fireplace itself could have accommodated a card table and four chairs with room to spare.

They followed Ava and continued through the vast room and entered a side room that would have been considered huge in any other house. Emelia almost coughed as she inhaled a lungful of cigar smoke and another odor she couldn't identify. She also realized that the room was not empty. There was a long U-shaped leather sofa with several ottomans next to it. A low, polished wood table sat in the center of the U-shaped sofa. It was covered with glasses and bottles of wines and liquors. Four men were sprawled across the sofa. Two of them had on dress shirts with ties hanging open. The two others were dressed casually in golf clothes. They had all obviously been drinking for a while. In front of the sofa were four chairs. Ava led the three girls to the chairs and told them to sit. Emelia was outwardly calm, but inside she was about to lose it the same as Selma had done as the men slowly turned their attention to the three girls now seated on the chairs.

CHAPTER 27
Tracking

Mark stayed on the patio until the tables had cleared out and he was assured of privacy before he called Roe.

"Roe, Samuel called and said he would be crossing tomorrow night. That's all he said. So far, other than two young men being delivered to the safe house, there's been no activity."

"I don't think you'll see any drug activity anywhere near the safe house. The people there are low-level members in the cartel. They'd be too vulnerable in such an obvious setting. If they plan to use anyone in the safe house as mules, the drugs won't be seen until it's time to cross over, just like Samuel's previous crossing. We're going on the assumption that this is a part of the Colombian Cartel, and no one will be challenging them. I think Samuel's vulnerability comes after they've used him as a mule to cross and taken all of his money. If they respond to the rich uncle story like we hope, that's when we step in."

"I hope you're right, Roe. I'm still pretty apprehensive about Samuel's well being. It's hard not to feel some degree of responsibility for Samuel. We're using him for our personal reasons."

"Samuel and his girlfriend were the ones who made the decision to start on this trip way back in Chile. We can't second-guess our decisions. After all, we are giving Samuel the only shot he has of ever finding out what happened to Emelia."

Mark couldn't help but laugh. "Roe, you've come a long way from the Bottom's Up Club in Tampa. You sound like the adult in the room now." Mark was referring to the time years ago when Roe worked in a nude strip club and was forced to help smuggle drugs into the country by the people who worked for Andre Mendez. And it was Mendez who was responsible for the death of his daughter, and indirectly for his wife's death as well. He just needed to focus on that fact alone.

"Mark, I think we need to be ready on this side of the border when Samuel comes across."

"I'll stay here until they leave the safe house tomorrow. Then I'll come back, and we'll be ready to follow Samuel wherever he goes or is taken."

Mark did stay in the hotel, spending most of the time sitting on the small hotel's patio. Two more young males were delivered to the house by the same van during the following day. Otherwise, there was nothing of any significance. A few times, some of the young men would leave the house to go into the small store across the street.

Mark had informed the old woman at the hotel check-in that he'd be leaving late to pick up his wife at the airport and he wanted to be sure he could get out of the parking area at a moment's notice.

Just after dark, the same white van approached the house. There were six men who exited the house and climbed into the back of the vehicle. Only two of them were carrying a backpack, one of whom as Samuel. As soon as the van had left the safe house, Mark drove out of the hotel parking area and into the alleyway behind the hotel. Almost immediately he was blinded by headlights coming straight toward him from both the front and rear.

He was forced to stop in the narrow alleyway and both vehicles pulled up to within inches of his car, trapping him. Two figures immediately exited the car in front of him and approached his car, one on either side, each clearly holding a gun.

Mark already had his gun in hand, and he didn't try to lock himself in his car but instead offered no resistance as the figure on his side pulled on the door handle and jerked the car door open. Without even raising his revolver, Mark fired a single shot upward and into the chest of the young man. As the man staggered backward with a shocked look on his face, Mark stepped out of the car and fired another round at the gunman on the opposite side of his car. This time he aimed more carefully, and this round hit the man in the forehead, causing his head to snap backward as he dropped like a rock. Without a moment's hesitation, Mark fired a shot through the windshield of the car in front, but it had already started backing up toward the street, where it quickly disappeared. The car behind him had begun to back out of the alley as well, leaving Mark standing in the alley, a gun in hand and two dead men on the ground. Getting back into his car, Mark quickly drove out of the alley and back toward the border. As he sped away and his breathing slowed back to normal, he realized he'd made a stupid mistake by displaying wealth when he registered at the hotel earlier. It did help him get a good room, but it also set him up to be robbed. He couldn't afford to do that again.

Before he reached the border crossing, he carefully wiped his fingerprints from his gun, unloaded the remaining shells, and dropped the revolver into a streetside trash can. By the time he reached the crossing, traffic was light and there was no holdup coming back across the border.

As soon as he'd reached his hotel he went straight to Roe's room. They had made sure they each had a key to the other's room; he knocked once, then went in. They had chosen this hotel because some of the rooms had a balcony with table and chairs. Roe was seated at the table on the balcony intently watching a screen that showed the movement of the Samuel's belt being tracked by a satellite.

Roe glanced up at Mark. "They're at the river but still on the Mexican side. They've been at the same point for almost an hour." There was some concern in her voice.

"I don't think that's a problem, Roe. It's only midnight. They're probably timing it with whoever is meeting them on this side." Mark pulled a chair around, so he had a good view of the monitor.

Almost immediately Roe said, "He's moving!" as they both hovered over the screen watching a tiny dot moving closer to the river. The dot they were watching on the map was located twenty miles north of the city. There were wooded areas on both sides of the river as well as numerous secondary dirt roads following the current and leading away from it as well. It would be an area that would take an entire army of Border Patrol to cover properly. The river itself made several sharp bends with sandbars reaching well out into it. Depending on the time of the year, there were spots that a person could easily walk across, with water being no more than waist-high. These details weren't apparent to Roe and Mark. The screen they were watching only showed the moving dot that was a reflection of the object embedded in Samuel's belt. They could see the exact location of the dot to within a few feet on the map. If they had been able to move fast enough, they might have been waiting for Samuel on the US side of the river. Without knowledge of the roads, terrain, and most importantly, where the receiving people on the US side would be waiting, it would be almost impossible—and also dangerous. Instead, Mark spread out a map of the area as well as a detailed map of the city.

They both breathed a sigh of relief. After having paused for a few minutes on the US side, the dot began to move rapidly toward the city. Mark continued to trace its progress as it reached the metro area, and he followed it on the city map. The dot continued through the city and into a commercial district in the southern part. Eventually, the dot slowed and after a small movement disappeared.

Mark opened his laptop and after opening a popular map on the screen, he located the spot where the tracking image had vanished. Switching to satellite imagery, they could look down on the location. The neighborhood was a mixed area of commercial and residential. It was probably a lower economic area because most people with a choice don't live next door to a salvage yard or a body repair shop. The dot had stopped in the middle of a walled compound that covered most of an entire block. There were only two other houses on the block, and one appeared to be connected to the compound judging from the roof lines. The aerial view of the compound showed a courtyard inside the entrance that might accommodate three or four cars. The rest of the compound was under a flat commercial type of roof. There had to be fifteen thousand feet under the roof.

Roe, being the most tech savvy, said, "We're lucky. We've got street view." She switched the map to street view. Immediately, it was as if they were standing on the street outside the compound. Roe continued to move the view and they were able to literally walk the streets around the compound. Two sides of the block were private homes, most of which had either walls or fences. On one of these sides were the two houses connected to the compound. The main compound wall seemed to keep them separated,

although one of them seemed to closely abut the compound wall. They both had tall chain-link fences separating them from the street. The third side was bordered by
a junkyard that was surrounded by a heavy, tall chain-link
fence. It had one large gate in the middle of the block
with a small shed next to it. The only entrance into the
compound was on the fourth side. It was a wooden gate
that was so heavy it had to have wheels on the opening
end in order to support the weight when it swung open.
Opposite the gate was a tire dealership that must have spe-
cialized in tires for large machinery. Tires that were taller
than a grown man were visible along the fence that closed
it off.

Looking up at Mark, Roe said, "What's next?"

Mark smiled as he replied, "As I told you once before,
I think it's time to go hunting again."

CHAPTER 28

1972

There was a lot of laughing and joking on the plane ride back. That is, all except for Mark, who hardly spoke a word. By the time the plane had landed and gear and weapons were stored, everyone was exhausted and headed for their rooms, save for Mark. He went into the bar and poured himself a glass of Tanqueray gin over ice after squeezing in a lot of lime juice before sitting alone on one of the soft sofas.

Mark had been sitting and brooding for thirty minutes before someone else entered the semi-dark room and went to the bar. Mark realized it was Rosa who walked over where he was sitting with a drink in her hand.

"Mind if I join you?"

"Have a seat." Mark said, as she sat on one of the arms of the sofa.

"Mark, I couldn't help but notice how quiet you were on the ride back. I thought everything went well. And, I might add, not one of us has yet to get a scratch."

"You're right, Rosa. It did go well. And yes, we've been lucky so far. I'm concerned for myself. I hesitated for a second tonight. I can't afford to do that. I'll admit that there's a conflict in my mind. I have no doubts about killing the drug people, but I don't know how far I can go with killing children. When that guy tonight said 'family,'

I hesitated for a second. I can't afford to put anyone in this group at risk by doing that."

"It's okay, Mark. As much as I want to see the people who killed my family hurt, I'm not sure I could intentionally harm a child. I have no doubt in my mind that you'll do what you have to do when the time comes. Tonight, we killed a cartel leader who has been responsible for hurting a lot of people, including children. If he had his family with him, then it's on him and not us."

As she spoke, Rosa moved from the arm of the sofa and sat next to Mark and laid her head on his shoulder. They sat for a while and finished their drinks in silence before standing up and going to their respective rooms.

The next day, as everyone slowly appeared in the lounge, Rosa had been at work for some time on a computer. After dinner, she said she'd gotten some feedback from some of their actions. There was chatter among the cartel's grapevines about the trouble the Plomeros were causing. A lot of finger pointing was going on along with a lot of confusion. No one had any idea who was responsible for the carnage that had occurred. The man in the Mercedes was a cartel leader, and he did have his wife and two adult children with him. It did bring some peace of mind to Mark to know that there had not been any young children in the car. The semitrailer was loaded with marijuana from Southern Mexico as well as twelve gang members from Central America being brought up to dispense drugs in US cities. No one seems to know what the lead truck was carrying, but it seems to have been the biggest loss whatever in was. Rosa also said that there was an unidentified message on the site that simply said, "Well done. Keep up the good work."

Rosa continued, "We're going into the oil drilling business next." She laughed. "No, not really, just pre-

tend. That's what our cover is going to be. We're going
to Phoenix. I'm sure none of you have ever heard of Sean
Caldwell. We normally think of drug dealers as mafioso
types or Hispanic males. This Caldwell character is very
well-known to authorities all over the country. He is the
son of a police officer, but he fell a long way from the tree.
He dropped out of school when he was in the seventh
grade. By the time he was fifteen, he had his own gang
and was stealing anything that wasn't tied down. He was
caught and spent over a year in reform school where he
continued his education in crime. He went through a series of jobs in the numbers racket and eventually became
an enforcer. Along the way he made connections with a
number of unsavory characters and was soon engaged in
the cocaine trade. He has proven to have superior orga-
nizational skills and has been unusually adept at uniting
different groups of dealers that you'd never expect to be
working together. He's remained untouchable even when
someone in his circle is taken down. His people are sup-
plying dealers at all major US military bases, even some in
Europe and Asia. Recently, some friction has developed
between his business and some other dealers. This is partly
due to what we've done. They're starting to point fingers
at each other. We've learned that he's called for a conference, including the people with disagreements. His ability
to bring all parties together just might be our opportunity
to hit the distributors here in the US. Our legal system
would never permit law enforcement to do what we're able
to do.

"Caldwell owns a home—one of many, I might
add—outside of Phoenix. The attendees are staying at a
resort hotel that's part of an exclusive golf country club,
but the meetings are being held at Caldwell's home. His
home is not within the confines of a club because he

wanted isolation on a large tract of land. The house is
huge, with plenty of parking, and can accommodate a large
group. The feds have an informer in the group of attendees, and from him, we know Caldwell has heavy security.
The house has a wall surrounding it and sits on a high
ridge surrounded by open desert. Getting in in the daytime
without being seen would be almost impossible. Caldwell
has planned a last night dinner party with entertainment.
That will be our opportunity."

Marcus asked, "What about the servers and so-called
entertainers? We hit them as well?"

Rosa answered, "I hope we can separate them from
our targets. We'll do everything we can to protect them.
But, as we've seen up to now, there's no guarantee that
there won't be some collateral damage. The conference is
scheduled for next week, so we've got several days to plan.
We'll fly into Phoenix two days before the final dinner
party. It'll give us time to observe and make detailed plans.
This may be our biggest challenge so far."

Chapter 29

Emelia

Emelia sat in the chair with her legs firmly crossed and her arms crossed tightly across her chest. She and Mariana were a stark contrast to Katrina, who smiled seductively at the men. As she leered at them, she assumed a blatantly seductive pose as she leaned back and made no attempt at modesty. One of the men said in a loud voice, "I thought there were supposed to be four of them tonight."

Ava, standing off to one side, said, "Don't worry. The fourth one will be here shortly." She'd hardly finished her statement when the tall man with the long ponytail and pockmarked face entered the room with Selma walking beside him. He was holding her arm to guide her, and she walked as if she had had far too much alcohol to drink. He led her over to the empty chair and helped her sit. Selma offered no resistance and only stared straight ahead with no apparent comprehension of her surroundings.

One of the men with a loose tie said, "I've got dibs on her first. I like dark meat."

"Wait one goddamn minute, Hoss. Not so fast. Let's do this fairly. After all, we've got all night. Right, Ava? Didn't Andre say we could have whatever we wanted?"

"Yes, he did, Mr. C, and we'll try to make it happen."

Mr. C was one of the men dressed in golf clothes, who again said, "Ava, why don't the ladies put on a modeling show for us? Let them show us what they've got."

Ava walked over and stood behind the four chairs. "All right, ladies, stand up."

There was no hesitation on Katrina's part as she rose from her chair with a flourish. Emelia and Mariana were slow to stand, and Ava had to help Selma to her feet. Ava spoke quietly behind the girl's backs, "Watch Katrina, girls. Just do what she does."

Katrina continued to smile at the men as she did a slow seductive turn, even bending forward and letting her scant see-through cover rise up high enough to expose her entire rear. Mariana seemed to have an easier time mimicking Katrina than Emelia, who could only turn around once. Ava had to rotate Selma herself, and as she did, she pulled up her cover, exposing her completely to the men who were now sitting on the edge of their seats and watching intently. Selma continued to only stare with eyes that were seeing nothing.

The man called Mr. C spoke to the man wearing the loose tie, who had laid claim to Selma, and said, "Mr. A, let's draw to see who gets to get first choice. Ava, get us a deck of cards."

Mr. A replied, "Okay, what about B and D here?" he said as he looked at the other two men. They both nodded an affirmative as one of them said, "As long no one gets piggish, it's all right with me."

By now Emelia was aware that the men were avoiding real names and were using letters as identification. The men's conversation about needing a deck of cards was lost on her, and she remained standing, confused, and humiliated in her scant, see-through garment.

Ava only had to walk across to a huge credenza and bring back a deck of cards, which she handed to Mr. C. He quickly shuffled the deck and shoved some glasses and bottles aside before spreading the deck out face down on the table in front of the sofa.

"Highest card gets first pick; lowest card takes what's left." Each man picked up a card and then all four men looked at each other and held out their cards.

Mr. A grimaced and said, "Looks like I'm getting third choice," while Mr. D smiled a huge smile and said, "And this ace says I get to go first. I'll definitely take her." He pointed toward Katrina.

Katrina smiled back at him and said, "You won't be sorry." She walked over to him and put her arm around his waist.

He picked up a bottle of opened wine and said, "Lets head upstairs to my room." And so they headed for the main staircase like two long time lovers.

"This is going to be a tough choice," Mr. C said as he held the second highest card, a jack of diamonds. He walked over to the remaining three girls and one by one he turned them around, looking as if he were at a livestock auction. When he reached down to raise Emelia's thin negligee, she abruptly pulled back and slapped at his hand. His face, which was already red from the effects of the alcohol, turned even redder.

"Forget this one," he spat out. "She needs better training. I'm not about to waste my time sparing with her. I'll take this one." He took Mariana by the arm and led her toward the stairs. She went obediently without a whimper, but she looked as if she were walking to the gallows.

Ava picked up an empty glass from the table, and with her back turned so Emelia couldn't see, she poured a powdered substance in the glass and then poured a little wine in. Turning, she got up in Emelia's face. Holding up the glass for Emelia, she said in a voice that was more order than request, "Drink this. It'll help your attitude." She watched carefully until she was sure Emelia had swallowed the last drop. Emelia gagged but held it down.

While Ava was focused on Emelia, Mr. A was having a hard time suppressing his delight in ending up with what actually was his first choice as he put his arm around Selma, whose mind was floating in a different universe. Afraid that he might have trouble walking her up the stairs, he led her toward the elevator, which led to the second floor, saying, "You can call me Dr. Livingston. We're going to do some exploring tonight."

That left Emelia and Mr. B, who was the only man who had not spoken. He was a middle-aged man in golf clothes, partially bald, and had a prominent gut hanging over his belt. Looking at Ava, he said, "Don't worry. If she tries to give me any lip, I'll beat the shit out of her."

Ava replied, "Just don't mess with her face."

Mr. B grabbed Emelia by the arm and pulled her toward the stairs, saying, "Let's go, honey."

By now Emelia was beginning to have an out-of-body experience. She was seeing two of everything and there was a roaring in her ears that sounded like a freight train. She was somehow able to reach the top of the stairs on her own, but Mr. B had to partially carry her the rest of the way down a long-paneled hallway to a bedroom. As Mr. B threw her across the bed, she felt her thin cover being pulled off her body, leaving her completely exposed. She was vaguely aware of Mr. B's fat belly hovering over her before she descended into darkness.

CHAPTER 30

The Stakeout

Roe and Mark used the beat-up Toyota. It blended well with the rundown residential and commercial area. There were parking spots on the street a short distance from the front gate of the compound. The Toyota looked good compared to some of the wrecks parked nearby. Mark brought a pair of binoculars and Roe had the laptop monitoring Samuel's location. It was still dark, but a glow in the eastern sky preceded an approaching dawn. Anticipating a long wait, they'd stopped at an all-night donut shop and bought coffee and food. Even before daylight, the tire business opposite the compound was waking up as lights came on and employees began arriving. Neither Roe nor Mark knew what to expect next from the occupants of the compound. By the time the sun was starting to rise, Mark told Roe, "I'm going to do a walk around the block. Keep an eye on the computer and the gate. If anyone comes out, drive around the block and pick me up as quickly as you can, and we'll try to follow whoever comes out. Mark was still wearing work clothes, and he looked like someone heading off to work.

Mark walked down the nearest side street bordering the compound. It was one of the streets lined with private homes. Looking at the wall surrounding the compound, he saw it was obvious that it would be difficult to simply climb over. Along with large shards of glass embedded in the concrete, a mesh of razor wire lay atop the glass. There was a sidewalk on the compound side, but it was so broken up that no one would be using it for skateboarding or pushing a baby carriage. The houses across the street were all protected by either a fence or wall. As he passed one house, two large pit bulls tried to climb a fence to get to him. *Southern hospitality,* he thought to himself.

The street that ran behind the compound was more of the same except that halfway down the street there were two small homes bordering the compound. Whoever built the compound either couldn't convince the owners to sell or the houses were left intact for a purpose. As he walked past, Mark could see that the two houses were connected, and they shared a parking area inside a tall chain-link fence. Each of them was backed up flush against the wall of the compound. A newer model pickup truck and a nondescript panel van were parked inside the fence. Mark could see a light inside one of the houses but no visible activity. As he walked on around to the street on the far side, there was a salvage/junkyard along the entire block. The employees were rounding up the guard dogs that had been roaming the yard all night and putting them in their daytime pens. Walking back toward the front of the compound where Roe was sitting, he saw that the tire business was a beehive of activity. It was also very noisy. Again, good cover for the compound across the street. Mark also observed cameras at both sides of the compound's gate.

Getting back in the car with Roe, Mark said, "I think we may be watching the wrong gate." At the same time his cell phone rang. He answered, "Hello."

"Uncle Martin! Thank God, I got you. I'm in the US, but these people are asking for more money."

Speaking in Spanish, Mark asked, "Who wants more money?"

"The people who brought me over the border. I paid them what they asked for, but now they say they've got to have a lot more or something bad will happen to me. They've got me handcuffed to the wall."

"How much more do they want?"

Mark could hear voices in the background instructing Samuel as he replied, "Twenty thousand US dollars."

Mark said, "I don't have that much cash."

Another voice spoke, saying, "Then you better find a way to get it. We'll give you two days. I'll call you back then and tell you how to transfer the money. If you don't have the money, your nephew will be floating down the Rio Grande without a head."

"How do I know I can trust you to let him go?"

The voice laughed, "You don't. Is it worth a chance?"

The last statement was followed by silence as the call was ended.

Mark looked at Roe and smiled. "We were right. They've taken the bait. We just have to find a way to get in. I think the houses in the back are connected to the compound. We need to watch both front and rear at the same time. Here's what we're going to do," he explained, as he began to detail to Roe what he had in mind.

CHAPTER 31

1972

The group landed in Phoenix in the afternoon at a private airfield on the outskirts of town. A commercial van was waiting and took them to a generic motel nearby. Rosa checked them in as part of a company called Global Energy. She paid in advance for the rooms with a credit card, but if anyone tried to trace the origin of the funds, it would be a blind alley. Rosa paid for three adjoining rooms, each with two queen beds. Their rooms were at the end of the one-story building.

Rosa apologized to Mark as they took their carryalls to their respective rooms. "Mark, I'm sorry, but in order to get connecting rooms, I had to double us up. I don't snore and I hope you don't either."

Mark laughed, "No, I don't snore, and even if you did, I could sleep through anything."

After settling in, they all met in Mark's room and looked at the satellite images and maps before getting back into the van and leaving the motel. They drove out to the periphery of the city where the rise in elevation was obvious and small rises of the terrain prevented viewing anything in the distance except the distant mountains. Caldwell's house was located in a newer subdivision, which reached well up into the hills and toward the mountains. He'd bought up all of the lots on the road leading to his home at the end of the street, leaving him a half-mile private driveway. The Plomeros did not enter the driveway but continued on the public road until if ended. From this point an old mining road that was used as a hiking trail led up into the mountains. There was an area at the end of the road for people to park before accessing the trail, where several vehicles were stationed. They then turned around and drove back toward Phoenix and into another subdivision. As they knew from studying the map, one of the subdivision's streets ended in a cul-de-sac located several hundred yards below Caldwell's home. The surrounding terrain didn't allow a view of Caldwell's house from the cul-de-sac. Returning to their hotel, they felt good about the plan that Mark proposed.

They spent the next day killing time and watching TV. Mark was a little uncomfortable being in the room with Rosa, especially when she acted as if he weren't even there. She had absolutely no inhibitions or modesty as she walked around in her panties and bra and once walked into the room completely nude to get something out of her satchel. Mark tried to avoid watching her, but he couldn't help himself. She was truly the most beautiful being he'd ever seen. He also sensed that she was well aware that he was watching her.

As dark approached, they all dressed in black before getting back into the van with their bags and driving the short distance to the airport and the plane. The plane had been parked inside a secure hangar in an area that was deserted after dark. Opening the locked luggage compartment of the plane, they retrieved the equipment they needed before driving on toward Caldwell's home. They passed the driveway leading to his house and continued on to the road that led to the hiking trail. By the time they reached the parking area at the trailhead, it was deserted.

Before leaving with the van, Ron waited until everyone had double-checked their weapons, making sure they were all locked and loaded. Each of them also carried a flashlight on a utility belt along with spare ammunition and grenades. Mark had an Ithaca Model 37 trench gun with a belt of twelve gauge high brass shells loaded with 00 buckshot. Mark's dad had the same model Ithaca in his gun store, which Mark remembered slam firing at bottles at the local dump when he was a kid. Marcus also carried the same gun. Rosa and Rich had their tried-and-true MP5s. Lou Croft had his sniper rifle strapped across his back. Each one of them carried a .22 long rifle suppressed High Standard pistol as a side arm. The small caliber would only be effective within a few yards, but it had been the choice of assassins for many years. Its silence was its virtue, and a close-up head shot killed a person as dead as a 357 Magnum would. As soon as they were all ready, Ron drove away in the van, leaving the five standing at the edge of the parking area. Mark called them together for a final huddle.

"From here on out we'll keep conversation to an absolute minimum. I doubt that they are so paranoid that they'd have someone on top of the ridge, but let's assume they do. Once we reach the top, we'll take another look before going down to the house."

Marcus laughed, "I'm more concerned about rattlesnakes than anything else."

"At least you'll hear it before it strikes so you'll know what's biting you," Rosa said.

"That's encouraging," Marcus replied as they started out across the dark desert toward the ridge.

The hike up the side of the ridge was difficult mainly due to the sharp cacti and thorny bushes that were hard to see in the dark. Fortunately, their pants were a ballistic nylon that offered protection from the rough terrain. When they had all assembled at the top of the ridge, they were looking directly down toward Caldwell's home. It was lit up like a circus. There were a number of vehicles parked around the front as well as three service trucks that were probably caterers parked at the rear of the house. Using his binoculars, Mark could identify at least five security guards posted at different points around the house. He could also make out two men standing by cars, smoking. Each one of the attendees was probably driven by a guard. There might be others sitting in a car. Each of them had a specific assignment as the five headed toward the house below, blissfully unaware that the Plomeros were about to suffer their first casualty.

CHAPTER 32

Emelia

Emelia woke up to bright light streaming through open drapes. Her head was pounding as if it were being beaten like a drum. Even the light itself was painful. She was so disoriented that it took several moments for her to remember where she was. The cold air conditioning was causing her to shake like a leaf. Her initial reaction was to try to cover her naked body with a sheet, but the sheet was tangled around the body of Mr. B, who was lying face down and snoring like a flushing toilet. Just looking at him caused her to gag; it required a supreme effort for her to not vomit. For a second, she had a thought that if she did throw up, she'd do it on him.

Looking around the room, she saw what must be the door to the bathroom. A chair near the bed had a small throw draped across the back, and she grabbed it and wrapped it around herself as she went toward the door. When she'd finished and came out of the bathroom, Mr. B was waiting for her. He was sitting up on the side of the bed. "Come on over here, honey. Now that I'm rested, I'm ready to have another go. How does that sound to you?"

Emelia immediately tried to go back into the bathroom and close the door, but Mr. B was surprisingly fast for a fat middle-aged man as he sprung off the bed and stopped the door from closing. He grabbed her by her wrist and pulled her back toward the bed. As he pushed her down on her back, she realized from his visible erection there wasn't going to be any foreplay. He held both her arms down and pushed his weight on top of her, leaving her with no way to fight back. Just when he had forced her legs apart there were a sudden scream and loud voices shouting. Mr. B halted at the noise and released one of Emelia's arms. Her hand shot up and she clawed at his face with her free hand. He yelled, "Bitch!" and slapped her across her face. The noise outside in the hallway grew even louder, causing him to forget her for a moment as he stood up. Reaching in a closet, he took out a robe and put it on. As he headed out the door, Emelia went to the closet and found another robe, which she immediately used to cover herself.

The door to the room was open. Emelia followed Mr. B out into the hallway, which was becoming crowded with people. All of the commotion seemed to be around the main stairway, with people looking down over the balcony on either side of the stairs and down to the marble floor below. What Emelia saw when she looked down almost made her throw up again. The distance from the balcony to the marble floor below was at least thirty feet, and sprawled out in an expanding pool of blood was Selma, lying on her back with eyes that were open but not seeing.

Mr. A, wearing a robe similar to Mr. B, walked up to the balcony and looked down. "What the hell happened? She passed out before I did. I never heard her wake up this morning."

By now, everyone from the night before had come out into the hallway. Ava, who had come up from the stairs after she'd thrown a covering over Selma's body, said, "Let's go girls. Now! Follow me." She led Emelia, Mariana, and Katrina through a series of hallways that led back to

the rooms over the garage. As she closed the door behind Emelia after reaching her room, she said, "I'm
going to deal with you later. You're a slow learner."

Emelia didn't think about what Ava was saying at
the moment as she rushed to her bathroom and turned
on the shower. She made the water as hot as she could
stand and tried to let it wash off the smell of Mr. B's
cologne. But no matter how hot the water or how long
it ran over her body, she still felt dirty, used, and abused.
It wasn't until she'd dressed and sat down on the bed
that she began to worry about Ava's words.

She didn't have long to wait. The door to her room
was opened and Ava was standing there with Mutt
and Jeff. Without saying a word, they walked over to
Emelia and with one on each side they walked her out
of the room and toward the stairs that led down into
the garage. The garage was large enough to hold several
cars. There were multiple doors leading off the garage
and all were closed. They stopped in front of a closed
door and Ava used a key to open it. The room was dark
until Ava flipped a light switch, illuminating the room
in a harsh glare. It appeared to be a storage room that
was maybe twelve by fifteen feet in size. At one end was
a large white freezer. Ava raised the lid of the freezer,
which was empty but not turned on, and without hesitation got right up into Emelia's face. "This will hold
enough air for about two hours. We'll try to watch the
time. We have been known to get distracted and forget.
Enjoy."

Emelia tried to pull away from the two men, but it was
a futile effort as she was lifted over and into the freezer with
the lid being slammed down, forcing her down into the
blackness. She tried to scream, but she was so frightened
that only a whisper came out. She heard a door slamming

closed, and then there was only the deepest silence and pitch-black darkness she had ever known.

CHAPTER 33
Mark's Plan

Although Mark had never shared his past military experiences with anyone, some of the weapons he'd used during that time were guns he was familiar with. Years ago, Mark's dad had owned the local hardware store that also served as the area sporting goods store. A bank in the town was being remodeled and Mark's dad bought the bank's old walk-in safe. He then had it built into his hardware store as a vault to store guns, coins, and other valuables. After his dad passed away, the safe was moved into his mother's garage, and then later after she passed, he had it moved to his home in Jacksonville. Mark built it into one end of the garage of his new home on the river and closed it off from casual view with a wall covered by hanging tools. The wall swung open to access the safe. When the safe's door was opened and you walked in, it was stunning. There were guns of all types, and some shelves were stacked with books of coin collections and other shelves had stacks of money. The guns and coins had been legally inherited from his parents, but the cash was drug money he and Roe had taken during an ambush of a drug transaction on the Florida Gulf Coast several years ago.

One of the many guns Mark had inherited from his father's store was an Ithaca twelve gauge trench gun as well as a suppressed .22 long rifle High Standard pistol. Each gun was a duplicate of the ones he'd used in the Army. The pistol was still wrapped in the same oilpaper he'd put it in when he had helped his mom inventory his dad's store.

One of the reasons Mark had chosen to drive to Texas rather than fly was so he could bring a few weapons with him. In addition to his Model 39 Smith & Wesson, he'd brought the shotgun and the High Standard pistol. He didn't know where the trip might take him, but he had learned from his military experience that it was always better to prepare for the worst and hope for the best. So, before he and Roe had left the hotel, he'd transferred the guns to the trunk of the beat-up sedan.

Soon after Mark and Roe had agreed on their approach, Roe drove the car around the block and parked in a spot that gave her a view of the entrance to the houses adjacent to the compound's wall. There were enough other vehicles parked along the street, so the beat-up Toyota looked like it had found a home. He left her there in the car to keep watching for any activity. He walked back to the front of the compound and sat down on the curb.

A passing and casual observer could see a homeless man half-sitting, half-lying on the ground in front of the tire business. A hoodie was pulled up over his head and he was holding a brown paper bag that contained an unknown beverage. He was sitting almost directly across from the gate that opened into the compound.

Fortunately for Mark, it was a cloudy day and it looked as if it might rain any minute. The clock had passed noon and still there had been no movement in or out of the compound. At one o'clock, Mark's phone rang.

"Mark, someone is coming out of the house and opening the gate."

"How many?"

"Two. One is opening the gate and the other is getting into the panel van."

"Roe, move now! Drive around and pick me up."

"Coming."

When Roe came around to the street in front of the compound, she stopped next to the curb where Mark was sitting, and he quickly slipped into the passenger seat. They waited, hoping the van would come out of one of the two side streets bordering the compound. It finally made a slow turn onto the street where Mark and Roe were sitting and with no apparent haste it continued on down the street. Roe's training with the agencies she worked for was apparent as she instinctively followed the van at a safe distance. They drove for several minutes before they entered a more upscale business district. The van entered the parking lot of a large members only shopping co-op. They watched as only one man got out of the van. Roe found an open parking spot close by as the man entered the busy store, which looked more like a warehouse. Mark got out and walked quickly by the van to make sure the second man who had opened the gate hadn't come along before coming back to the Toyota.

"Roe, how we get inside will depend on a lot of variables. First, will this guy panic and alert them? Also, is there video surveillance of the courtyard, and how many actual cartel people are there? What this guy brings out of the store will tell us if he's the one we should be following. Let's stay gloved and masked from now on. Both our fingerprints are easy to find and there's no reason to help anyone who might want to ID us later."

When the man exited the big box warehouse, they knew they had the right person. With one arm he was pushing a huge grocery buggy that was piled, to the point of overflowing, with food. With his other arm he was pulling another buggy that was half-filled with food, but the rest was beer and bottles of liquor. He could only be shopping for a large group of people. He was a short squat man with browned skin and dark hair. As he struggled to pull the buggies up to the driver's side of the van, Mark walked several cars down and then back up to the van's passenger side where he couldn't be seen by the man. He pulled on the door handle to be sure it had unlocked when the man opened the side door. When the man had finally finished unloading the buggies, he just left them where they were sitting and opened the driver's door and climbed into the seat. Mark timed it perfectly, and as the man slid into his seat and before he could start the engine or lock the doors, Mark opened the passenger side door and sat in the seat.

Startled, the man tried to open his door, but Mark beat him to it by shoving his pistol into his ribs and quietly saying, "It's okay. Just be calm and you're not going to get hurt."

"What do you want?"

"First of all, what's your name?"

"Arturo."

"Okay, Arturo, I know who you work for, and I know where you're going with all these groceries. I need your help. I told you that you won't be hurt. I was lying. I should have said that it depends. If you help me, I'll help you."

"How do you know who I work for? I'm not even sure myself. I know they are bad people. I am only a cook. They helped me get into the US, but when they learn I can cook, they tell me that unless I work for them, they'll kill my family in Mexico."

"Who exactly is telling you this, Arturo?"

"Diego Cano! El Carnicero!"

When Mark heard Arturo say the name El Carnicero, he felt a wave of elation knowing they had found the people that might lead them to Mendez.

"How often do you see this Diego?"

"Almost every day. I cook for him and the others."

"How many men live with him in the compound?"

"It depends. Sometimes only three of four. Sometimes more."

"How many are there now?"

"I think six."

"Is there video surveillance of the courtyard?"

"No."

"Are there cameras anywhere?"

"Yes, a camera at the back door at the wall and cameras covering the front courtyard. These are the only ones I know of."

"Okay, Arturo. Start the engine and drive back toward the compound. I'm going to ask you some more questions on the way. Do not lie to me. If you try to warn anyone, just remember that you'll be the first to die. Now here's what you're going to do."

CHAPTER 34

1972

A dry stream bed ran down from the mountains behind them and passed close to the wall on one side of the house. Mark worked his way down the ridge, moving around outcroppings of large boulders until he reached the dry stream bed. The bed was depressed enough that he was able to easily work his way to the house without being visible. Rosa and Marcus went straight down toward the rear of the house, carefully watching for the presence of guards. There was a lot of activity at the rear of the house where the cooks and servers were busy caring for the guests.

One of the delivery trucks left, leaving only two trucks parked at the service area. One of them was a panel truck with a caterer's sign on the side. The other truck was a refrigerated truck. Rosa and Marcus were eventually able to get to the wall surrounding the home without being seen. They were protected by the dark of night and the dark clothing they were wearing. Rosa had had dark face paint, as they all had, except for Marcus, whose darker skin enabled him to skip the oily face paint. The group had all agreed that face paint was good enough to serve as mask. They both sat behind the wall and waited for everyone to be in place.

Lou Croft had moved halfway down the slope before he reached a pile of boulders that provided a perfect spot for him to lie prone and support his rifle on his backpack. He had a good view of the back of the house as well as the parking area and the driveway leading in. He watched as Rich Holtz moved down the slope toward the parking area and driveway entrance.

Mark carefully moved up to the wall and cautiously looked over. There was no one toward the rear, but he could see the glow of a cigarette toward the front corner. Staying well below the top of the wall, Mark eased forward until he'd almost reached the corner. He carefully reached for the suppressed pistol, and planting his feet in a shooter's stance, he raised the gun up to the top of the wall and slowly stood up. The man was facing toward the front of the house. He carried a rifle of some sort hanging on his back. One minute he was peacefully smoking a cigarette and a second later he was dead as a .22 long rifle lead bullet entered his head, just behind his ear. Mark was rolling over the wall before the man's body had settled to the ground. In one fluid motion Mark lifted the man and pushed him back over the wall into the darkness. The only windows on this end of the house were contained within small patios, and he was able to quickly move to the rear. He looked at his watch as the last thirty seconds ticked off, and he came around toward the door where all of the servers were located. At the same time, Rosa and Marcus were coming over the wall into the service area. Marcus made sure there was no one inside the cabs of the trucks, and the three moved into the kitchen area. The occupants were staring at the three in complete surprise as Mark held up his hand.

"Everyone, stay calm and no one's going to get hurt. We're just part of the entertainment tonight. Your ticket to safety is your cell phone. Lay them here."

There were five people in the cooking area when they came in. Mark quickly moved to one of the doors leading out of the room and Rosa moved to the other. Marcus took the five occupants who were staring at the shotgun he pointed toward them out the back to the caterer's truck and herded them inside, telling them, "Stay here and you'll be okay."

While he was moving the first five out of the kitchen, three more came in all carrying trays with empty glasses, plates, and saucers. Marcus moved them out to the truck as well after taking their cell phones. The three then started down the hall toward the sounds of loud music and laughter. A man suddenly came down the hallway directly toward them, saying in a loud demanding voice, "Where the hell are those drinks?"

Rosa shot him in the face with her suppressed pistol—not between the eyes as it was supposed to be—but instead dead into his right eye. As they approached the double door, Rosa put her pistol back in its holster and took her MP5 off her back. Mark and Marcus each held their shotguns with safeties off. When they stepped through the double doors, they were looking at a large room with wood paneling and heavy oriental carpeting partially covering a dark wood floor. The centerpiece of the room was a long teak table ringed with upholstered chairs. There were four chairs on either side and one at each end. But what the three of them paused to stare at were the three naked girls dancing—or rather gyrating—to the loud pulsating rhythm of the stripper's music.

"Get off the table," Mark yelled. "Come over here."

Surprised and frightened by Mark's words, the two girls closest to them jumped off the table toward the open doors. The third girl hesitated as one of the men sitting on the far side of the table directly behind her brought a small compact pistol up in his hand, aiming it toward the three in the door. There was no hesitation by Mark this time. He understood how the slam fire pump shotgun would continue to fire as long as he held the trigger, and the effect was devastating as he fired eight rounds of double 00 buckshot within a couple of seconds.

Marcus was a little more deliberate with his eight rounds, actually aiming carefully with each shot. Mark's first round cut one of the stripper's legs almost in half; as she fell onto the table, another of Mark's shots hit her chest. The man who had raised his pistol was hit in the head with another of Mark's shots and killed instantly. Rosa had her MP5 set on selective fire and unloaded three rounds each time she pulled the trigger. Several of the men seated at the table tried to stand up and run, which only made them better targets. One heavily bearded man tried to hide under the table, but Marcus casually knelt down and fired a blast under the table, hitting him square in the bald spot on the top of his head. Rosa inserted a second magazine in her gun and casually walked around the table, placing three bullets into anyone who showed signs of life.

As she reached the far end of the table, she said looking down at the figure lying on the floor. "This is Caldwell." She placed another burst into his head. "This is for the lives he's ruined."

CHAPTER 35

Emelia

Even if she survived, Emelia knew she'd never recover from the experience. She had been taking in deeper and deeper breaths, but it was becoming more difficult with each breath. She was hyperventilating, but no matter how hard she tried to breath, there was no oxygen entering her lungs. She accepted that she was going to die when she heard a door open followed by the freezer lid being raised. The sudden rush of oxygen that filled her lungs was the most wonderful thing she'd ever experienced. Ava and the same two men were looking at her, wondering how she would react. Emelia started screaming at the top of her lungs as she stood up and tried to climb out of the freezer. The two men lifted her out, and Emelia stood there shaking like a leaf and sobbing uncontrollably.

Ava smiled at her without a trace of sympathy. "I hope you've learned something. I warned you before. The next time you go in, you won't be coming out. Now, let's go upstairs. You've peed on yourself. You need a shower before you finish your night's work."

Ava led Emelia back to her room where Katrina was sleeping in her bed and watched her undress and get into the shower. When she had finished showering, Ava helped a still trembling Emelia dry off.

"You are a beautiful girl. I may want to spend some time with you myself," she said as she ran her hand down Emelia's flat stomach. "Let's get you dressed," she said as she went to the closet and came out with a sheer cover that hid nothing. It only reached her hips, and Ava offered Emelia no underwear. "Okay, follow me," she told Emelia, leading her back towards the main house and down a familiar hallway. Emelia couldn't help but look down as they passed the main staircase. There was no indication of what had occurred the night before.

Emelia's fears were confirmed when they stopped at the door to Mr. B's room. Ava knocked on the door, which was opened by a smiling Mr. B. Ava pushed Emelia into his room, saying, "I don't think she'll cause you any problem now." She turned, closed the door, and left.

From the moment Emelia had come out of the freezer, she realized only one thing: She wanted to live. She realized that as long as she was breathing, somehow there might be a way to get out. She had no doubt that Ava's threat to let her die in the freezer was real. When they'd just passed the stairwell and she'd had a vision of Selma, lying on the cold marble floor in a pool of blood, she knew she would have to compromise if she wanted to stay alive. She thought of Carmila back at the compound in El Paso and how she couldn't understand at the time how Carmila could let herself be so used and abused by Diego and the other men. Now she understood. She could be a martyr and die or she could compromise all she'd been taught and stay alive. She couldn't help but wonder what Samuel would say to her now if he were still living. She would probably never know. But Emelia did know one thing for sure. She was going to stay alive.

Mr. B was wearing the same robe he'd worn earlier in the day. He had a drink in his hand, which he sat down on the nightstand. Throwing off the robe left him completely naked. Sitting down in one of the upholstered chairs in the room, he spread his legs and told Emelia, "Get down on your knees and crawl over here." Emelia did as he ordered and obeyed the rest of his demands until he was finally satisfied and fell asleep on the bed.

Emelia sat in one of the chairs and covered herself with the robe he'd thrown on the floor. Thinking of the things Mr. B had made her do, she thought about her compromises. In a strange sort of way, she felt some relief. She was not in the freezer, and she was alive. She'd never again question someone's motives for their actions.

CHAPTER 36

Breaching the Compound

Roe followed the van back, and before they had reached the compound, Mark called Roe's cell phone and explained what the cook had told him. Learning that Emelia had been there was almost more than they could have hoped for.

As they passed a large hardware store, Mark pulled into the parking lot and waited while Roe went inside and soon came out with a plastic bag containing three rolls of duct tape and a fifty-foot length of heavy hemp rope.

Before they drove away from the hardware store, Mark told Roe more of what he'd learned from Arturo.

"Arturo here tells me that when he left the compound, three of the men were still sleeping inside the house next to the wall. The fourth one was the one who opened the gate for him to leave. Arturo is expecting him to be the one who'll open it for him again. Diego is inside the compound with one other man. Park on the street and bring the stuff you bought up toward the gate, but wait down the street until I signal for you to come in."

Before they reached the rear of the compound, Mark moved into the back of the van just behind the two front seats.

"Arturo, my friend, whether you live or die depends on how well you follow my orders. If I have the slightest feeling that you're warning anyone, you're a dead man."

"Señor, I believe you. But I say to you again, these are very bad men. They will show you no mercy."

"I believe you, Arturo. That's even more incentive for you to help me. If I fail, they'll consider you a traitor. Let's not fail."

When they reached the gate at the back of the compound, Arturo sounded his horn in three short honks. It took almost two minutes before a man came out of the house and unlocked the gate. Mark stated crouched low behind the driver's seat as Arturo drove into the parking area. The man closed and locked the gate and was headed back into the house when Arturo yelled at him, "Amigo, how about some help here! I've got a lot of stuff to bring in."

"You're the cook. It's your job."

"That's true, my friend, but I also make sure no one spits in the food or gets a bad case of diarrhea. I know you want to get the liquor inside as fast as possible. Right?"

The man rolled his eyes in exasperation, but the mention of liquor got his attention. He did an about face and approached the side of the van as Arturo opened the sliding door on the driver's side.

Mark knew that they'd only get one good chance to get inside the compound, and he wasn't going to leave anything to chance. As the man leaned into the van to pick something up, Mark fired one shot from the suppressed .22 into the man's left ear, causing him to fall forward into the van. Mark quickly pulled him all the way into the van before he took the key out of the man's pocket and handed it to Arturo, who was staring with wide eyes at Mark's sudden action. If he had any doubts about Mark's resolve, it quickly evaporated.

"Arturo, unlock the gate and let the lady in. Then close the gate back but don't lock it. Understand?"

"Sí," was all Arturo could muster as he headed toward the gate.

As she entered the gate Roe was carrying the rope and a bag with the duct tape. She had pulled a three-hole balaclava over her head similar to the one Mark was wearing. They were both wearing gloves. Letting Arturo lead the way, they entered the door of the larger of the two houses and went down a short hallway. Arturo pointed to a door that was partially open. Looking in the dim room, they heard snoring, but nothing was moving.

Mark whispered to Roe, "Let's keep one alive," as he eased into the room. There were four beds in the room, three of which were occupied. So far, Arturo had been honest with his information. Mark approached one bed and fired one shot into the sleeping man's head before pivoting and firing another round into the second man. Although the shots were not audible outside of the room, the noise was enough to cause the third man to rise up in bed with a quizzical look on his face. Roe swung her pistol, a heavy Beretta, striking the man in the back of his head. It stunned him enough for Mark to wrap duct tape around his mouth, followed by his hands and feet. They left him in a hogtied position on the floor. As soon as they were sure he wasn't possibly going to be able to move, they turned their attention back to Arturo, who had watched in wonder as they finished.

"Okay, Arturo, how much can they see on the camera from the inside?"

"They can see the person standing there next to the entrance and down the hallway behind the person."

"What if you had an arm full of boxes of groceries. Would that block out the view of the hallway?"

"No. The camera is mounted high up in the corner."

"Okay, well take a different approach. Here's what we'll do."

After explaining what he had in mind, they went back out to the van and stacked boxes of food in the arms of both Arturo and Roe. The boxes were arranged so that Arturo's face was easily visible, but the boxes Roe carried were stacked so tall that all of her face and upper body would be obscured to a casual viewer.

The main hallway that ran between the two houses ran straight through, and where it would have probably at one time opened onto a back porch or patio, it now ended at a cinder block wall and a single heavy metal door. In addition to the camera on the wall, there was a single peephole in the door. An electric cord ran down the wall next to the door and was connected to a button.

Arturo came down the hallway carrying his armload of groceries. A few feet behind him, Roe, who was about the same size as the man who'd open the gate, followed with a stack of boxes that rose over the top of her head. Arturo had to lean in close to the wall in order to push the button. There was along pause before Arturo said in a loud voice, "We need some help here, Bruno. This stuff is heavy."

The sound of a key rattling in the door was followed by a grinding sound of metal on metal as the heavy door swung outward on large rusty hinges.

"What took you so long?" a guttural voice asked as Arturo took a step through the door. As he did, he appeared to stumble and fall, piling cans, bottles, and boxes of different products over the floor. Bruno, the man who'd opened the door, cursed loudly as he leaned over to pick up something from the floor. By now Mark had moved into the hallway—and still obscured from Bruno's view by Roe, who was standing in front of the door holding the pile of boxes—he stepped through. Before Bruno could react, he hit him on the side of his head with a can of beans. Bruno dropped like a rock. Within a few seconds, Mark had him trussed up with duct tape like a pig being carried to the market.

By now Roe had entered the small room, which was completely bare except for a small computer table with a monitor providing the view of the hallway. She dropped the boxes she was holding and had her Beretta in her hand. Arturo held the door open and Roe watched him carefully as Mark ran back down the hallway and back to the room where the men had been sleeping. He dragged the man they'd tied up through the metal door and into bare room where Roe was waiting. They left him on the floor next to Bruno, who was finally regaining consciousness. The hatred coming from his eyes was intense, but the duct tape across his mouth prevented him from speaking.

Arturo explained the layout of the rooms to Roe and Mark. Probably the last threat inside the compound would be Diego Cano, alias El Carnicero, himself. They passed through the empty kitchen and to a doorway leading into the main room where the men ate, played cards, and abused whichever females were available at the moment.

Diego was lying on his stomach on a couch. He was nude and sitting on his back was Carmila, who was also totally nude. Diego was giving Carmila instructions on how to massage his back when Mark entered the room. Carmila was the first to be aware of the presence of strange people, and she paused for a moment. Mark held his fingers over his lips, indicating silence. She understood and continued her work on Diego's back. Mark came up behind the sofa, reached over and placed his gun's muzzle against Diego's ear, and whispered, "If you move or even blink, your brains will be all over the furniture."

Diego froze as Roe walked around the sofa. After motioning Carmila to get off his back, she wrapped first his wrist, and then his legs and feet with duct tape. He resembled an Egyptian mummy by the time Roe finished securing him. Only then did Mark remove his gun from Diego's ear.

During the drive from the grocery warehouse, Arturo had told Mark some of the things that Diego and his men, especially Brutus, had done to some of the people that had passed through the safe house or compound. He'd detailed the brutality that they'd inflicted, especially on Carmila. For some reason, Diego had singled Carmila out as his own personal doormat.

Roe had already gone through Diego's clothes and had a set of keys in her hand. She handed the keys to Arturo and told him, "Go and open all of the rooms. Bring everyone back here."

By now Arturo accepted the fact that this was going to be his way out. Somehow, he sensed that he wasn't going to have to be in fear of El Carnicero for very much longer.

CHAPTER 37

1972

For a moment there was silence when all three stopped firing. The room was a nightmare. It resembled a scene of a bomb blast with splinters of the table and furniture spread around torn and bloody bodies. The two fortunate strippers who'd made it out of the room in one piece were huddled on the floor outside the room and were trembling in abject terror, expecting the worst.

The sudden sound of gunfire outside the house caused Mark, Rosa, and Marcus to suddenly refocus their attention toward the front of the house. When they reached the large foyer at the front of the house, they were met by two men in dark suits holding handguns. When they saw the three figures dressed in black, their surprise caused them to pause for only a second. It was a second too long, as both Marcus and Mark, who were ahead of Rosa, each fired a blast from their shotguns. Rosa stepped up and fired a three-round shot into each one as they passed by the two men and out the front door. Their goal now was to go over the wall across the front of the house and follow the slope down toward the neighborhood below where Ron would be waiting with the van. Rich had already crossed the line of parked cars, but before he crossed the road, he threw a grenade into a car that was trying to turn around in the driveway. The explosion created enough distraction for Mark, Rosa, and Marcus to climb over the front wall.

As soon as they were over the wall, they watched and waited for Lou and Rich. By now, Lou Croft was following Rich around the end of the parking area and past the burning car that Rich had just demolished. As he passed the burning car, he was outlined in the light from the fire and a man stepped out from behind a parked car and fired a burst from an automatic weapon. Lou fell to the pavement, dropping his sniper rifle as he fell. Although he'd already crossed the driveway, Rich was close enough that he fired several three-round bursts toward the man who then disappeared. Rich ran toward Lou as the other three saw Lou fall. Staying behind the wall, they ran toward where Lou was lying. Mark told Rosa and Marcus, "Stay behind the wall and keep firing to keep anyone else down."

By the time Mark reached where Lou was lying, Rich was kneeling by his side. As Mark approached, Rich looked up at Mark and shook his head. Lou had been hit several times, but the one in his head left no doubt. Mark tried for any semblance of a pulse, but there was nothing.

Mark acted quickly. "Help me move him."

Dragging Lou over to one of the cars whose windows had been shot out, they put Lou into the driver's seat.

"Do you have an incendiary?" he asked Rich.

Rich, the explosives expert, handed Mark an incendiary and another frag grenade.

Mark said, "Take Lou's rifle and head for the wall. I'll be right behind you."

He threw the fragmentation grenade as far as he could toward the house before sliding the incendiary grenade under the driver's seat where they'd placed Lou's body. Mark then ran like hell toward the wall where the others were still firing toward the parked cars. He dove headfirst over the wall and rolled on the hard ground but luckily didn't hit a boulder or cactus. The remaining guards were smart enough to stay hidden, and as both grenades exploded, they had added incentive to stay out of sight. The fire produced by the incendiary created a flame so hot that it ignited the cars parked nearby. The only thing left would be a piece of metal, and Lou's body would be reduced to ashes. The Plomeros, their number now reduced to four, headed down the hill to the cul-de-sac where Ron waited in the van. As they exited the neighborhood, the noise had brought some people out of their homes, curious about the distant sound of fireworks. They were so focused on the fires and sounds from up on the ridge they ignored the van that rapidly left the neighborhood. When the van reached the airport, the plane was out of the hangar and ready to go. Within minutes they were airborne and heading back to El Paso. There was no celebration on this flight home.

Chapter 38

Emelia

Emelia sat in the chair for what seemed to be hours before Mr. B started to wake up. Bracing herself for more of the same, Emelia held her breath, but he looked at her as if he couldn't remember who she was. Then he said, "Get out. I need to sleep." Breathing a sigh of relief, she pulled the robe around herself and went out into the hallway. Trying to remember which direction to go, she started down the hallway. Before she could reach the end, Ava seemed to materialize out of nowhere.

"Well, I can see there's been a huge improvement in your attitude. Let's get you back to your room and you can rest. We need to have you well rested before the weekend. The Big Man will be coming then."

"Big Man?"

"Yes. The Big Man will be coming. You'll want to be looking good for him. If you're lucky he might want to spend some time with you."

Emelia didn't want to ask any more questions. Somehow, she thought that the less she knew about anything, the better off she'd be. When she went back into her room, Katrina was awake and watching TV.

"You know I told you not to cause any trouble. You're only still here because you are really good-looking, and they see value in that. What happened to you this morning?"

When Emelia told Katrina about the freezer, she turned white for a moment. "I heard Ava mention something about the freezer being a big help, but I had no idea what she meant."

"What did Ava mean by the Big Man and a party?"

"I didn't tell you this, but she means a Mexican guy named Mendez. He's the rich man who sets all this up. It's how he rewards his business associates. Don't say his name out loud. You never heard it. He's only known as Mr. M around here. One of the men I was with one night was drunk and bragged about how he provided rental vehicles for Mendez. He didn't say what for."

The name Mendez was somehow familiar to Emelia, but she couldn't quite place it. She shrugged it off as she showered again and lay down on her bed. With the smell of Mr. B washed off her body for the second time, she was overcome with exhaustion from the day's trauma. As she drifted off to sleep, she thought of Samuel and her parents back home. She realized that she'd probably never see any of them again.

Emelia did have a few days to rest. Apparently, Mr. A, B, C, and D had left, and the estate was empty except for Ava, Mutt, and Jeff, as well as the cooks and gardeners. Emelia, Katrina, and Mariana were allowed to move around the estate under the close scrutiny of Mutt and Jeff or Ava. The three girls spent a large part of the day lying by the pool. Ava wanted them all to get a little tan. "The men like the tan lines," she told them.

One day the three girls were lying by the pool with Ava watching them like a mother hen. Emelia couldn't help but feel Ava's eyes focusing on her. When Ava stood up and told Emelia to come with her, she was a little bit confused, but when she followed Ava into one of the rooms in the pool cabana, she realized immediately what Ava's intentions were. The room was a small dressing room with a chair and sofa. Ava closed the door and turned to face Emelia. She reached behind her back and unsnapped her top and stepped out of her bikini bottom. "Take yours off," she said.

Emelia was turning red and hesitated. Ava stepped up to her, and turning Emelia around, unhooked her top. Without pausing, she pulled Emelia's bikini bottom down. She turned Emelia back around so she was facing her and pushed her back onto the sofa. It was midday, and the sofa was lit up with direct sunlight shining in through the open blinds, leaving Emelia exposed like an ancient offering to the gods.

"I've wanted to do this from the first time I saw you. Just relax. You might even like it," she said as she dropped to her knees between Emelia's legs.

In the next few minutes, Emelia experienced an endless succession of emotions. They started with shock and embarrassment, but the fear and memory of the freezer overrode her thoughts of resisting. When she experienced a moment of carnal, blissful pleasure it only added to her feeling of shame and degradation. It was not that Ava was female. Emelia had once had a brief affair with one of her girlfriends back in Chile. But that was voluntary. This was not and was no different from being subjected to Mr. B's attentions.

When Emelia returned to the pool area, Katrina was smiling at her. "So, you had a session with Ava? I should have warned you."

Emelia was still in shock and could only nod in reply.

Over the next few days, Emelia had to submit to Ava's attentions several times and once Ava had Katrina join them.

Katrina seemed to be comfortable with whatever Ava wanted. Emelia only wanted to avoid the freezer at any cost.

On Saturday afternoon, they were eating in the small area reserved for meals when Ava said, "Tonight's the night. Be ready by nine and look good."

When they returned to their rooms, Emelia tried to relax and soon drifted off to sleep. She was rudely awakened by Katrina, who said, "Time to get ready."

Katrina was already wearing one of the see-through outfits from the closet and she threw one toward Emelia.

"This one will look good on you. Hurry up. Ava will be here any time now. I tried to let you sleep as long as possible."

Emelia had no idea how long she'd been asleep, but she was aware that it was dark outside. She quickly put the scanty things on, and Katrina used a hairbrush to take a few kinks out of her hair.

"You want to look nice for Mr. M."

Ava opened their door soon afterward, and Emelia and Katrina followed her to the door of Mariana's room. Mariana came out, and they followed Ava along the usual route down the back stairs and into the room that Emelia had learned was called the "playroom."

The room was set up similar to the previous time. The only real difference was that there was only one individual sitting on the large U-shaped sofa. There were two men standing at a distance behind it. They were both large men dressed in dark suits with open-collared white shirts. Their heads were close shaven, which only accented their dark short growth of facial hair, creating a sinister look. They stood with arms crossed, their faces devoid of any emotion, watching everyone that came near the man on the sofa.

This time there were no chairs for the girls, so they stood in front of the man sitting on the sofa, not quite sure what to do next. It was Ava who spoke first, "These are the girls we currently have here in the house."

The man on the sofa set his wineglass down and stood up. He was maybe five foot ten with a slim build and within fifty to sixty years in age. His hair was dark and pulled back in a short ponytail. He was dressed in a cream-colored linen suit with a pink silk shirt open at the collar, exposing a hairless chest and a heavy necklace of gold. The gold Rolex on his wrist sparkled with a ring of diamonds surrounding the bezel. As he slowly walked around the coffee table, he said, "I'm only interested in one girl at the moment."

At that moment, Emelia recognized the voice. It was the man who had come to her room with El Carnicero back in El Paso.

He spoke again, "You are called Emelia. I thought you would be a valued asset back here, but I've not been able to get you out of my mind. I know you suffered a terrible loss when your boyfriend was killed. I am sorry. My name is Andre. I want to make it up to you. Your future here is maybe not so good. I am going to help you if you'll let me."

Emelia didn't know whether to try and scratch his eyes out or to drop to her knees in gratitude. But when he said her boyfriend was dead, a dagger went through her heart. What difference did anything make now that she knew for sure that Samuel was dead? She did want to get out of this place, but at what cost? Again, her sense of self-preservation took over.

He reached out his hand and led her a few steps away from the others. "Ava, I wanted to see her with the others just to remember how beautiful she is when compared to other beautiful women. She is truly a diamond."

The two other girls and Ava stared at Emelia, who was the Cinderella of the moment. Katrina seemed pissed, as if she'd lost her chance at the lottery. And Ava, who was having a hard time saying anything, could only force a smile and keep her mouth tightly shut.

Speaking directly to Ava, Andre said, "Take her and get her some proper clothing. Quickly though, my plane is waiting."

"Come with me," Ava angrily muttered through clenched teeth as she led Emelia away.

So much for choices, thought Emelia as Ava took her to a room in the main house that had a closet full of designer women's clothing. Throwing some things on the bed, she told Emelia to get dressed. Emelia didn't pay a lot of attention to what she was putting on. Anything was better than the scanty see-through costumes she'd been forced to wear. When she was dressed, Ava took a couple of other things and put them in a small carry-on bag. They went back by Emelia's room, and Emelia put in a few toiletry items. Katrina had already returned to the room and sat on her bed, sulking but not speaking, until Emelia was walking out.

"He's probably taking you to a high-end whore-house."

Emelia only said, "Just like this one?"

Ava took Emelia back to the main house and to the opulent front entrance where a long black limousine waited under the huge portico.

I guess this is called progress, thought Emelia. *In through the garage and out through the front door.*

Andre was waiting in the limo with the driver and the two bodyguards. No one said a word, and Emelia was afraid to ask any questions as they drove south on I-95 toward the Opa-locka airport.

CHAPTER 39
Carmila and El Carnicero

While Arturo was bringing in the people locked in rooms throughout the compound, Mark dragged Bruno and the man from the house outside into the larger room and spread them out on the floor. When Arturo returned with the captives being held by El Carnicero, Samuel ran to Roe and hugged her as if she were his long lost mother. He then turned to Mark and shot him a thumbs-up salute with a huge smile. Mark held his hand up in a cautionary sign and said, "No names." There were only two others whom Arturo had brought back into the room. One was an older woman who appeared to be in shock and a young girl not more than fourteen who was shaking like a leaf. Arturo pointed toward her and said, "They have treated her very poorly."

Carmila spoke up as well, "They have raped her many times. Mostly Bruno."

Mark looked at Arturo and told him, "Arturo, I want you to take all these people back to another room well away from this room. Explain to them that we're not going to hurt them, and we plan to help them to go to a safe place. Leave the keys with Roe."

As Arturo was leaving the room with them, Carmila defiantly said she was going to stay and help with whatever

Mark planned to do. "This man is a pig, and he deserves to be gutted like a pig."

Mark answered her, "Don't worry. Be patient. You just don't need to hear our conversations with these others. You're better off not knowing what they say."

Carmila left reluctantly with the others, leaving Mark, Roe, and Samuel in the room with the three men spread out on the floor.

Mark pulled them to a sofa and sat them down, side by side. The sofa was small, and the three men were wedged tightly against each other like three calorically challenged people in the economy section of a commercial airplane. They could hardly move even if they were not bound so tightly.

Both Bruno and Diego the Carnicero were glaring with hatred as Mark ripped the duct tape off their faces. The third man who knew what Mark had done to the other two men who'd been sleeping in the room with him was not quite so confident. Diego let loose a long stream of obscenity and Mark laughed at his blustering. Samuel pointed toward Bruno.

"This is the shithole who hit Emelia and forced her into the van."

Bruno looked at Samuel and said, "Yes, and I'd have fucked her, too, except for Diego here who wanted to save her for Andre."

Diego looked toward Bruno. "Shut up, you dumb shit. Don't say another word."

Mark looked toward the third man, who'd been silent.

"What can you tell us about the men you killed on the river? Were you there?"

"Yes."

"Did you help to bring a girl back here?"

"Yes."

"Did anyone harm her while she was here?"

"I don't think so."

"Where is she now?"

"I don't know."

Without a moment's hesitation, Mark placed the end of his gun barrel against the man's ear and pulled the trigger. The man jerked once before his head dropped forward onto his chest. A small stream of blood spurted out of his ear, wetting Bruno's shoulder with blood. Bruno tried in vain to twist away, but the three were wedged too tightly for him to avoid the blood.

"Wrong answer. Let's move on to you," and he placed the gun barrel against Bruno's head.

Mark had suddenly gained the attention of both Bruno and Diego as he said, "Now think very carefully before you answer my questions. What is your name?"

"Bruno."

"You want to tell me more about the girl called Emelia? Did you touch her?"

"No! I only helped bring her here."

"Where did you keep her?"

"In one of the rooms in back."

"Arturo said she helped him in the kitchen."

"Yes. We were instructed by Diego to not touch her."

"Where is she now?"

"They took her."

"Who took her?"

Bruno was starting to sweat profusely now as Mark continued to press him. "Answer me. Who took her?"

"Someone gave the order that she was being taken somewhere else."

Looking at Diego, Bruno blurted out, "Ask him. I only do what he tells me to do."

"Bruno, I'm only going to ask you one more time. Who took her from here?"

Visibly shaken as Mark pressed the gun barrel harder into his ear, he blurted out, "Señor Mendez!"

"You mean Andre Mendez?"

Diego exploded. "Shut up, you fool! Don't you know what will happen to us?"

Mark was looking at Roe, who nodded back and said, "Bingo."

Mark couldn't keep from laughing at what Diego said. "My friend, I think you need to reprioritize your problems."

Mark was looking up toward the open beams running across the open ceiling. There was still a piece of rope hanging partway down. Mark took the rope Roe brought, unwound it, and threw it up and over where the old rope was hanging. Grabbing Diego by the legs, he pulled him forward and onto the floor. He carefully tied the rope around the duct tape holding Diego's wrist together.

"Okay, I'm going to need some help here." Both Roe and Samuel helped Mark pull down on the rope draping across the beam and Diego was raised up into the air. They tied the end of the rope around a heavy pipe that was exposed on the outside wall, leaving El Carnicero hanging naked and vulnerable like a fat ugly piñata. His fat belly hung down and his testicles had shrunk up into his groin.

Turning back to Bruno, who was watching, Mark asked again, "Where did they take her?"

"Señor, on my mother's grave, I don't know. I only follow orders. Only Diego talks to Señor Mendez. They never tell me such things."

"Let me ask him," Samuel said. "Can I borrow your gun?"

Mark handed his gun to Samuel. "It's ready to fire. All you need to do is to pull the trigger."

Samuel stood in front of Bruno. "Tell me where she is, you bastard."

Bruno pleaded, "I do not know where she is!"

Samuel placed the tip of the gun barrel on Bruno's knee and pulled the trigger. The resulting howl of pain from Bruno was much louder that the sound of the gun.

Pleading again, Bruno repeated, "I don't know where they take them!"

Mark took his pistol back from Samuel and looked at Bruno, "I don't see where you are any help to us. There's no reason to keep you around anymore," he said as he raised the gun barrel toward Bruno.

"No, no! I can help you! I'll tell you where we keep drugs and the money!"

Mark paused and said, "So tell us."

"Diego keeps the only key in his pocket. One of the back rooms has a tall cabinet. Behind the cabinet is a door to a small room. That's where the drugs and money are held until someone collects it for Señor Mendez."

"Where is this room?"

"It's the last room in the back hallway. The door is painted green. The same key opens both doors."

Roe looked at the keys she'd taken from Diego's pocket along with a cell phone. She was already headed out of the room. "I'll check it out."

She soon returned and nodded. "There's cash and a shit pile of heroin."

Mark nodded, took one step toward Bruno, and fired point-blank into his head. A small dot appeared in the center of his forehead as his head suddenly flopped to one side. Mark turned toward Diego, who'd seen everything he'd done. By now, Diego was in considerable pain from hanging by his arms.

"I'll make a deal with you."

Mark only smiled and asked, "What did you have in mind?"

"I can tell you where they were taking the girl called Emelia. You must promise me that you or your friends here won't kill me."

Mark appeared to think for a minute before replying, "I'll accept your offer. I give you my word that neither I nor my two friends here will harm you. Now tell us where they took Emelia."

Thinking to himself that he was going to be okay, Diego began to talk. Somehow, he'd find a way to get back at these people later as he said, "Señor Mendez is always looking for beautiful women to help him entertain at his home in West Palm Beach. He makes some of them work at his gentlemen's clubs in Florida."

"Where is his home in West Palm Beach?"

"I once drove the van that carried two girls to his home. It is really a castle on the ocean. There is an iron gate with the letter *M* built into the metal. The house can't be seen from the road. You don't want to go there because there are many guards. I've only been as far as the garage, never into the house."

Roe asked, "I thought Mendez operated out of Mexico. Why does he have a home in West Palm Beach?"

"Oh, he has many homes. I think he has businesses in Florida, and he likes to go there."

"That's not enough, Diego. Give me a name of someone who works for Mendez in Florida."

"I only know of one name. A woman who works as a maid at his castle was married to my cousin. Her name is Esmeralda Gonzales."

"Okay, this is all good to know. Let's go talk to Arturo and the others, but first, Roe, take us to the hidden room."

As they were starting to walk out of the room, Diego bellowed, "Wait a minute! What about our deal?"

Mark replied, "Don't worry, we will be honoring my promise. Just be patient and hang tight." Samuel missed the humor, but Roe laughed as she led them toward the hidden room. "You have a way with words, Mark."

They took the cash from the room but left the drugs. They left the doors open so the room was no longer a hidden room. They returned to the room where Arturo was waiting with Carmila and the other two women. Mark gave each one of them a sizeable amount of cash. For each of them it was more than they'd ever had in their lives.

Mark told Arturo to take them out through the kitchen so they wouldn't see Diego hanging from the ceiling. "Dump the body out of the van and all of you use it to drive far away from here. I'd encourage you to forget this place and move on."

Carmila was angry. "I wanted to talk to him while he was tied up. You promised me."

"Roe, you and Samuel help these people out the back and into the van. Ask them to wait for Carmila. Come with me, Carmila."

Carmila followed Mark back to the room where Diego was hanging like a fat hog. Carmila let out a gasp, followed by a laugh that lacked any semblance of humor. She looked at Mark and asked him, "Are you through with him?"

Mark smiled. "He's all yours. You've got fifteen minutes before the van leaves."

Diego shouted at Mark, "You promised me!"

Mark's grin grew even wider. "Yes, I did promise you that neither I nor my two friends would hurt you. I didn't say anything about anyone else."

"Mr. Carnicero, I'll be right back," said Carmila, heading toward the kitchen. She returned a moment later carrying a large tin washtub and a gleaming butcher knife. She positioned the tub under his feet as she looked up at him.

"Do you remember what you did to my friend Gloria when she tried to escape this place?"

The wall of the compound was made of thick concrete, and with the high level of commercial activity from the adjacent businesses, Mark wasn't worried about anyone outside hearing any sounds from within the building. However, the screams that started coming from El Carnicero made him cringe. He made a quick exit out the back just as Roe was helping Arturo and the other two into the van.

Just as they were about to leave without her, Carmilla came out of the house, wiping her face and arms with a wet towel. Her dress that she'd hurriedly put on after Mark had tied Diego up was stained with multiple dark splotches. She had a huge smile on her face, and as she climbed into the van she smiled at Mark and mouthed a big, "Thank you."

As soon as Arturo had driven the van out of the parking area and disappeared down the street, Mark and Roe removed their face coverings and gloves. With Samuel following, they walked casually down the street to the old Toyota and drove away from the compound.

Before they reached their hotel, Mark stopped at a convenience store for Roe to use a payphone outside to make one quick call. The DEA would soon be making a gruesome discovery at a cartel safe house.

CHAPTER 40
1972

The flight back to the hangar base in El Paso was a long one. No one spoke, and each of them were lost in their own thoughts. They all knew the risks they were taking, but Lou's death really made it a reality. Mark especially was second-guessing everything they'd done. What could he have done differently? In the end though, he knew there was nothing he would have done differently. The images in his mind of the things he was doing were starting to build. The image of the family in the Mercedes being blown to pieces, the stripper's leg being severed by his shotgun blast, and especially of Lou being consumed by the incendiary played over and over in his mind on an endless reel.

By the time they were home and everything was packed away, they all went to the bar. Rosa had maintained the role of leader partly because of her knowledge of their targets. She was also the one who had a line of communication with the ones who could be called their "handlers," but even she had no idea who exactly those people were. Everyone had accepted her emergence as the default leader of the group. The people responsible for selecting the group had chosen well. There were no egos questioning her assumption of leadership and neither did anyone question Mark's tactical planning. Everyone had a voice and had no fear of speaking up. So, after everyone was settled in a seat with a drink, Rosa pulled over an upholstered chair and placed a hat in the seat. "This was Lou's chair. It will continue to be his chair. A toast to Lou." She raised her glass.

After the toast, Rosa asked, "Do any of you have any doubts about our mission? If anyone of you questions what we're doing and wants out, say so now. We all knew from the start of the risks we would be taking. Any doubt or hesitation on the part of anyone simply can't be tolerated."

No one spoke or moved.

"Okay, then. Let's move on."

One by one they each drifted off to their respective rooms. Mark had returned to his room and was stepping out of a long hot shower when he realized that he wasn't alone. Rosa was in his bed under a sheet.

"I hope you don't mind. I just don't want to be alone tonight. If you'll just hold me. That's all I need."

Mark only nodded and finished drying himself off before turning out the lights. When he got into the bed, he realized that she wore nothing. Mark did indeed hold her, with her small body molding perfectly into his much larger frame. What began as a comforting embrace slowly turned into a passionate one. It was as if they both were looking for relief from the mental trauma of the mission. For a while all their troubles were forgotten before they collapsed into a long and dreamless sleep.

Mark woke in an empty bed. He was surprised that he was never aware of her leaving the room. When he finally entered the meeting room, Rosa was working at the computer desk. There was no mention of the previous evening as she smiled and said, "Good morning,"

Soon everyone was up and watching the morning news on television. Marcus Jefferson laughed and said, "Talk about a shit storm. Look at this."

The story of what the news was calling "The Phoenix Massacre" was on every channel. It was being described as the result of a major drug war. Events such as this didn't create much news in the US when it happened in Mexico, but when it occurred in an American resort city, it suddenly became headline news. Sean Caldwell was fast becoming a cult hero as the news media began to look closely at his life. The talking heads were predicting major upheavals within various criminal organizations. As to the perpetrators of the massacre, the only thing reported in the media was that a gang of Spanish-speaking men were responsible.

Rosa had to laugh, "So only men can do such things? I can't get any respect. Seriously though, let's hope that's all they really have. I think our cover at the motel was good and the van we used was taken care of. We had masks and we wore gloves so there shouldn't be anything to point back to us. Besides, we don't exist. I know how well our government can screw something up but, so far, we've been backed up pretty well. The news I'm getting is that we're creating a lot of angst among the cartels. They're really starting to become paranoid and pointing fingers at each other. Our job is going to become more dangerous just because of that paranoia. They're going to be looking over their shoulders more and more. They just can't keep taking everything for granted. And in fact, that means we're succeeding in our mission. Someone sitting in the Pentagon or maybe even the White House at this moment, is patting themselves on the back, thinking about how brilliant they are to have devised this plan."

The missions did continue, and they did become more and more difficult. The drug production facilities were better hidden and better guarded as time passed. On several occasions they flew deep into Mexico to attack a drug facility. There were times when they would go several weeks between missions. During these periods, they agreed to periodically take short leaves. Mark visited his mother once during his time with the group to prove to her that he was alive and well. She had to promise to only tell anyone who asked that he was stationed somewhere in Southeast Asia.

Over time, Mark and Rosa's relationship deepened. The others in the group were aware as it became apparent, but no one seemed to consider it to be a problem. Rosa would occasionally talk about her brother and parents. It was obviously a difficult topic for her, but Mark was a good listener and it seemed to help her cope with the loss she couldn't let go. She described to Mark the anguish she'd felt when she returned home to find her home engulfed in flames. By the time the fire had died out, there was simply nothing left. The police only told her that the cartel had sent body parts of her parents to them, and the fire had burned so hot and for so long that her twin brother had been totally consumed in the fire. That Rosa and her brother were very close was apparent, as she would talk about him endlessly. Like many twins, they had been inseparable. Her parents did sometimes refer to them as "our child." Mark soon realized that the loss of her brother had affected her far more than the loss of her parents. It seemed that half of her identity had been literally torn from her. It helped Mark understand her passionate search for the leaders of the cartel responsible, and until she found them, she considered any cartel an open target. And even though she was Mark's first true love, he was constantly perplexed at how she could be so soft and tender but at the same time she could turn on a dime and become brutal and ruthless toward the people they were targeting.

Months passed, and the group had bonded as much as any on the battlefield possibly could have done. One morning, Rosa stood up from the computer, walked over to the bar, and poured herself a large amount of whiskey. It was uncharacteristic for her to be drinking in the morning. She had a faraway look on her face. She walked over to where Mark was sitting in a chair reading and looked down at him before she spoke quietly to him.

"I've got them now. Finally."

Mark knew what she was referring to. What he didn't realize was, that without realizing it, she was setting the Plomeros up for their final mission.

CHAPTER 41

West Palm Beach

After leaving the safe house Roe, Mark, and Samuel returned to their hotel and checked out. Roe drove the Toyota to the airport and left the car in a long term parking lot after wiping it down as much as possible. When Mark had bought the Toyota from the lady, he'd not used his real name, and she had just signed the title to release it to whoever wanted to register it so it couldn't be traced back to him. Roe locked the car and kept the keys. Then she bought a ticket to West Palm Beach.

Mark and Samuel started driving east toward Florida. Mark knew that even if he could drive nonstop, it would take him at least twenty-four hours to drive to West Palm Beach. Although Samuel was capable of driving, He didn't want to chance being stopped with Samuel behind the wheel. That would be a complication they didn't need. He thought that if he stopped at a rest stop about halfway, he could sleep for five or six hours and be okay to drive through. As soon as Roe arrived in West Palm, she was to get hotel rooms. Then she was to drive along the coast and locate the oceanfront estate so they wouldn't have to waste any time looking for it.

It was after 10:00 PM when Roe landed at the West Palm Beach airport. After renting a car, she reserved three rooms at a hotel just outside the perimeter of the airport.

After putting her things in her room, she called Mark. "Hey, I've reserved rooms at the airport Hilton. How's the driving?"

"I gave Samuel a rolled-up newspaper. His job is to hit me if I start to nod off. We're making good time, and we should be there by late tomorrow afternoon. Just be careful if you start looking for the estate. Once whoever's in charge hears about what happened in El Paso, they'll be looking over their shoulders."

"Right. I'm going to get something to eat and then a good night's sleep. I'll see you tomorrow. Drive safe," she said and went down to the hotel bar, which was busy and still serving food. After a burger and two glasses of wine, she borrowed a phone book from the front desk, went back to her room, and looked up the name Esmeralda Gonzales. As might be expected in South Florida, there were a huge number of Gonzaleses. By now, all she wanted to do was to crash, which she did.

Early next morning, after a large breakfast from room service and a hot shower, she looked at the phone book again.

It was going to be a daunting task to filter Esmeralda out of these names and she didn't know for sure that she would even be listed in the phone book. There were three listings with Esmeralda as a part of the listing and one simple E. Gonzalez. There was no answer on the first Esmeralda and an older-sounding man answered on the second. Roe asked if she could speak to Esmeralda, but the man simply said, "She's gone back to Ecuador," and abruptly hung up. The third try was answered by a woman speaking Spanish. Roe said, "Esmeralda, I was told that you are looking for other house cleaning jobs."

The woman started laughing, and when she finally stopped, she said, "I suspect you've got the wrong number.

Between my husband and two kids, I don't need another house to clean. I can't keep up with the one I've got. Besides, I'm a schoolteacher. Just out of curiosity, how much does a house cleaner make? It's probably a lot more than a schoolteacher."

Roe had to laugh. "You're probably right. Sorry for the wrong number." She hung up. When she dialed the E. Gonzales listing, a woman answered in heavily accented English, "Yes?" Roe knew as she spoke that what she was doing was not the smartest thing to do. And she was right.

"Esmeralda, a relative of your husband told me to call you. He told me that you might be able to help me."

There was a pause before the voice replied in a hesitant voice, "My husband has been dead for three years. What relative do you mean?"

"Diego Cano."

Roe could sense the woman's reaction just from the sound she made at the mention of Diego's name. There was a sharp gasp followed by what sounded like a moan. Answering in a whisper, she asked, "What do you want?"

Roe had to struggle to contain her excitement and remain calm as she tried to reassure Esmeralda that she meant no harm. "I only want to ask you some questions. I don't mean to upset you in any way. If I could meet with you for only a few minutes you might be able to help me."

"Why didn't Diego help you?"

"He did help me, but there were many questions that he couldn't answer. I don't think Diego can help me anymore."

Reluctantly, Esmeralda said, "I have to be at work by noon. Can you come to my home now? I will only be able to talk for a short time."

Still struggling to contain her excitement, Roe replied, "Is your address the same as the phone book?"

"Sí, there is a blue car in the carport and a large limestone rock in the yard."

"Esmeralda, I should be able to be there within thirty minutes," Roe replied as she was already looking at a Google image of the address on her laptop. "You don't know how much I appreciate your help."

Before leaving her hotel room, Roe had the presence of mind to write a note for Mark. She wrote down where she was going along with the exact address. She started out the door but suddenly reversed her course and went back into her room. She rummaged in her suitcase and came out with one of the satellite tracking devices. Placing it inside her bra, she made an addendum to the note before finally leaving the room. When she reached the lobby, she placed the note in a hotel envelope and left it at the front desk addressed to Mark.

Leaving the hotel, she went east on Southern Boulevard to US 1, or South Dixie Highway, as it is called by locals. After passing SW 10th Avenue, she went a few blocks before turning into a neighborhood with a mix of closely packed homes and an occasional business. The variation in houses was amazing. They ranged from wooden boxes to elaborate Spanish stucco hacienda styles. The dense tropical foliage surrounding many of the homes indicated the age of the neighborhood, with many homes totally hidden behind dense overgrown vegetation. Some of the houses and duplex apartments were well-maintained, but many others had zero landscaping and instead had a large concrete parking pad jammed with older model cars and trucks. The neighborhood definitely leaned toward a Hispanic population, as every person she saw could have just arrived from Central America. Roe couldn't help but notice how they avoided eye contact, thinking she might be an agent from ICE who, they wanted to avoid at all costs.

Her plan was to talk to Esmeralda and then drive to the coastline and try to identify the estate that Diego had described. Intellectually, she knew that she should wait for Mark and Samuel before meeting with Esmeralda, but she felt like she was on a roll, and she needed to forge ahead. She should have listened to her instincts.

CHAPTER 42
1973

In the beginning, the next mission seemed to be no different than the many missions they'd already done. As usual, the Plomeros gathered in the lounge. Lou's chair, with his hat still resting where Rosa had placed it, remained untouched. As Rosa began to disclose the target, Mark wondered if he was the only one to sense the difference in Rosa as she began to describe the people they would be going after. He could see the level of fervor and excitement in her as she spoke. She always expressed resolve and determination with every mission, but this time it was more than just that. This was personal, and he hoped it wasn't so obvious to the others.

Over the previous months, their missions had taken them into Mexico on several occasions. They only stayed within the chopper's range in each one. This time the target was too far without refueling at some point. There were no airports near the target that they could safely use, so the plane was out of question as well. They would have to travel on the ground from the border both to and from the site. As Rosa pointed out, it was going to expose them to additional risks from both the Mexican authorities as well as the possibility of unexpected encounters with random gangs or cartel members. Rosa spent a lot of time explaining why this mission was so important.

"The damage and chaos that we've caused the cartels over the last few months has been significant. Our success is partially why this opportunity has opened up. If you remember how much reaction we created in Phoenix, then multiply this by ten. The paranoia among the cartels has resulted in actually bringing them closer together. The old axiom, 'Keep your friends close but keep your enemies even closer' was never more apparent than in this case. There is going to be a wedding. Cartels are extremely family-oriented. Members do not intermingle with other families in other cartels. That's why this wedding is an anomaly. A son of one cartel is marrying the daughter of another. The family of the son are the dominant cartel from Mexico City and up the east coast to our border. The girl's family from Sinaloa controls most of the west coast. Groups from Coahuila, Sonora, and Chihuahua and others will be attending. It will be a who's who of cartel leadership. The boy's family owns a large exclusive beach resort near Tampico. They plan to open its doors so that all the guests can stay there since there's nothing else nearby with the same luxury and capacity. There is an airport in Tampico for guests to fly into. There's no way we would be able to fly into the airport with our equipment. Our only option is to drive down the coast from Brownsville. We'll fly to Brownsville. There's a landing strip west of the city that is used by DEA and Border Patrol. We'll go south from there."

Everyone in the group listened intently as Rosa spoke.

Marcus asked, "Won't we be standing out like a sore thumb?"

"Hopefully not," Rosa replied. "As always, we'll be creative. We know by now that someone from the top is watching us and making sure we get whatever we ask for. I do need to say up front that this wedding is going to be a family affair. Families of both the bride and groom will be involved. There will be a risk of far more collateral damage than we've experienced so far," she said as she looked directly at Mark.

Mark spoke in a quiet voice, "Yes, I'm afraid she's right. For this mission to be effective, we have to hit them at the most vulnerable moment. It has to be at a time the principals are all together and are momentarily distracted."

Rich Holtz, the explosive expert who was the quietest member of the group, spoke. "I think I see where this is going. It has to happen during the actual wedding, and it has to be a cataclysmic event, like maybe involving explosives."

No one spoke. Each member of the group absorbed the implications of the suggestion.

"It's war," Rosa said. If we can drop bombs on Hanoi, these people are probably a far greater danger to our country than any North Vietnamese could ever be."

With that statement Rosa brought out maps and satellite images and laid them out across the table. She also had brochures advertising the resort. The brochures actually were the most helpful because there were numerous photos of both the exterior as well as the interior. The resort sat on a small hill that dropped sharply to the ocean on the eastern side. There was a gradual slope toward the north and level toward the western side. The building seemed to consist of three different sections. Toward the ocean side were the hotel rooms, providing a magnificent view of the ocean. The center building contained the reception area, restaurants, and the entertainment areas, including a large banquet hall on the second floor where the actual wedding and reception would be held. The westernmost part was made up of service areas such as kitchen, laundry, and maintenance. There was a parking garage that extended underneath the entire complex. The resort was accessed by a secondary road from the south, north, and a main road approaching west from the mainland.

Rosa said, "We have one advantage. The wedding is planned for 7:00 PM. It will be getting dark by then. Now let's get suggestions from you all."

She set up a whiteboard on a stand and started writing down suggestions. Without realizing it, the entire group seemed to feed off Rosa's intensity. It didn't take long before the board was filled with suggestions. As fast as ideas were added to the board, some were removed when it became obvious they were impractical. When he glanced at his watch, Mark realized how late it was and how long they'd been working. They eventually ran out of any new suggestions and Rosa said, "Okay. I'll sum this all up and tomorrow everyone can take a final look before we submit our request for hardware."

The session seemed to have sapped the energy out of everyone, and as they headed to their respective rooms, Rosa turned to Mark.

"Go ahead and get some sleep, Mark. I want to finish this while it's fresh in my mind."

Mark had no problem going back to his room and crashing into a fitful sleep. Flashing images of the exploding Mercedes at the bridge wouldn't go away. He awoke with Rosa's hand on his chest and her breath on his ear.

"It's okay, Mark. It's okay."

His breathing and pulse slowed as he became fully awake. His pulse rate began to rise again as Rosa positioned her body over him and wrapped her legs around his hips. Images of exploding cars were replaced with sensations that he wanted to go on forever. It became the most intense and profound sexual experience of his life. As their bodies melted together, Rosa took him to a different dimension and for a short time they both seemed to escape the physical bounds of earth and float in a cocoon of pleasure. Afterward, as they both struggled to regain their breath, Mark was somehow overcome with a wave of sadness as he wondered if he would ever again be able to match this experience. By the time his breathing had subsided, Rosa had curled into his side and was sound asleep. It was as if Rosa had suddenly found a new intensity with the realization her lifelong mission of revenge was now in sight. Mark feared, and rightly so, that like the honeybee that dies after stinging its enemy, Rosa's sting might be her last.

CHAPTER 43

Roe

As Roe slowly regained consciousness, she couldn't comprehend where she was or what was happening. She was in total darkness, and she was unable to move. As she tried to cry out, something in her mouth prevented her from making any sound other than a weak moan. As the massive pounding in her head slowly receded, she realized that she was tightly bound and gagged. She knew from the sounds and vibrations that she was in the trunk of a moving vehicle. She had no idea how long she'd been in the trunk, and she was still trying to remember why she was here. Fortunately, her hands were tied in front of her and judging from the feel, probably with duct tape. As the fog in her head continued to clear, she tried to move, but there was no room to even try to roll over. As the rotten egg smell of the car's exhaust filled the trunk and her lungs, a wave of nausea washed over her. Terrified, she knew that if she vomited with the gag in her mouth, it would be fatal.

She tried to feel for some kind of release that might open the trunk, but she was lying on her side facing away from the rear wall of the trunk. She was wedged in tightly by something pressing against her back. For a brief moment she was overwhelmed by a panic attack. Somehow, she was aware that she had been in a similar position sometime in her past and the outcome had not been good. She tried to take deep breaths, although the gag made it difficult to do. She was still unable to remember where she had been before or what had led to her being in this position. Finally accepting the fact that there was nothing she could do, she tried to pay attention to the sounds and movement of the vehicle. Instead, she slipped back into a semiconscious state. She was awakened again as the vehicle hit a series of sharp bumps that might have been railroad tracks. Soon the vehicle stopped, and she could hear a clanking sound like a metal door opening. The vehicle moved a short distance and stopped abruptly, throwing her against the front of the trunk. She could hear voices yelling, and the trunk lid was suddenly opened. Rough hands pulled her out of the trunk, and her eyes tried to adjust to the light. The face that was staring at her suddenly jolted her memory and she realized the magnitude of her mistake.

She had followed the directions of the woman she had called. It was a house in the south part of the city only a few blocks off South Dixie Highway. The further she drove from South Dixie, the more the neighborhood had deteriorated. The house was a small frame home with an open attached garage. An old model—a large blue sedan just as the woman had described—sat on the cracked concrete driveway. The back half of the car was inside the narrow carport. The car's paint was faded so badly that the original color was almost indistinguishable. Other than three teenage kids kicking a soccer ball a couple houses down the street, there was no sign of movement around the house. She parked on the street in front of the house and walked up to the front door, which was open. She'd knocked once on the open door before a small woman with dark brown skin in faded jeans and T-shirt appeared.

"Are you Esmeralda?"

"Sí. Come in."

Thinking back, she should have paid attention to the warning signs. But she hadn't and she had followed Esmeralda into the house. As she passed through the threshold, the woman was shoved aside and a man who was no taller than herself and was completely bald had appeared. At the same moment the door behind her slammed shut and an arm went around her neck in a chokehold. The bald man moved forward at the same instant and shoved a large rag on her face with a pungent odor that she instinctively knew was chloroform. Her next conscious moment was waking up in the car's trunk.

As she was unceremoniously dragged out of the trunk by the bald-headed man, she realized why she had been wedged in so tightly. Esmeralda was also lying on the floor of the trunk. She recognized the car as the one that had been parked in the driveway of the house. She tried to look around at her surroundings. She could tell that she was in a large metal warehouse. The short man was helped by a tall man with a pockmarked face, goatee, and long ponytail.

They lifted her up by the arms and half-dragged, half-carried her toward the rear of the building. She could tell that the entire rear of the structure consisted of a concrete block structure with several metal doors. She was taken through one of the doors and down a dark musty smelling hallway before being dragged into a small windowless room. She held her breath as the tall man pulled out a switchblade knife that made an ominous click as it flipped open. She closed her eyes as he reached toward her with the knife but immediately breathed a sigh of relief as he cut through the duct tape binding her arms. The short man quicky snapped a handcuff on her left wrist and wound the other cuff around one of several heavy iron pipes that ran down the concrete wall. Only after she was secured to the wall did the man with the knife cut through the tape around her feet and legs. Both men left the room, leaving the door open. So far neither of them had uttered a word. Moments later they carried Esmeralda into the room and secured her to another pipe a few feet away. The woman's T-shirt was covered in blood, and she was still unconscious. This time, as the men left, they closed the door, and she could hear a bolt being closed.

As her eyes slowly adjusted to the dark, she was finally able to see some of her surroundings. There was a gap between the top of the wall and the ceiling of the room, with some sort of metal screening rather than a solid material. It allowed some dim light to filter into the room. She knew that unless the inside of the warehouse was lit up at night, there would be no visibility in the room after dark. She began to take in every detail of the room while she at least had some limited vision. The pipe she was locked onto appeared to be quite secure. It was supported by brackets anchoring it to the wall. Without the right tools, she knew that it couldn't be loosened. The room was approximately eight by ten feet and was probably a storage room. There were several boxes stacked at one end and some cleaning supplies were faintly visible. It really didn't matter as long as she remained handcuffed to the wall. She was sure of one thing though. The fact that no one had made the faintest effort to cover their faces and that they had put Esmeralda in the same room with her with whatever information she might have could only mean one thing. They had no intention of ever letting her go.

CHAPTER 44

Searching for Roe

Driving down the Florida's Turnpike, Mark tried to call Roe as they passed the Stuart exit. His call was immediately forwarded to her voicemail, and he left a message for her to call back. He was curious to know if she'd identified the beach compound. They had been driving for so long with only a few hours of sleep and short breaks for gas and fast food. His butt hurt and his eyes looked like two piss holes in the snow. He talked a lot with Samuel, and the more he learned about the young man, the more he liked him. Mark was able to appreciate Samuel's depth of love and concern for Emelia. He also was aware that the search for Emelia had added additional motivation to their goal of finding Andre Mendez.

When Mark turned off the turnpike onto Southern Boulevard in West Palm Beach, Mark called Roe again. Still no answer. Now Mark felt growing concern that Roe hadn't answered. As soon as they'd reached the hotel, Mark checked them both in and asked the clerk if there were any messages. The clerk handed an envelope to Mark, which he opened immediately. Inside the envelope was the note from Roe giving him Esmeralda's name and address. The envelope also contained a key card for her room and information on the tracker with a key to her room.

"Follow me," Mark told Samuel as they headed for the elevators. They went straight to Roe's room, where they found the computer that Mark and Roe had used to track Samuel earlier. Mark turned the computer on, but as soon as the computer booted up, Mark realized he didn't know how to activate the correct screen.

"Let me," Samuel said as he immediately began to hit the keys. Mark realized that his knowledge of computers was very limited compared to Samuel's, who quickly opened a screen with the pulsating location of the tracker winking at them.

Still not knowing whether Roe was really in trouble but still fearing the worst, Mark looked closely at the location of the tracker on the map. Because he had owned a condominium on the ocean at Boynton Beach for several years, he was familiar with West Palm Beach, which was only a short drive north of his condo. He'd flown in and out of the airport many times and he'd visited many of the great restaurants in West Palm Beach. He recognized the tracker's location immediately as being in an area of warehouses near the airport. There was a well-known gun shop where he'd used the shooting range within just a few blocks of the pulsating dot on the screen.

"Samuel, you'll need to come with me. If there is any movement of the tracker, I'll need you to be watching for it while I'm driving."

As they went back down to his car, Mark had forgotten his sore butt and lack of sleep as his concern for Roe had his adrenaline pumping. The signal was only a short distance from the hotel on the other side of the airport. The area was a jumble of warehouses made mostly of corrugated metal, but there were newer buildings of brick and cinder block. By now it was dark, and most businesses had shut down. The area was quiet except for a few barking dogs guarding some fenced-in areas. The building that appeared to be the one where the signal was located was a combination of cinder block and metal. There was only a faint glow of light coming from a single window at the front. There was a large bay door which was closed. In a small parking area just off the street Mark could see two vehicles. One was an old beat-up sedan of unidentifiable color. The other was a large black SUV with dark tinted windows.

Mark backed up and parked on the street leaving a good view of the entire front of the building.

"Samuel, you stay in the car and watch. I'm going to try to go around the building and see if there's another way to get in. If anyone comes out the front, blow the car's horn once. If anyone else drives up and parks in the lot, blow twice." He took his Model 39 S&W out of the center console, checked to be sure there was a shell in the chamber, and got out of the car.

There was a narrow alleyway along both sides of the building, and he followed the closest one toward the rear. There was enough ambient light from streetlights and the adjacent building's floodlights, so he had no trouble finding his way along the building. There was a lot of discarded lumber and broken cinder blocks, so he had to be careful with every step. There were no windows or openings of any kind along the length of the building, but when he turned the corner and started across the rear, he found a window set into the concrete wall. It was so dusty and covered with years of accumulation of grime that it blocked all visibility of the interior, although there was a faint light visible on the inside. The window was an old type that opened outward by turning a crank handle. It had probably never been opened, and Mark wasn't sure it could be opened now. Looking around, he found a piece of concrete block and used it to break out one of the lower panes of glass where he thought the handle would be. Reaching inside, he located the handle and put pressure on it. It turned once and the widow opened a couple of inches. That's when he heard an agonizing scream coming from somewhere inside.

Doubling his effort, he put his weight into turning the handle, and with a sudden loud snap, the handle broke completely off.

CHAPTER 45
Esmeralda

As the effects of the chloroform wore off, there was enough faint light coming through the open ceiling for Roe to look around the room. It was definitely a storage room with a sundry of items stacked at one end of the room. Anything she might use was well out of her reach. At the same time, Esmeralda was beginning to regain consciousness. When Roe saw her try to sit up, she cautioned her, "Esmeralda, don't try to move too fast. You may have broken bones."

In a voice that was barely more than a whisper, Esmeralda said, "It is my soul that is broken. I am dead and probably now my family back in Mexico is going to die as well."

"You're not dead yet, Esmeralda. If you'll help me, maybe we can get out of this place. Your hair is fixed in a bun. What's holding it in place?"

Esmeralda tried to raise her hands to her head but was hit with a wave of pain. Both of her hands had handcuffs just like Roe's that went around the back of a heavy pipe on the wall. "It's a hairpin."

"Okay, Esmeralda, listen to me. Try to crunch up in a ball so that your hands can reach your hair. Try to get the hairpin out. Just go slow and maybe it won't hurt so badly."

Esmeralda slowly repositioned herself so that her head was near where her hands were secured to the wall. It was slow, but she eventually had her head even with her hands. After some searching, she triumphantly held out a long hairpin.

Suddenly they could hear voices approaching the door. Esmeralda had the presence of mind to let the pin fall down between herself and the wall. The sound of the sliding bolt on the door could be heard, and when the door opened, a tall well-dressed woman with dark hair and sharp features entered the room. The short bald man stood behind her.

"This is a real mess," she said as she looked at Esmeralda in disgust. "What in hell were you thinking? You know you shouldn't be talking to anyone without our permission. You haven't figured out by now that we monitor your phone?"

Esmeralda nodded as tears streamed down her cheeks.

"I'm sorry. I meant no harm."

"Well, Esmeralda, it's a little late to be sorry," the woman said as she turned her attention toward Roe. "Who the hell are you and how do you know Diego?"

Roe wanted to buy as much time as possible, and she hoped that this woman hadn't yet heard anything about what had happened to Diego. "My name is Roe. Diego was helping me find someone. I paid him well for his information."

"Helping you find who?"

"I'm looking for a relative of mine who disappeared crossing the border into Texas."

"What is their name?"

"Her name is Emelia Rojas."

Roe could hear Esmeralda's sudden intake of breath, and the woman took a step back. She was quiet for a moment before she turned to the short man.

"Enzo, I want you and Carl to watch these two. I'm scheduled to talk to the boss later tonight and I'll get his instruction on what to do with them. I'm sure he'll let you and Carl work on this woman a bit. I think there's a lot she's not telling us."

Without saying another word, she turned and left the room with Enzo close behind. They could hear the bolt in the door close again.

Roe looked back at Esmeralda, who looked as if the wind had been knocked out of her for a second time.

"Esmeralda, focus! Let's get back to the matter of the hairpin. Feel behind you and find the pin."

Soon Esmeralda had the pin in her hands again. "Great job. Now, use your hands as much as you can and throw the pin toward me. Then try and use your feet to push it closer to me."

After some awkward movements, Esmeralda was able to push the pin across the concrete floor toward Roe. They were at least eight feet apart and now it was Roe's turn to stretch out flat on the floor and reach as far as possible with her feet to tease the pin closer and closer toward where her hands were locked around the pipe. After a series of contorted stretching movements, Roe had the pin in her hands. It only took her a second to unlock one of the handcuffs, and that allowed her use of both hands to free her from the wall.

Not knowing how soon one of their captors might return, Roe quickly went to the area where there were mops, brooms, and other cleaning materials. Taking an old broom that had a wooden handle, she put her foot on the broom end and using all of her body weight, she broke the handle. As she had hoped, the break in the wood caused the handle to split almost halfway up. She was left holding what was essentially a wooden spear. She rummaged around and found a short heavy iron pipe which she laid next to the broken broom handle where she should be sitting. After removing the handcuff from her other hand, Roe moved over and unlocked Esmeralda's handcuffs.

"Esmeralda, keep the handcuffs in your hand. When we hear someone opening the door, sit back down put the handcuffs around the pipe like you're still attached to the wall. Can you do that?"

"Sí."

"Now, while we're waiting for someone to come back, let me ask you a few questions. I saw you react when I mentioned Emelia's name. Tell me what you know about her."

"Not much. I'm only a maid. I clean whatever they tell me to clean. Emelia was not in the house very long. I heard that she was treated harshly because she refused to do as they told her."

"Refused to do what?"

"The girls that are brought into the house are required to provide services to the guest. When she refused, I heard that they put her in the freezer."

"Freezer?"

"Yes, it's what they do to any girl that causes a problem."

"What happened then?"

Esmeralda continued to tell Roe everything she knew about the girls—the guest and especially how ruthless Ava could be. Ava being the woman who'd just been there. Roe listened to Esmeralda, and as she did, her anger toward these people continued to grow. There was no doubt that the head of the snake was Andre Mendez, who seemed to stay just out of their reach.

More than an hour had passed when Roe heard footsteps approaching outside. "Quickly, Esmeralda, remember what I told you. Lean back up on the wall and stay still."

The door opened and bald-headed Enzo walked into the room. When he quietly closed the door behind him, Roe sensed that his intentions were not good. But she was thankful that he was coming in alone. She had curled herself up so that it appeared that her hands were still locked to the pipe on the wall. The broom handle was hidden under her body.

Enzo smiled down at her. "You are a pretty woman. You might want to experience some pleasure while you still can." He bent down and reached for the belt on Roe's pantsuit trousers. Roe offered no resistance, and that seemed to encourage Enzo even more as he leaned forward over her, his garlic-loaded breath almost causing her to gag. In one fluid motion, Roe's hands moved to the broom handle under her. Rotating her body slightly and bracing against the concrete floor, she pushed the broken end of the broomstick upward and into Enzo's soft belly.

The look on Enzo's face went from smiling anticipation, to confusion, and then to sheer terror as he tried to get back up, but because of the position he was in, he couldn't. The more he struggled, the deeper the broom handle went into his stomach. Roe pushed herself out from under him, put her foot on his back, and pushed hard. The sharp end of the broomstick came out of his back and pushed into his shirt, creating what looked like a tent held up by a single pole. He turned his head and looked at Roe as he uttered his last words, "Why would you do such a thing?"

Esmeralda watched with wide eyes and a growing respect for Roe. Maybe they did have a chance to get out alive.

Roe checked Enzo's pockets for a gun, but no luck, so she picked up the iron pipe and quietly opened the door. She could see a faint light down the hall and some sounds coming from a room with an open door. Easing down the hallway, she slowly looked into the room. The room was a break room with a small TV, worn-out leather sofa, and a couple of battered lounge chairs. There was a Formica coffee table in front of the sofa covered in beer cans and empty fast food containers. Sprawled out in one of the chairs was the ponytail man. He was fast asleep. He had left his gun lying on the table almost hidden by the beer cans. Without hesitation, Roe entered the room and hit him across his forehead with the iron pipe. His head rolled to one side as blood poured out of his scalp. She tucked his pistol in her belt. Looking around the room, Roe looked for something to tie him up with, but seeing nothing, she suddenly ran from the room and back to where Enzo was lying in a growing pool of blood, grabbed the handcuffs, and went back to the room where ponytail hadn't moved. She roughly pulled him out of the chair and onto the floor before cuffing his hands behind his back. She took his belt off and used it to lock his legs together.

By now Esmeralda was standing in the doorway watching Roe tie him down. Roe left the room and told her to watch the man and to call her if he moved. Roe went down the hallway to where it opened into a large open warehouse. On one side there was what looked to be a shop with workbenches and a lot of tools. She looked around the shop, nodded to herself, and went back to the room where the man lay on the floor, still unmoving.

"Help me move him," Roe told Esmeralda. Together they each took an arm and dragged the man out into the open area and over to the shop part. "Let's lift him up and lay him over the workbench next to the vise." Roe found a key for the handcuffs in his pocket and unlocked the handcuffs. The vise was a large commercial apparatus bolted onto the bench, and they positioned him close to it so that his right arm was next to it. Roe opened it and positioned his arm so that it was cradled by the vise. She then closed it so that his elbow was positioned in the middle. After tightening it down, she found a roll of duct tape and bound the arm even tighter to the vise so that there was no possibility that it could be pulled out. She again used the handcuffs and stretched his left arm across the workbench and locked it to a heavy metal bolt at the back of the bench. It left him with his upper body lying across the bench with his arms spread out as if he were trying to fly. He was beginning to wake up, and at some point, as he became aware of what was happening, he let out a scream of anger and pain which only increased in crescendo as Roe tightened the vise on his elbow.

CHAPTER 46
1973

The night before they left their quarters in El Paso, they all gathered together for a final review of the mission. They had submitted their request for the things they thought they'd need, and all their request had been satisfied. It was time to roll. There was no doubt that this mission created more concern and anxiety than any previous one had done. Mark hoped that it wasn't a result of Rosa's demeanor, but rather from the simple fact that this operation was taking them much deeper into Mexico and involved far greater risks than any one so far. But like American solders now and in the past, they only focused on the mission ahead.

After there was nothing left to say, Rosa said, "I want to offer a toast." Opening a bottle of champagne, she continued, "First for Lou and then for us all. I know that I'll never have better friends than the people in this room."

Everyone responded with a "Here, here."

Mark had already opened another bottle, and the toast continued as they laughed and toasted everything they could think of until they ran out of champagne.

They left El Paso early the next morning and flew to an airfield near Brownsville. The field consisted of a single runway set in a field of cactus. There were a couple of hangars with a few small planes parked nearby. The entire area was enclosed by a tall chain-link fence with only one entrance gate. Just inside the gate was a low cinder block building with a faded sign in front. A couple of brown cars covered with dust with some type of official decals on the doors sat next to the building. There was no one in sight.

Ron taxied the plane toward the furthest hangar and cut the engines. On the far side of the hangar, out of sight of the cinder block building, was a large panel truck. Faded letters on the sides read *Aire Acondicionado*. They all began to remove baggage out of the plane and into the truck. Tied down in the center of the cargo area of the truck was a wooden crate with the letters *COOLAIR* stenciled in black lettering on each side. Rich Holtz went to the rear of the box and used a large screwdriver to pry the corners loose. The back side of the box opened, revealing a huge hidden area. Instead of an air conditioner, there was a carefully supported stack of C-4 explosives along with detonators. There were also four MP5s with multiple loaded clips secured to the inside walls of the box. There was a bench across each side of the truck's cargo area, and each contained a storage area underneath. Inside were several uniforms with the same lettering as on the outside of the truck. There was no wall separating the truck's cabin from the cargo area. It only took a few minutes to transfer their personal items from the plane and into the truck. Soon they were heading toward the Mexican border.

Continuing his role of being in charge of transportation, Ron Lassiter drove and Marcus Jefferson rode shotgun. Growing up on the border, Marcus was the only one of the five who had actually driven down this route. He explained to the group that Tampico had once been a tourist destination. The city was a major port for shipping oil out of Mexico. As the oil dried up, the oil industry was replaced by drugs, and with that came the cartels. As the cartel increased its grip on the city, the crime rates rose, and even though Tampico was a beautiful city populated by wonderful people, it had become a dangerous place to visit. Even the major highway taking them south from the border involved some risks. It was not an unusual occurrence for a vehicle to be stopped and held until a "fine" was paid in cash. The truck had Mexican plates and had all necessary documentation, but even so, the police might stop them anyway. It was the roving gangs of opportunists who posed the greatest threat.

The drive was uneventful until they passed through the town of Soto La Marina. They had only stopped once before to pee by the side of the road along a deserted stretch. They were running low on gas as they passed through Soto La Marina, but Ron, who was still driving, had hoped to find a station in a less populated section south of the city. After passing through the city and realizing there were no gas stations, he drove a few miles. The area was desolate. "Folks, I made a miscalculation. It looks like there are no stations outside the town. It's too far to the next town to risk running out of gas. We may need to turn around and go back and find a station."

Marcus was looking intently forward. "Just go on around this curve first. I think I see something."

Sure enough, there was a small fruit stand and grocery store just ahead. It had two tired-looking pumps advertising regular and diesel fuel. While Ron filled the tank, Mark and Marcus walked to the side of the store where a sign read *Baño*. Just as the two of them walked around the building, a pickup truck, jacked up high on oversized tires skidded into the parking lot, stopping just in front of the truck. Two young men jumped out of the truck's cab and two more came out of the back. One of the men held a cheap assault rifle, and two of the others were holding revolvers that looked to be left over from the Spanish-American war. As far as they could tell, the only occupant of the truck was Ron Lassiter, who was pumping gas into the truck's tank.

The man holding the rifle was small and brown, with greased black hair parted down the middle. He approached Ron, who was ignoring them, and demanded to know where he was going. Ron didn't look up but only said, "South."

Not getting the respect he thought he deserved, the young man prodded Ron with the tip of the rifle barrel. "Answer me or you'll get hurt. Where are you going this far out here?"

Ron looked up for the first time and calmly said, "How about letting me finish filling this tank?"

Meanwhile, the other three men—or to be more accurate, boys—walked around to the back of the truck where the doors were open. All three eagerly leaned into the back of the truck to see what kind of bounty they were going to confiscate. What they saw was not what they were expecting to see, as Rosa and Rich Holtz placed the muzzles of their MP5s up against their faces.

Rosa quietly said in Spanish, "If any one of you moves a muscle, your mamas will never recognize you when she is burying you." They didn't move as Rosa and Rich climbed out of the truck, keeping their weapons locked on the trio.

At the same moment, the rifleman's anger was increasing by the second as Ron finally finished topping off the gas tank and casually replaced the hose on the gas pump. Turning toward the young man, he calmly asked, "Who do you work for?"

Flustered, the kid replied, "Nobody," as his empire collapsed when he felt the cold metal of a gun barrel pressed into the back of his neck. At the same time, a strong arm reached out and took the rifle out of his hands. Mark handed the rifle back to Marcus, who was standing behind him with a smile on his face. Mark checked to be sure the kid had no more weapons before grabbing him by the collar and forcibly leading him around to the side of the truck, where Rosa and Rich were holding the other three at gunpoint. Ron had gone into the back of the truck and returned with four sets of plastic ties, which they used to tie the hands of the four behind their backs. While Mark and Rosa led the four boys over to a ditch running behind the store, Ron and Marcus slashed all four tires of their jacked-up truck, which sank down onto its rims like a deflated rubber duck. The four boys watched in fear as Rosa approached them and had them all kneel in a row in the muddy drainage ditch behind the store. They feared the worst when she opened a knife and came up behind them. Using the knife, she sliced a long piece of each one's shirt off. Taking the pieces of shirt, she wrapped them tightly around each of their heads, covering their eyes.

By now, Marcus had approached the group and handed Mark the rifle they'd taken from the leader. Mark made a big deal of working the action of the rifle. "Now is your last chance to get right with your maker." Then he began to fire the weapon close to the ears of the kneeling boys. One of them simply fainted, and the other three were close behind as the rounds passed by their heads. When the magazine was empty, Mark and the rest quickly got back into the van where Ron had it running after he'd left money for the gas on the counter inside the store.

As the truck drove away, the four boys were left in the ditch wondering what the hell had just happened, but they were also grateful to still be alive.

It was well after dark when they reached the outskirts of Tampico. It was definitely a low rent area with open desert just beyond the many commercial businesses lining the road. They chose a place that had no visible name, only a large sign that said *HOTEL*. Outside its walls was a large dirt parking area filled with large trucks. Their truck seemed to be at home parked among the array of others parked in the lot. They paid cash for two rooms with the plan that one of them would sleep in the truck as security.

Mark and Rosa shared a room, but neither felt like sleeping. They lay on the bed, which sagged in the middle, with Rosa cradled in Mark's arms. Neither of them spoke for a long time, each absorbed in their own thoughts. It was Rosa who spoke first.

"Mark, regardless of what happens this time, it's going to be my last mission. I'm already feeling a letdown. I'm beginning to question my obsession for revenge. It's not a way to live. I'm ready to move on with my life."

"Does moving on include me?"

Rosa looked up at Mark and kissed him softly on his cheek. "You are part of my reason for moving on."

"I've tried to be a good soldier and do my job. I'm not questioning the importance of what we're doing, but I'll admit that it's getting harder and harder to ignore the collateral damage we're causing. I'm also worried about how hard it's going to be to forget the damage we've done to so many. I'm with you. Let's think about what kind of life we could have if we end this."

"I already have, Mark."

Both of them seemed to sense a tidal wave of relief knowing that they shared the same feeling. Rosa snuggled even tighter into Mark's arms and drifted off into sleep, blissfully unaware of what the next day would bring.

CHAPTER 47

Emelia

Emelia was silent as the limousine drove down I-95. She was devastated after hearing the confirmation that Samuel was dead. She'd suspected the worst but had still clung to a thread of hope that he was alive, and they'd be together again. Now she was confused and afraid. How much should she resist this man who was taking her to parts unknown? What was his plan for her? Now that Samuel was dead, would she ever see her parents again? But even as she faced an uncertain future, she still had a great sense of self preservation. She would survive and maybe, if she was lucky, she would see some justice for the people who had killed Samuel.

As if sensing her fear, Andre spoke, "Emelia, you have nothing to fear. I'm not going to hurt you. If you stayed back at that place, your future would not have been good. Most of the girls who are brought there are eventually used up and move on to the modeling and strip clubs. It's all downhill from there. I sense that you are well-educated on top of being exquisitely beautiful. I suspect that you come from a well-placed family in Chile who would pay well for your safe return. I don't want the money. I want you. I want to bring you into my home. My business is not a pleasant one, but I am not a bad person, as I hope you'll see."

Emelia was at a total loss for words. She could only nod and look away.

It was an hour drive to the Miami Opa-locka airport. The airport was located in a heavily congested area of low rent subdivisions mixed with various commercial businesses.

The airport was an aviation facility that catered to private charter aircraft and some old commercial cargo planes. At one point the airport developed a reputation as being very lax on monitoring ingress and egress of both passengers and cargo. It was still a friendly airport for private planes even though US Customs and Border Protection regulations officially required a detailed travel manifest for all passengers as well as arrival and departure information.

They drove into the airport and straight up to the side of a plane. Emelia could only tell that it was a jet, and the interior was all soft leather and polished wood. Someone from customs came to the door and spoke to the pilot, who had some papers in his hand. The door was quickly closed, and the plane rose into the sky within moments. Emelia didn't ask where they were going, as she realized it really made no difference. She was going whether she liked it or not. A waiter in the cabin offered her food and something to drink, which she eagerly accepted. In a short time, she could see that they were flying over water with no land in sight. She dozed off to sleep and was awakened by the popping in her ears as the plane descended. They were still over water as the plane came down and then they were over a town and dropping rapidly. As the plane rolled down the runway with engines roaring in reverse, she could see the main terminal building with the name *TAMPICO* on its side.

The plane taxied up to a hangar well away from the terminal building where a man waited for the door to open. The pilot met the man on the steps, spoke for a moment, and handed the man an envelope that quickly disappeared into a jacket pocket. As the man walked away, a large black Mercedes sedan stopped at the foot of the steps. The driver got out and opened the doors for Emelia and Andre.

As they drove out of the airport and city, Emelia was alert but also remained both curious and fearful as the car took them into the countryside. She noticed that there was a car leading them as well as a car closely following them. When they turned off onto a side road, the scenery changed dramatically. There were white fences with vast areas of beautiful countryside. There were what must be purebred cows as well as many horses, all in different pastures as they drove on.

They drove for several miles with the same scenery on both sides of the road before approaching a tall gate. The double iron gate was supported by a tall thick sandstone archway. The sandstone extended out from the gate and continued on both sides. It gave the impression of driving past a moat and into a medieval castle. The gate was opening as they approached, and they hardly slowed down as they passed through. Ahead of them the driveway split, and the Mercedes went straight ahead as the two other cars left the main driveway. Ahead, Emelia saw a massive hacienda that seemed to rise up out of the open desert. It was made of the same sandstone as the gate and wall, and it blended with the surrounding desert as if it were a natural part of the landscape that had been there for a long time. The driveway led up to a large porte cochere larger than many hotels. A man dressed in white was waiting to open the car's doors and greeted Mendez as an old friend, "Welcome home, Señor Mendez."

"Thank you, Alex. It is good to be home."

They went up several steps to a landing where Alex was opening one of two massive mahogany doors for them to enter. Emelia forgot her immediate concerns when she stood inside the foyer. If she was impressed by the mansion in Florida, this house made it look shabby. The floor was a polished dark marble. There was a round table in the center of the room with a heavy wood base and a thick stone tabletop made of an exquisite, polished stone. On the surface of the table, a huge bronze statue of a man on a horse dominated the room. The walls were mirrored glass that accented the imposing statue. Three hallways led off the circular foyer.

Andre led her down one of the hallways lined with paintings that ranged from Picasso styles to Rembrandt Renaissance. Emelia sensed that they were not knock off copies but originals. They passed several rooms on either side before the hallway opened up onto a large room that simply said *comfortable*. One wall was glass overlooking a pool and patio area. A bar made of rosewood with glass shelves lined with liquors from around the world lined one side. Another wall was made up entirely of the native sandstone surrounding a fireplace. Surprisingly, the furniture was all a soft beige fabric with no visible leather, adding to the soft and comfortable feeling of the area. Even in her current state of uncertainty, for Emelia, the room exuded a sense of comfort and tranquility.

When they entered the room, a small figure rose up from a chair near the fireplace and laid down a laptop computer onto the chair.

Andre approached her slowly in a submissive and respectful manner. "Hermana, this is the girl I've told you about. I want you to meet Emelia."

The woman who walked to meet them was roughly five foot eight and one hundred fifteen pounds. Her skin was a light bronze, but the contrast with her jet-black hair and expressive dark brown eyes made it appear even lighter. Her facial features were a mixture of classic Spanish and Aztec aristocracy. Because of her slight figure and smooth bronze skin, it was difficult to guess her age. She was dressed in a casual silk pantsuit that exuded wealth and with it the confidence that great wealth can bring.

"It is good to meet you, Emilia. Welcome to our home. When Andre told me he was bringing someone, I knew it had to be someone exceptional. And I see that you are truly beautiful. I hope coming to our home can make up for some of the misfortune that you have endured. Andre, please leave us. I would like to talk to Emelia alone. I'm sure you have many business concerns to address. You and I will talk later."

And with that statement, there was no doubt that Andre had been dismissed leaving Emelia alone with this beautiful woman. Considering how she had been treated up to this point, she was even more confused than ever.

Motioning for Emelia to sit, she sat down opposite Emelia before speaking again. "Everyone calls me Hermana. Now tell me how you ended up here."

Emelia took a deep breath and told the lady how she and Samuel had left Chile and traveled to the US looking for a better future. She told her about the massacre at the river, her time in the safe house in El Paso, and her time in the oceanfront mansion in Palm Beach. Hermana showed no outward emotion as she listened to Emelia and didn't speak until Emelia had finished.

"Emelia, I am saddened that you lost Samuel and for everything you've had to endure. I have told my brother that Diego Cano, or El Carnicero as he fancies himself, is a liability. His methods are not good for business in today's world. That will be corrected. Now, about my brother, you are not the first woman he's brought to this place. You should know that he loses interest very quickly with each one. How you respond to him is up to you, but I can assure you of one thing. In this house you are under my protection and if and when Andre is done with you, I'll send you safely on your way out of here."

By now tears were streaming down Emelia's face as her mind swirled with conflicting emotions. After her experiences at the Palm Beach estate, she felt as if her degradation couldn't descend any deeper. Her debasement was complete. Submitting to Andre Mendez couldn't make it any worse. Just as she'd felt after her time in the freezer, her survival instincts overrode her sense of honor. Besides, without Samuel, what difference did it make?

Hermana escorted Emelia down a hallway and left her in a lavishly decorated bedroom. She lay on the bed and closed her eyes, overcome with fatigue. When Andre entered the room without knocking and began to undress, Emelia braced herself for the inevitable.

CHAPTER 48

Gentle Persuasion

When Mark realized he was holding the broken window crank in his hand, he grabbed the window frame with both hands in frustration. Placing both feet against the wall and using all of his body weight as leverage, he pulled with all of his strength. Because the metal was severely rusted, the entire window frame suddenly gave way, sending Mark crashing backward. Quickly recovering, he squirmed sideways through the opening it created and rolled onto the concrete floor. He saw that he was at the end of a long hallway with doors on either side. The sounds were coming from somewhere toward the end of the hallway. Carefully moving down the hallway through an open door, he saw a body on the floor in a pool of blood. Looking closer, he was relieved to see that it was a man and not Roe.

The body lay face down and he looked like he'd been skewered with a pole. The rank odor of oozing intestines permeated the room. The end of the hallway opened onto a cavernous room. On the far side of the room, he saw a strange sight. It was a shop area, and sprawled across a workbench was a tall screaming male figure whose head was bobbing up and down in severe pain. Looking closer, Mark could see that his arm was locked in a large vise. Standing over him, Roe was slowly turning the handle of the vise. Standing near her was a woman with long black hair cascading down her face and shoulders, giving her the appearance of someone you'd expect to see in a horror movie. She was holding a two-foot piece of iron pipe looking as if she wanted an excuse to use it.

As Mark walked across the room, the two women became aware of his presence. The wild-haired woman raised the pipe in a defensive motion, but Roe held her hand up to indicate Mark was not a threat. "What took you so long?"

Mark only said, "I think we need to talk."

Nodding, Roe told Esmeralda to watch the man locked in the vise but not to beat him with the pipe unless he looked like he was getting loose. She and Mark walked to a corner of the room where they could talk without being heard. Mark had to bite his tongue to keep from asking Roe how she could be so stupid, but Roe was a step ahead of him when she said, "Mark, I'm sorry. What I did was dumb. I just got excited, and I really underestimated these people."

Mark could only nod. "Okay, start from the beginning and tell me what happened."

Roe told Mark what had happened and all that she'd learned form Esmeralda. Mark listened quietly to everything Roe was saying before he finally said, "We can't stay here. I have an idea, but it depends on this guy." He explained to Roe what he was thinking before they returned to the workbench where the man locked in the vise was shouting at Esmeralda.

"Esmeralda, you cunt. You can't imagine what we'll do to you."

"What, Carl? Will you take me on one of your midnight boat rides where three go out but only two come back? You don't think that after all the time I've worked in that hellhole of a house that I don't hear and see what's going on? I think maybe you've crossed the wrong people this time."

As Mark approached, he smiled at the man before speaking. "So, your name is Carl. Carl, I'd like to make a deal with you."

"Fuck off. You're a dead man walking."

"Carl, that could apply to all of us, but at the moment you're a lot closer to being dead than you know. Roe, does this thing turn clockwise or counterclockwise?"

"Clockwise to tighten."

Before Carl could say another word, Mark pulled on the handle of the vise. There was a distinct pop as Carl's elbow was crushed, followed immediately by a wail of anguish.

When Carl stopped screaming and had stopped hyperventilating enough to hear what Mark was saying, Mark addressed him again. "Here's the deal, Carl. If you do as I say, I won't turn your arm into hamburger. There's still a possibility you can save it. But more important than your arm is your life. While he was speaking, he had taken out his pistol and stepped closer to the struggling man, placing the gun against his forehead. Your choice."

With the pain pulsing through his arm, Carl could only nod a yes. "I'm telling you though, you're making a huge mistake. You should run while you still can."

"Carl, we do appreciate the advice."

In addition to the large rollup door in the front of the warehouse, there was a single door as well. Mark went out the door and walked to his car parked down the street. He drove it up to the front of the warehouse and parked next to the large SUV. He gave Samuel an abbreviated version of what he'd learned, especially that Emelia had been here in West Palm Beach. While Mark was bringing Samuel inside, Roe was also telling Esmeralda how Samuel was

connected to Emelia and that it might be better for him
to not know everything that had happened to her at the
ocean compound. Esmeralda seemed to understand what
Roe was telling her, and she agreed to limit what she said
to Samuel other than the fact that she had seen Emelia at
the house.

They left the warehouse in two cars. Esmeralda drove
her old car with Samuel and headed back to her house
where they were to wait for Roe and Mark. Roe drove
Mark's SUV to their hotel, which was nearby and left it
in the parking lot. Mark and Carl followed Roe in the
black SUV and picked Roe up. Mark drove. They'd used
the duct tape to wrap Carl's damaged arm and to lock
his legs together. He was in a lot of pain, causing him to
grunt every time the car hit a bump in the road. They'd
left Enzo's body where he'd died with the broomstick protruding from his body. There was no way these people
would be calling the police in on this scenario. Dealing
with the police was the last thing they'd want to do.

They drove past the entrance gates to the compound
once without stopping. Mark could see security cameras mounted on top of the entranceway columns. They
turned around in a dark driveway, and before reentering
the highway, they questioned Carl about the compound.
Roe gripped Carl's injured arm and put pressure on it
with each question. Sweating heavily from the pain, Carl
appeared to be answering truthfully when he answered,
"The Big Man is out of town and there aren't any guests
currently staying at the house. There's only one guard
at the house tonight. He's probably asleep in the control
room where all of the security controls are located. Then
there's Ava and two girls in the servant's quarters over the
garage. All of the other employees won't be back until
tomorrow morning."

Mark and Roe had already gotten a description of the main floor plan of the house from Esmeralda, and Carl only confirmed what they already knew.

"Carl, you're going to drive a couple of blocks with your good arm. Roe and I are going to be behind the front seats. I'll have a gun aimed at your lower back, and if you do anything stupid, I'm going to blow out your spine and you'll never walk again. Do you understand me?"

Carl muttered a "Yes" through gritted teeth.

This time when they approached the compound, Carl turned into the entrance and pushed a button on the speaker. A sleepy voice answered, "Carl, what are you doing here? I thought Ava had left you and Enzo at the warehouse."

"Don't worry. Everything is okay. I just need to get my insulin meds. I didn't realize I'd be staying at the warehouse all night. They're in a refrigerator in the garage."

"Whatever. Come on in. Just be quiet. We'll never hear the end of it if you wake Ava up."

The gates slid open, and the SUV rolled through. As they approached the garage area on the side of the compound, Mark had Carl stop and let him out of the SUV. The car continued on around to the entrance doors of the garage. Only one door was open, and Carl drove in and stopped. As he was stopping, a door opened and a uniformed guard came out and approached the SUV. His potbelly hung over his gun belt and his hat was sitting at an odd angle on his head where strands of hair were sticking out as if he'd just woke up from a long nap. But before he reached the car, Mark seemed to suddenly be standing behind him and had his arm around the guard's neck in a choke hold that cut off blood to his brain. The guard blacked out in only a few seconds. Mark used the duct tape they'd brought from the warehouse and quickly had him secured with tape over his eyes and mouth. Looking around, Mark walked over to a Lincoln Town Car in the adjacent space and popped open the cavernous trunk. With Roe's help, they dragged the guard over and lifted him into the trunk. They then pulled a cringing Carl out of the SUV. Mark pulled Carl's head up close to his and stared hard into his eyes. "Carl, if anything happens to Esmeralda, I'll put your head in a vise and watch it pop like a cantaloupe." After taping his mouth shut, they forced him into the trunk next to the still unconscious guard.

Roe was smiling as she helped Mark force Carl into the closed space. "Let's see how you like spending time in a trunk," she said, slamming the lid closed.

They both went quietly up the stairs and into a hallway with several side doors. Following Esmeralda's instructions, they stopped at one of the doors. Mark put his ear up against the door and listened. He could hear sounds and assumed it was coming from a TV. Thankfully, there was no peephole in the door, so Mark gently knocked on the door. The sounds stopped and there was a long pause before a loud voice said, "Who the hell?" Another long pause before the door opened and Ava was standing there wrapped in a thin see-through robe that hid little. Her hair looked as if she'd been riding a fast motorcycle.

Before Ava could express surprise, and with no hesitation, Mark hit her square in her face with a blow that knocked her back into the room. Both Mark and Roe followed her into her room. Sitting up in the bed and trying to cover herself, a blonde girl with eyes wide with fear watched.

Roe picked up a robe lying on the floor and threw it toward the girl in the bed. "You must be Katrina. Put this on and go to your room and wait for me to come back. Don't worry, we're here to help you. Where is Marianna?"

"She's asleep in our room."

"Both of you need to get dressed and put some clothes in a bag. We're going to help you get to a safe place."

Katrina didn't have to be told twice, as she grabbed a robe and headed out the door.

Mark bent down, pulled the unconscious Ava up, and threw her over his shoulder. He and Roe then went back down the hallway to the stairway and back down to the garage level. Again, Esmeralda's description of the house was spot on. They easily found the room with the large freezer. Mark dropped Ava on the floor next to the freezer as she was waking up.

Roe walked over to an industrial sink, found a small plastic bucket, filled it with water, and came back where Ava was lying on the floor. When the entire bucket of cold water hit her face, she was immediately alert.

"What the fuck are you doing? Who the hell do you think you are?"

Mark knelt down next to her before he replied, "Ava, who we are doesn't really matter. What matters to you is how you answer our questions. Now I'm only going to ask you once. You only have to answer two simple questions. First, where is Andre Mendez, and second, where did he take Emelia?"

Ava looked at Mark and Roe with eyes filled with hate. "Do you really think I'm telling you anything? You can both go straight to hell. You have no idea who you're dealing with here. You'll never leave this place alive. And even if you did, there's no place you can hide."

Mark had a sudden repressed memory rise to the surface of his mind when he repeated a line he'd used under similar circumstances years ago. "Ava, to quote from an old movie, 'I think what we have here is a failure to communicate.'"

Before Ava had a chance to protest, Roe had opened the freezer lid and they both bodily lifted Ava and dropped her unceremoniously into the empty compartment, which emitted a gagging odor of feces and urine the moment the lid was lifted. Ava tried to hold onto the edge of the freezer with one hand, but Mark closed the lid with such force that it crushed Ava's fingers. Mark raised the lid enough for a screaming Ava to pull her hand back inside before closing the lid tightly and muffling the screams coming from inside. The freezer had a lock with the key protruding. Mark turned the key to lock the lid, and speaking loud enough for Ava to hear, said, "They'll let her out when they look for her tomorrow."

Mark and Roe left the room and went back up the stairs and into the main house. After finding what must be an office of the owner, they looked through the huge mahogany desk for anything connected to Andre Mendez. Ava had done a remarkable job of keeping anything connected to Mendez well hidden. There was one drawer that held two stacks of hundred dollar bills, which Mark stuck in his pocket. They needed Ava to talk if they were going to find him.

They went back to the rooms over the garage to find Katrina and Marianna. Both girls were dressed and waiting. They each carried a small laundry bag filled with clothing looking as if they were standing at a Greyhound bus station eagerly waiting for the next bus leaving town. They took both girls downstairs and seated them in the back of the SUV they'd come in. By now, Mark estimated that Ava was getting low on oxygen. Hoping he'd not left her for too long, he and Roe went back to the room with the freezer. When the freezer was opened, they were met with the same odor that would gag a maggot. Ava was not moving, but she was still laboring to get oxygen into her lungs. Once she was outside the freezer, she rapidly came to life as she breathed in the precious oxygen.

This time Ava's attitude had changed dramatically. There was no belligerence but instead a pleading look in her eyes.

"Okay," Mark said. "Answers to the two questions. Where is Mendez and where is Emelia?"

Still pulling in large gulps of air, Ava said, "One answer for both questions. They're together. Andre is somehow attracted to her, and he's taken her back to his ranch in Mexico."

"Where in Mexico?"

"His family owns a huge ranch outside Tampico."

Mark's reaction surprised Roe. In all the time she'd known Mark and through all the challenges they'd faced together, she'd never seen Mark react like this. He looked as if he'd seen a ghost. He turned white and sat in a trance until she actually reached out and shook him by his shoulders. He quickly regained his composure and asked, "What's the name of the ranch?"

"It's called Rancho de Rio Sinuosa."

Mark closed his eyes and shook his head as memories long suppressed fought their way into his mind. "What does Andre plan to do with Emelia?"

"He wants to screw her. He'll use her until he gets tired of her. Then he'll get rid of her."

"Get rid of her how?"

"I don't know what happens when he gets tired of them. They never come back here."

"How long will Andre stay in Tampico?"

"Usually, he stays for a couple of weeks at a time."

"Have you ever been to the ranch?"

"Yes. Once I delivered a girl from here to his ranch."

"Tell us about the ranch."

After Mark and Roe had gotten all the information they could out of Ava, they exchanged glances. Nodding in unison, they knew that they couldn't take a chance on Ava warning Andre that they know about him. They once again surprised Ava by lifting her up and forcing her back into the freezer. Locking the freezer again, they left the room leaving Ava screaming and banging on the lid. This time there would be no one to let her out.

Again, driving the SUV out of the compound, they drive back into the city and back to South Dixie Highway. Turning off onto a side street, they drove a few blocks before stopping at a nondescript building with the name *Central American Rescue Center* over the door. When Mark stopped the SUV, Roe turned to Katrina and Mariana sitting in the back seat and looked directly at them before she spoke.

"Listen very carefully to what I'm telling you. Unless you want to end up in a place far worse that that house you were in, you won't remember me or this man with me. Wait outside this place until morning. The people who are in charge here are good people and they'll help you get to a safe place."

As soon as Karina and Mariana were out of the SUV, Mark drove away and following Roe's directions, headed to Esmeralda's house, which was only a short distance from the rescue center.

When they reached her house, Mark told Esmeralda, "I'd recommend that you just go to work tomorrow as if nothing has happened. I don't think you'll be high up on their agenda after tonight. Just like the warehouse, they'll do everything possible to keep the authorities out of this."

They left Esmeralda's house with Samuel sitting in the rear seat. Samuel said, "Esmeralda wouldn't tell me if anything happened to Emelia while she was there. I think she knew a lot more than she was telling me. I don't think it was good. I wish I could have questioned them myself. Maybe I'm better off not knowing what happened. I'm not sure I could handle it well.

Roe turned back to look at Samuel. "Don't worry, Samuel. Regardless of whatever did or didn't happen to Emelia, the people from that place have paid a heavy price."

Samuel only muttered quietly to himself, "It couldn't have been heavy enough."

CHAPTER 49

1973

They spent the morning in Mark and Rosa's room going over the plans for the hundredth time. For one last time they reviewed the maps, satellite data, and all of the pictures of the resort that they had been provided. Afterward, they all dressed in the uniforms they'd brought. The outfits were gray one-piece coveralls that had a well-known air conditioner company logo displayed prominently in the front. The coveralls were fitted loosely so that there was ample room to hide anything on the inside close to their body. The caps had the same logo on the front as well. Finally, there was nothing left to say. They all looked at each other and nodded in unison as if to say, "Let's go."

Leaving the motel, they traveled down Highway 80 and entered the city before turning onto the freeway that took them east and then south along the coast. They passed multiple resorts before they reached the Naturista Resort. It was easily visible from the main highway as they approached. The resort sat alone on a high bluff, providing an expansive and unimpeded view of the ocean. There were three roads that approached the resort: two secondary ones from the north and one leading directly east from the main highway. Both roads from the north were completely closed off as they had anticipated.

As soon as they turned off the main highway onto the road leading into the resort, it was obvious that it was well-protected. What would have been tight security at any other time was intensified because of the nature of the guests and the events planned for the weekend. They had to pass through two checkpoints before they even reached the hotel. They felt as if they were entering a secure prison every time a gate closed behind them. Each time they held their breaths, hoping their disguise would hold up. As they had hoped, there was a lot of traffic going into the hotel. At each checkpoint, the traffic was split into two lanes. One lane was for guests and the other was for all of the commercial traffic entering the resort. At the first checkpoint they sat for a long time behind a food truck that had aroused some suspicion from the guards at the gate. Ron Lassiter finally got out of the driver's seat and approached the guards with an angry look on his face. When one of the guards raised his hand to stop him, Ron released a string of invectives that set the guard back on his heels.

"One of the units cooling the ballroom isn't working. When they complain about the heat during the reception, I'm going to give them your name and tell them you said, 'A little sweat will be good for them.'"

The guard backed down and went back into the guard shack and came back out with a yellow sticker that he stuck under a windshield wiper. He then directed them around the food truck and on toward the hotel.

As hoped, the guards assumed that a broken cooling system was an urgent matter. When they reached the second gate, they were quickly waved through when the guards saw the yellow sticker. They were directed to a driveway that led off the main entrance road and led around the rear of the complex to a large service staging point. The whole area was a chaotic scene of activity. There were service vehicles of all types, and they reminded Ron of a disturbed ant's nest. In the middle of the activity, Mark, Rich, and Marcus used the confusion to climb out of the rear of the truck and began to untie the heavy dolly on the roof of the truck. Ron was able to play chicken with other vehicles as he skillfully backed the truck into a loading dock. Two men stood on the dock holding short automatic weapons as they carefully observed the activity. Ron stayed in the driver's seat while Rosa climbed out of the cab of the truck holding a sheaf of papers and headed toward a set of steps leading up onto the loading dock. She immediately attracted the attention of the two guards as she came up the steps. The fact that she had unbuttoned the shirt under her coveralls, making a large part of her breast visible, immediately attracted their attention. Smiling at the men, she asked, "Which way to the manager's office?"

"Through here, down the hall, and on the right," one of them said. Rosa followed the instructions the guard had given her only partially. The group knew that the resort consisted of three parts. The ocean side was a multistory building that contained the guest rooms and provided the ocean views. The middle section of the complex was two stories with the lobby, reception area, restaurant, administrative offices, and workout center on the main floor. The second floor consisted of a large area that could be divided up into multiple areas or left open as a huge ballroom. One small part had been sectioned off and had been furnished to resemble a small chapel where the actual service would be held. The third section of the complex where they were, held the kitchen, laundry, and everything involving maintenance. There were two levels of parking below it.

As soon as Rosa entered the wide hallway that opened onto the dock, she turned to the right and followed the hallway, which continued through the entire length of the building. There were signs along the way indicating where the doors that connected to the hallway led to. It was an efficient way to move services along the length of the complex, allowing the hotel guests to have minimal contact with the people who were serving them. Rosa followed the hallway until she found the service elevator that served the middle building. The top level was listed simply as *Roof*.

By the time Rosa had returned to the loading dock, Mark, Rich, and Marcus had maneuvered the large crate with the air conditioner markings onto the loading dock and onto the dolly. Nodding to the three, she indicated for them to follow her. As they pushed the large crate down the service hallway, they had to maneuver around the constant stream of service people who all seemed to be in a hurry and didn't even acknowledge the presence of the air conditioner workers. When they reached the service elevator door that led to the roof, they were relieved to see that it was large enough for the dolly holding the crate and all of them as well. When the door opened at the roof level, they were looking at a large expanse of asphalt covered in a fine gravel. In the very center was a collection of air conditioner units. They pushed the box around to the far side of the units to provide some concealment from anyone coming out of the elevator door before Rich and Marcus opened the crate. Mark and Rosa stood guard next to the elevator door.

By the time they'd opened the crate, the marriage service was starting on the level below. The MP5s and multiple loaded magazines for each person were handed out and were quickly concealed inside their overalls. Then Rich Holtz took out blocks of C-4 explosives. All were already armed with a receiver. Marcus helped Rich fill a laundry bag with the blocks and carried them slung over his shoulder. He followed Rich as he placed the blocks at different spots around the roof and two next to the pad that held the air conditioning units. He placed two blocks on the roof where he estimated the entrance to the chapel would be located. They carried the dolly back to the elevator and went down to the second floor where the marriage ceremony was taking place. Rich placed another explosive in a trash can in the hallway. Rosa, Rich, and Marcus stayed in the hallway on the second floor while Mark went back down to the first floor. In his arms he carried an air conditioning filter and a folded sign. He followed a hallway that led past the restaurant area and into a large lobby. A wide staircase led up to the second floor. The area underneath the winding stairway was open and Mark casually opened the folding sign which had *SUPERFICE MOJADA* printed in red letters. What was not visible were the two flat blocks of explosive concealed in each side of the sign.

The plan was to first set off the explosives over the entrance to the ballroom area as well as the explosives under the main stairs leading up to the ballroom. When the occupants ran away from the explosions toward the rear hallway, they would be met by Rosa, Rich, and Marcus, who would selectively assassinate any adult males with the possible exception of the priest. Mark would eliminate the guards on the loading dock and also prevent any other guards from entering from the rear. Even though they would be focusing on the adult males, they all knew there would be considerable collateral damage. After eliminating as many cartel members as possible within a two-minute timeframe, they would retreat to the dock area at the same time the explosives on the roof would be timed to detonate. They hoped that the ensuing panic would give them cover to escape the resort since all attention would be focused on the area of the explosions.

As Mark came back out onto the loading dock, he glanced at his watch and knew it was time. He felt the vibrations of the first explosions before the heard them. A constant stream of gunfire could then be heard amid screams of panic. The two guards on the loading dock headed toward Mark, ignoring him until he leveled his MP5 at them. At the same moment, several children ushered by a matronly woman ran out onto the dock between Mark and the guards, who ignored the woman and children and began firing their short automatic weapons. Fortunately, the children were small, and the rounds flew over their heads, but the woman, who presented a much larger target, was not so fortunate. As she was hit by multiple rounds meant for Mark, she pitched forward, and her flailing arms knocked two of the children to the floor. It was enough of an opening for Mark to fire several bursts, hitting one of the guards in the chest. The second guard had stupidly emptied his magazine with one long automatic burst and was attempting to insert another magazine when Mark fired two three round bursts from his MP5, cutting him down. By now all the children were safely off the dock and running for their lives.

Mark realized that two guards were coming up the steps onto the dock. He tried to raise his gun, but something was wrong. Blood was pouring across his face and eyes, blocking his vision. Everything was starting to spin, and his knees turned to rubber as he sagged to the floor. He could only watch as both guards raised their automatic weapons. But before they fired, Mark watched as they both pitched forward onto the steps. Standing directly behind them was Ron Lassiter, holding his Colt Python. Ron ran up the steps and pulled Mark to his feet and started to drag him toward the open doors of the truck, which was still backed up to the loading dock. As they reached the rear doors of the truck, Marcus came running out of the building. Marcus was bleeding but was still able to move without assistance. His face was ashen-colored as he said, "Let's go."

Mark seemed to regain strength as he pulled away from Ron, who was trying to push him into the truck.

"Wait! Where's Rosa?"

It was Marcus who replied, "She's gone, Mark. We need to leave now if we want to make it out."

Mark screamed and seemed to summon strength from somewhere as he started toward the hallway leading into the building. That's when the entire building seemed to erupt in a blinding flash that almost knocked them off the dock. Debris flew out of the doors leading into the building. Both Ron and Marcus took Mark by both arms and threw him into the rear of the truck. At that point, Mark mercifully blacked out.

CHAPTER 50

Pieces of the Past

Mark, Roe, and Samuel returned to their hotel and found a quiet table in the lounge. After ordering food and drinks, Mark said, "We need to plan our next step carefully. Even though we know where he is, getting to him will not be easy. Roe, how do you feel about talking to Angel without revealing too much of our past? Do you think he'd have any information on Mendez that might help?"

"I'm not sure, Mark. Tampico is a known smuggling center that's controlled by cartels. The town once had a thriving tourist industry when it was a major oil center. I do know that our government knows a lot more about the individual cartels than they'll publicly admit. Angel has gotten pretty far up the ladder, so he might know something specific about Mendez's operation. I don't have a problem talking to him. I'd need to go back to El Paso because I don't want to ask any questions on a phone. This would need to be face-to-face."

"I agree, Roe. I've also got someone I want to talk to in El Paso. When I'm on my deathbed I may be able to tell you about him. He might be able to help."

Samuel, who had remained silent, finally spoke, "I'm ready to go to Tampico if that's where he took Emelia."

Mark put his hand on Samuel's shoulder before replying, "One step at a time, Samuel. Let's try to move the odds toward our favor. We'll go back to El Paso first. Let's go back to our rooms and make reservations for the first flight we can get."

They were able to get early bird tickets that included only one changeover. After arriving at El Paso International, they retrieved the Toyota from long term parking and found a hotel located on the perimeter of the airport. Roe called Angel Ruiz and arranged to meet him outside his office later in the day. Mark used a taxi to take him to the university campus main administration building. Samuel would have to sit alone with his anxiety and wait.

Because Mark had been a tenured professor himself, his familiarity with the academic bureaucracy enabled him to find what he was looking for with ease. Walking a short distance across the campus, he entered a building, and after looking at the directory at the entrance, he found a reception room with an older gray-haired lady sitting behind a desk. Her hair was pulled up tightly in a bun and her glasses were hanging on her chest.

"Can I help you?" she asked as Mark entered the room.

"Yes, you can. I'm here to see Dr. Jefferson."

"Do you have an appointment?"

"No. But I think he'll want to see me."

"He's still in a class, but he should be back any time now. You're welcome to wait."

"Okay, I'll try not to disturb you while I'm waiting," he acquiesced, as he sat in one of the three chairs near the desk.

She was right about the timing. Within five minutes, a tall, distinguished man walked through the door. Marcus Jefferson had aged well. He was dressed in khaki slacks with a white shirt and tie that emphasized his dark brown skin. He had remained in good physical condition even though he was definitely heavier than Mark remembered him. When he first saw Mark sitting, he had a curious expression on his face that suddenly changed as he recognized him. His brown features turned almost white for a moment as he blurted out, "Mark."

Mark stood up and reached out his hand. "Marcus."

Instead of shaking Mark's hand, Marcus enveloped Mark in a huge bear hug as he said, "It's been a long time. You haven't changed much."

"Maybe not on the outside, but a lot on the inside."

"Haven't we all?" Marcus replied. "Come on back to my office."

After they were seated in his office, Marcus said, "I've followed your career and I know you lost your wife and daughter. You sort of went off the academic radar afterward."

"It's a long story, Marcus. Being chair of the Department of Psychology, you could have a field day with me. I often blame our past deeds for what happened to my family."

"Mark, the things we did, I have to shut them out of my mind every day. So, you're not alone. You know what happened to the only other survivor, Ron Lassiter?"

"No. I've followed your career like you've done mine. It's not hard to follow others in the academic world, but I lost track of Ron Lassiter almost immediately after we left the military."

"He had a problem with heroin within a year after our last mission. It's ironic that what we'd been fighting was his nemesis. Fortunately, the military was true to its word and supported him through it all. He's now working undercover for the DEA on the border."

"I'm glad he came out okay. You and he together saved my life. The last few minutes at that place are still like a vague dream."

"We each did all we could for each other. You kept those guards from going into the building. If they'd gotten past you, maybe none of us would have made it out."

"When I woke up, I was in an intensive care ward at Fort Sam Houston. There were so many unanswered questions, but there was no one I could talk to that could have helped me. There have been times over the years that I've come close to calling you. After General Hinson came to my hospital room and told me that the mission had been accomplished but I was to never speak to anyone including other members of the group, I've been reluctant to call you. Not for fear for myself, but fear of what might happen to you."

"I think enough time has passed that you and I can safely talk. I will never tell anyone what we did, and I know you feel the same. There's not a lot to tell you about Tampico. When the first charges under the stairs and the ones toward the front of the roof went off, there was total bedlam. As we could identify men through the smoke, we shot them as fast as we could. Rich had already set the timers for the rest of the explosives when one of the figures coming out of the chapel area unloaded his automatic rifle toward Rich. He took most of the rounds dead center. One of the rounds hit me in my left shoulder, but I could still move okay. Rosa was off to my right and took out the man who shot Rich. But there was nothing we could do for Rich.

"There were bodies everywhere and no one else was coming out. That's when Rosa screamed and ran directly into the smoke and toward the chapel. I tried to stop her, but she was like a wild thing. I guess she wanted to kill one more of them. That's when the next charge on the roof exploded. At that point I couldn't see anything, so I ran back toward the loading dock. I was hoping that Rosa would be right behind me, but she wasn't. By the time I reached the dock, I knew that the rest of the charges were going off at any moment. That's when you tried to run toward the entrance and Ron and I both pulled you back toward the truck. When the rest of the explosives detonated, it was devastating. No one inside that building could have survived.

"We were lucky that the truck was still operable. We had no trouble driving out of the area because all of the police were heading toward the resort. We stopped after we were well north of the city and Ron did what he could to bandage us up. When we got close to the border, Ron called ahead, and we were met at the border by an ambulance. I wasn't in such bad shape, but we were surprised that you were still alive. You'd lost a lot of blood and your face was split open. Looking at you now, I'm really amazed that your face is normal." Marcus smiled and added, "Well, almost normal. There must have been a pretty good plastic surgeon at Fort Sam."

Mark could only smile at Marcus as he continued, "I was only in the hospital for two days before Hinson came into my room and told me I was being honorably discharged but only on the condition that no one would ever know anything about what we'd done. If we ever did talk, we would be considered a threat to the country's national security and we would have to be sanctioned. You know what that means. I was not allowed to see you and Ron was already gone. Later, I did some research and found that the attack at the resort had been a major news story. Over a hundred people had been killed, including civilians. It did indeed turn the cartels upside down and had a dampening affect on the cartel's drug activity at the time."

Mark had almost been holding his breath as Marcus described the events. He let out a deep breath when Marcus finished.

"Marcus, after I left the hospital, I went back to El Paso and to the hangar that had been our headquarters. It was occupied by a kitchen remodeling business. It looked as if they had been operating out of the building for a long time. When I talked to a couple of people there, they seemed to have no idea who the previous occupants had been. We had been effectively erased, just like they said we would be. The discharge papers they gave me only listed my assignment as 'Central Command.' The Army did follow up with the money and education perks they'd promised."

"Same for me, Mark. I was able to get my PhD and I ended up here because I grew up in South Texas and my wife was from here. Probably, mostly because of my wife. Now, tell me, why after all this time did you decide to visit me now?"

Mark gave Marcus a sanitized version of what had happened to his wife and daughter, leaving out incriminating details of what he'd done in the aftermath. He finished by telling Marcus that Andre Mendez was the leader of the group that was responsible for the death of his daughter and had surfaced after they were sure he was dead. He included the plight of Samuel and Emelia. It was when Mark told Marcus that Mendez operated out of Tampico and had taken Emelia there that Marcus started to shake his head.

"No, Mark. Don't tell me that you're thinking of going there. I wouldn't think about going to Tampico with a company of Marines. Living here on the border, I follow all of the news both north and south of it. It's just not safe. And after what you went through before in Tampico, why could you ever think of going back?"

"I've asked myself the same thing. Why can't I just let it go and enjoy my life? Is revenge the answer? Will I be at peace by killing Mendez? I don't know. I only know that I made a promise at the graves of my wife and daughter that I would never stop until those responsible for their deaths were rotting in hell. I intend to keep that promise."

"You must think I can help you in some way or you wouldn't be talking to me. I will tell you that I'm not going to Tampico with you if that's what you're thinking. Maybe if you talked to Ron, he might be able to help you. I am truly sorry for what you've lost, but my family is still dependent on me. The last I heard of Ron was that he was working on the Texas border, but I have no idea where."

Smiling, Mark replied, "There's no way I would ask you to help me with this. You asked why I'm here talking to you after all these years? It's because the question of what happened to Rosa at that resort in Tampico has kept me awake so many nights. Just hearing what you've told me explains a lot. I don't blame you for her death. There was nothing else you could have done. Why she ran back towards the chapel, we'll never know. I suppose it's a good thing I wasn't the one inside the building with her. I would have probably followed her back inside. I did truly love her. I just had to hear the details from you before I go back to Tampico. I wanted to finally have closure on that part of my life. I thank you for talking to me, Marcus. It's good to see you doing well."

"I wish I could change your mind, Mark. I'm not sure what I'd do given the same circumstances, but I respect your decision. When I remember what you were capable of doing back then, I suspect that this Mendez character should be looking over his shoulder."

The second Mark left Marcus's office he called Roe's cell phone. She was waiting to meet Angel in a coffee shop.

"Roe, when you talk to Angel, ask him how to get in touch with an agent named Ron Lassiter. Just tell him that I knew him from basic training in the Army and I'd like to touch base with him while I'm in Texas."

Mark returned to the hotel and waited at the bar for Roe to return from her meeting with Angel Ruiz. Mark ordered a Tanqueray on the rocks with a wedge of lime. Sitting and sipping on his drink, he tried to digest what Marcus had told him about Rosa. Even after all the years that had passed, including a marriage and a child, there was a hole in his heart that had never healed. It was a hole that was left when he lost Rosa. Going back to Tampico would be like visiting a loved one's grave. He was starting on his second Tanqueray when he saw Roe enter the lobby. He stood up and waved to her, and she joined him at the bar. She ordered a glass of wine before she started to talk about her meeting with Angel.

"We're in luck. Our people are aware of the Colombian Cartel that's based in the state of Tamaulipas. Most of the attention has been centered on the capital city, Ciudad Victoria. That's where most of the smuggling across our southern border originates. Only recently have our people become aware of what's going out of the city of Tampico. Like flowers from Colombia being used to smuggle drugs, limes and lemons coming out of Tampico are being used and are shipped all over the world, including the US. It's gone unnoticed for a long time, but the DEA is starting to take notice. Apparently, we have well-placed informants in Tampico, plus there are citizen groups who are fed up with living under the threats from the cartel. Angel said our agencies were aware that a major drug cartel controlled Tampico. They also knew that this was a Colombian organization run by a man and his sister. The family is expanding their influence along the entire border. When I told him what I knew about Mendez, he was impressed, but he really lost it when I suggested that I wanted to go to Tampico. It took a lot of talking to convince him that it was something I had to do. He explained that I would be on my own if anything went south and that I was putting my career at risk, etcetera, etcetera. When I mentioned Ron Lassiter's name, he only shook his head. He said it would be better if we stayed away from Ron, because he was known throughout the agency as a loose cannon. But he did tell me he worked out of the office in Brownsville. He has a bad reputation because he has a habit of losing his partners. The last thing Angel said was that we'd never had this conversation. Whatever I did would be on me alone."

Mark had a flashback to the time in the Army when he'd been told the same thing. "You don't have to go, Roe. Samuel and I will go. Angel is right. There's no need for you to put your career at risk. I am going to try and talk to Ron Lassiter, but I'd rather not let anyone know I've talked to him."

Roe smiled and reached for Mark's hand. "We have no choice. Maybe you and I are like two snowballs headed to hell. We have to finish this together and let the chips fall where they may."

Mark smiled back at her. "Roe, you'll never know how proud I am of you. If Kim could see you, I know she'd be smiling. Let's go to Tampico."

CHAPTER 51
Déjà vu

Not wanting to waste time driving, they booked a flight to the Brownsville airport. Although he didn't want to have any connection to the trio, Angel did do two things to help them. The Border Patrol had a compound near the airport where they stored confiscated vehicles. When Mark, Roe, and Samuel got off the plane in Brownsville, they went to the short term parking lot and found the car that Angel had provided. He'd given Roe a description and plate number. Someone had brought the old Toyota 4Runner from the impound lot and left it unlocked with keys under the seat. It was dented in places, covered in dust, and smelled like a pair of old shoulder pads. The tires looked okay. Most important though, it had current Mexican plates for the state of Tamaulipas.

Leaving the airport on Boca Chica Boulevard, they checked into a cheap motel, and with Roe's help with phone numbers, Mark finally reached the office that Ron Lassiter worked out of. Mark had paid in cash for the rooms and had used an ID that he'd taken from one of the men from the safe house in El Paso, so he had no fear of the number being traced back to either Roe or himself. Speaking in Spanish, he asked to speak to Señor Johnson. When asked what he wanted, he simply said that he had the information that Señor Johnson wanted. There was a long pause before a voice from the past said, "Who is this?"

Mark replied, "No names. You saved my life in Mexico and brought me safely home. I've never had the chance to thank you properly. I'd like to do that now."

Again, there was a long pause before Ron answered, "Yes, it has been a long time. Where are you calling from?"

"I'm calling from a thrift store on Boca Chica."

"There is a small bar called the Blooming Cactus, just a block from where you are. Can you meet me there in thirty minutes?"

"I'll be there."

Mark left Roe and Samuel at the motel and drove to the bar Ron had described. It was a real dive bar. He couldn't help but marvel at the debris covering the upswept floor. It was deserted except for two men sitting at the bar protectively huddled over their drinks as if the drinks might run away.

Mark ordered a bottled beer, not wanting to risk an unwashed glass, and sat in a chair facing the door.

Ron Lassiter had not aged as well as Marcus had. He was dressed well. He was almost too dapper. His pallor was pale gray, and he obviously had avoided any time in the sun. When he saw Mark, he approached and stood still, looking at him as if he were processing all that had passed years ago. He held out his hand. "Hello, Mark. You're looking good."

"You haven't changed much yourself, Ron."

Ron made a gesture to the man behind the bar. "Double Scotch," he said as he sat down facing Mark. "What brings you here after all this time? I really didn't do anything heroic. I was trying to save my ass as much as yours."

"I guess what I'm looking for is closure. I remember so little of what happened in Tampico. I guess I just wanted confirmation on what happened to Rosa and Rich as well."

"I can only tell you what I witnessed from the dock area. You shot two guards. I shot two guards and then Marcus came out of the building alone. You started to go back into the building but Marcus and I both stopped you. If you'd gone back inside, you'd never have come back out. The explosion was massive. No one inside the building could have survived. You passed out the minute we pushed you into the truck. You'll never know how lucky we were that I was able to drive out of the service area. It was total bedlam everywhere. Once we got back out on the road, we stopped, and I tried to stop your bleeding. Marcus's arm wound was easy to bandage, but your face was a mess. Marcus and I were both amazed that you were still breathing when we finally reached the US border."

"I do thank you for getting Marcus and I both back safely. You always did your part well. It seems ironic that you're still fighting the same battle that we did back then. It makes one wonder if what we did was just a waste of lives."

"Mark, every day that I wake up I look at my face in the mirror and ask the same question. We're fighting a massive game of whack-a-mole."

"I understand what you're saying, Ron. I've heard that the state of Tamaulipas where we went is now a huge Colombian stronghold."

"Yes, it is. The main cartel is now being run out of Tampico by a Colombian named Mendez and a woman whom we know very little about. I'll work undercover anywhere along the border, but I'd die before I ever thought about going back to that place."

Mark's instincts had always served him well, and a little voice told him to not press the conversation. They made some more small talk before Ron looked at his watch and said, "Mark, it was good seeing you again. I've tried to bury the ghost of our past and sometimes not so well. I wish you the best, but I don't think we should meet again. I don't want to be reminded of what we did." And with that statement, Ron abruptly stood up, tossed down the last of his Scotch, and walked out without a backward glance.

Mark returned to the motel and picked up Roe and Samuel. They drove to a nearby gun store that had been recommended by Angel. Mark bought a compact tactical shotgun, two Glock 19s, and lots of ammunition. Roe had still been able to fly with her sidearm.

Next to the gun store was a local thrift store. Going into the store, all three picked out worn clothing that would help to lessen any attention. Roe and Samuel would blend easily, but Mark would always stand out because of his size. Hopefully the loose, baggy clothing he chose would help. Angel had advised Roe to look as un-North American as possible.

Next, they stopped at a big box store where Mark bought two ten-gallon gas tanks, a small cooler, and an armful of preprepared sandwiches. Remembering his previous trip to Tampico, Mark wanted to avoid stopping any more than absolutely necessary. He still had the two stacks of bills he'd confiscated from the Palm Beach estate. As soon as they'd filled the tanks and car with gas, they crossed the border into Mexico and headed south.

It was late afternoon when they left, and the plan was that they'd just drive through the night. Mark hoped they'd have enough gas and wouldn't have to stop at all, but he finally realized that the 4Runner was using a lot of gas, so after they'd emptied the cans, they started looking for a secluded station. At a point where Highway 101 split with 180, going south toward Tampico, a huge *ASTER* sign lit up the night. It was a large truck stop with a restaurant and motel. They pulled into the pumps and Mark filled up the 4Runner's tank as well as the cans. Roe and Samuel stayed in the car.

They thought they'd gone unnoticed, but when Mark got back into the driver's seat, a police vehicle drove up in front of the 4Runner and stopped, almost touching their front bumper. Another police car stopped within a foot of their rear, blocking all possibility of leaving. Both of the police cars left their bright lights on, making it difficult to see the figure that got out of the driver's side of the car in front. By the time he'd reached the driver's side window, Mark could see he was large—as in fat. His potbelly hung down, obscuring his thick gun belt. His right hand rested on a large revolver hanging at his side. He had a thick neck and a wide brown face. If he hadn't been worried, Mark would have laughed. He reminded Mark of a character in a movie about a country cop chasing an elusive Pontiac Trans Am. Mark rolled his window down and waited for the man to speak. The cop had a flashlight in his left hand that he used to look into the car, keeping the light shining on Roe for an uncomfortably long time.

He finally spoke, "Where are you headed?"

Mark smiled and replied, "Home."

Not smiling, the cop asked, "Where is home?"

"Tampico. We've been working in Texas for the last six months. We pooled our money to drive home. We don't want to spend our hard earned North American money on a motel. This is my daughter, and the man in the back has been working with us."

"So it must be very profitable working in Texas."

Mark knew exactly where the conversation was headed, and he replied, "Yes, it has been profitable. Maybe profitable enough that we could share some of it with the good people in Mexico who keep us safe."

The man smiled for the first time. "My friend, you are a wise man."

Mark had anticipated what was happening the moment the police had appeared and had five hundred-dollar bills in his hand which lit up under the beam of the flashlight. His right hand finally left its grip on his gun and reached into the car. The bills disappeared into his fat hand as if by magic.

"Have a safe trip my friends," the cop said as he returned to his car.

Mark let out a sigh of relief and Roe released her grip on the gun she held concealed in her lap. As they drove out of the truck stop, Mark kept a close eye on the rearview mirror, half-expecting the police to appear behind them. But they drove south into the night alone. Mark suspected that the cop was too busy trying to hide the money Mark had given him, from his compatriots.

Faint light was beginning to appear in the east as they approached Tampico. Mark recognized the motel where they'd stayed just north of the city. He slowed as they drove past. It appeared to have been frozen in time with dozens of big rigs parked in the front and a sign that simply read *OTEL* because the lights in the *H* were burnt out. He tried to shut out the flashbacks that were trying to fill his mind. Mark had looked carefully at a map, and he knew the directions Angel had given Roe would take them to a motel just past the resort where Rosa and Rich Holtz had died. They entered the city and then went east on the same causeway before turning south along the coast.

Mark tried to ignore the sense of déjà vu that he felt as they approached the turnoff to the resort. How much of a coincidence would it be that he would be returning to the place of his worst nightmares? Knowing it was the last thing he should do, he was drawn like a moth to a flame. When he reached the turnoff, he slowed and turned toward the site of the resort. Roe gave him a quizzical look and Mark only said, "I want to look at something."

The changes were dramatic. The once grand road-way entrance was almost completely covered by the shifting sands along the side of the road. There was no sign of a guardhouse, and the road was littered with years of accumulated waste. Discarded tires, rusted mowing equipment, bottles, rotting lumber, and bags of trash made the road nearly impassable. As they got closer, the imposing structure rose up like an Egyptian monolith. It almost resembled a mountain because of the growth of vegetation that was claiming the entire complex. There were literally trees growing on the roof. Vines crept up all sides, competing with green growth reaching out of windows like fingers reaching for the sky. The surfaces of the building that were visible were blackened and covered in soot, resembling the inside of an old fireplace. Graffiti was scrawled on every exposed wall. Mark was able to drive up to the entrance leading into the loading dock area, but the ground was so filled with debris he couldn't get any closer. A rusted hulk of a delivery truck sat next to the dock.

It was the sight of the rusted hulk that broke whatever barriers he'd erected in his mind. A sudden image of a florist truck unloading flowers flashed in his mind, and it was followed by the image of children being herded by a matronly lady who seemed to explode in a burst of red directly in front of him. He pressed both his hands tightly against his head, trying to shut out the agony the memory was causing.

Roe was confused, not only by Mark driving to this place, but especially by his reaction to a burnt-out hulk of an old derelict building. Mark's reaction was so uncharacteristic. Samuel, sitting in the back seat, seemed to be equally confused.

"Mark, what's going on?'

"I'll tell you about it later, Roe. This is not the first time I've been to this place. I never, even in my wildest imagination, thought I'd see it again. But I've seen more than I want to see. Let's go."

CHAPTER 52

Local Assistance

The motel they were looking for was only a short distance down the coast. It was located on the main highway several blocks removed from the beach. It was typical of many motels in that it was a walled compound with a gated entrance and exit. They got a room for Roe and a double room for Mark and Samuel. Since they weren't supposed to meet the contact until the evening, all three of them slept for most of the day.

By evening, all three were rested and hungry. Following the instructions Angel had provided, they found the restaurant only a short drive away. It was just inland from the beach area and was on the first floor of one of many small hotels. They were met at the door as they entered by a small, old, and very wrinkled smartly dressed man. Roe said, "We were referred here by Señor Marin."

Without hesitation, the old gentleman said, "Follow me," and led them through a door and into a closed-off section at the rear of the restaurant. After they were seated at a table for six, the man said, "Please order something to eat and drink. Someone will be here soon that you will want to meet."

The food was excellent, and they had just finished eating when a well-dressed lady entered followed by two middle-aged men. One of the men was wearing a suit and the second one was dressed in nice slacks and an open-collared dress shirt. The woman seemed to be the spokesperson for the trio.

"For obvious reasons, you don't need to know our names. I'll just say I'm in education, the man in the suit is connected to medicine, and this man"—she pointed to the man in the shirt— "is a businessman. We are taking a great risk meeting you here tonight. But as we've learned, you three are taking an even greater risk just by being here. I will commend you for maintaining such a low profile. We were holding our breaths when we were told you were coming mainly because most US visitors coming to Tampico are easy to spot. You've blended in very well. We've had you under constant surveillance since you checked into the motel. We're confident that no one from the cartel is aware of your presence. Turning to the older man who had greeted them earlier, she made a drinking motion and he immediately brought out a bottle of tequila and six glasses. We may as well enjoy a drink while we talk. The old man poured a generous portion for them all, set the bottle on the table, and discreetly left the room."

What followed was a long history lesson given by the woman educator. "We've had some cartel presence here for the last hundred years. For many years it was mostly low-level and had a minimal effect on the city. The real drug problems started in the Sixties and corresponded with the rise of drug use in the US. But even at that time, the cartels were so busy fighting each other that the local population hadn't been affected. Everything changed in 1972 when what we call 'The Great Massacre' occurred."

Roe raised her hand. "I'm sorry, but what do you mean by the 'Great Massacre'?"

"That is something of a local legend. There was a marriage between members of two different cartel families that was supposed to occur here in Tampico. Drug families from all over Mexico were invited to the resort. A temporary truce had been agreed upon between the cartel families just for this event. There was an attack during the wedding and dozens of cartel members as well as many innocent civilians were killed. To my knowledge, no one has ever claimed responsibility, but it left a huge void in the leadership of cartels all over Mexico. That's when the Colombians moved into the void and took over. The main beneficiary was the person you're interested in, Andre Mendez, and his sister. She's ultimately the one with control. You actually passed within a short distance of the site where the massacre occurred. It was once a fine hotel, but no one has touched it since the massacre. People only go there to scare themselves or to play paintball."

Roe looked at Mark, who was staring straight ahead and holding his breath. Fortunately, she had the good judgment to remain silent.

"Anyway, the Mendez family has its finger in almost every business and governmental agency in the region. Any opposition is met with beatings, kidnappings, and death. Most of the population wants relief. We can't count on the Mexican government to help us. In fact, they have no idea that we're working with anyone from the US. We are effectively acting on our own. We think that if the Mendez family was eliminated, then the general population might have a chance to put our people in power. We have mutual interest. You want the girl and Mendez. We want Mendez erased. We were told that you have experience in this sort of thing. We can help you."

Mark asked, "Is Mendez here in Tampico right now?"

"Yes. And so is the girl he brought with him."

Samuel was almost hyperventilating at the possibility of seeing Emelia again. Roe put a hand on his shoulder to calm him.

Roe appeared thoughtful and asked, "So the sister needs to be eliminated as well?"

"Yes. Maybe even more so than Andre."

Mark continued to question the woman. "What can you tell us about their security?"

"They have so much power in this area, they've gotten casual with their protection. They have many locals on their payroll, and I think they believe themselves to be untouchable. There is a guard gate with a twenty-four-hour guard at the main entrance to the ranch. There is also video surveillance at the gate and at the front of the house. But here is where we can help. Over the years, the family has hurt so many people here. For example, their trusted butler's son was kidnapped and killed by the cartel because he refused to work for Mendez. The father who is now their trusted butler lived in Mexico City and came here using a different name and worked his way into the home as a trusted servant. Alex is a source of information from within the house. One of the guards who lives on the ranch in the bunkhouse was also hurt by the Mendez family when his father was killed because he refused to sell his property to them. He has access to the surveillance controls."

Mark nodded. "That all sounds good, but how do we actually get past the guarded gate and into the main house without being detected? If we are going to have any chance of getting out safely, we've got to do it without alerting the guards that are living on the ranch."

The woman nodded and pointed toward the man in the shirt who spoke for the first time. "I own a large wholesale grocery warehouse. A truck from my business delivers food supplies to the ranch at least once a week. They don't even check the truck's cargo at the gate any longer. You'll be able to be drive to the service area at the back of the house. You'll leave the same way. The truck will be found abandoned and burning later. There will be a burnt body with bullet wounds found in the truck. Don't worry. We're not going to kill someone to put in the truck. We'll have an unclaimed body from the local morgue that we'll shoot up and put in the truck. I'll claim that the truck was hijacked, and the driver forced to drive it. This way I won't be blamed for being a part of whatever happens when the local police, who are an arm of the family, investigate."

Pointing to Mark, he continued, "You'll be a new driver who just got hired if the guard at the gate questions you. I hope you know how to drive a truck."

CHAPTER 53

Shock

The delivery was scheduled for late the next afternoon. They thought that if they went in late enough, they might have the cover of darkness when they left the ranch. The delivery truck had been left sitting outside the walls of the motel. Mark drove while Roe and Samuel rode in the rear of the panel food truck. They had been given detailed descriptions of the route to the ranch as well as how to access the rear service area of the main house. As a backup, the truck was equipped with a GPS system routinely used by the delivery trucks. Mark was wearing work clothes supplied by the food warehouse. Mark had one of the Glocks stuck in his waistband, while Samuel carried the other one. Roe had her gun as usual, and the shotgun was hidden in the back of the truck.

Before they left the motel the three of them made a pact. The goal of course was to enter the ranch, rescue Emelia, and euphemistically eliminate—meaning kill—Mendez and his sister. Hopefully they would then exit the ranch without drawing any undue attention. They all agreed without hesitation that if it came down to an all-out shootout with the guards at the ranch in order to accomplish this, there would be no backing out. It was to be all or none, regardless of the consequences. Mark and Roe both did have some doubt about how effective

Samuel would be if he had to use the Glock he carried. They had no doubt that he would use it. They just hoped he wouldn't shoot the wrong person.

It was late in the afternoon when they finally approached the guarded gate. The single guard approached the driver's side door and looked quizzically at Mark.

"I haven't seen you before."

"No, you haven't. And you probably won't see me again after today. I've fucked up almost every delivery I've made. That's why I'm so late. The boss told me that if I screwed up this delivery, I'd better not come back."

The guard laughed and replied, "I understand. The difference is that if we screw up, we're not fired, we're just killed."

With that, the gate started sliding open, and the guard waved the truck through. Mark hoped that the security cameras had been disabled as promised.

Even though they'd been given detailed instructions, Mark was surprised at the distance between the entrance and the actual house. It was obvious from the expensive fencing, and the animals he could see, that a lot of money had been spent to build the place. As he approached the main house and followed the service road around toward the rear service area, he had a hard time comprehending the amount of wealth required to build and maintain a place like this.

The service area at the rear of the home was hidden by tall walls of the same stone used on the house. It was covered in well-manicured ivy. Mark turned the truck around as he'd been instructed to do and backed up within several feet of a set of large double doors. As soon as the truck was stopped, a man dressed in an immaculate tuxedo was opening the double doors. Mark climbed out of the truck and approached the man, who simply said, "My name is Alex. The way is clear."

Mark opened the rear doors of the food truck and Roe and Samuel got out. Mark, Roe, Samuel, and Alex huddled up just inside the doors. They were in a hallway with swinging doors at the end. They knew the floor plan that Alex had previously provided to the contacts in the city showed the house to be over twelve thousand square feet, all on one floor. The maze of hallways that ran through the center of the house and around both sides was a logistics nightmare. Not sure how Samuel would react under the circumstances, they planned to leave him at the service entrance with orders to not allow anyone to enter the house behind them. They had spent a lot of time preparing Samuel for meeting Emelia. He had to know that she had been abused by her captors and no one could predict what her state of mind might be. How he would react to her would be critical for them both.

Roe was going to follow the hallway leading to their left, which led to most of the bedrooms. Mark was going toward their right, which led past the kitchens, dining room, and to the study. Alex whispered to Mark when they first arrived that Andre had just left Emelia alone in a bedroom. He wasn't sure where he'd gone when he'd left her. Alex thought that Hermana was alone in the study. He volunteered to watch the front entrance.

Moving to his right, Mark passed through swinging doors from the kitchen and into an expansive dining room. From there he followed a short hallway that opened into a huge room that he realized must be the study. To his left was a long bar made of a heavy polished wood. The longest outside wall was stone with a fireplace that was almost large enough to sit in. The rear wall was all glass and overlooked a patio and garden area with a pool that looked as if it were a natural part of the landscape. The only light in the room was a small reading lamp coming from a sitting area near the rear windows. Mark stepped into the room and had gotten as far as the fireplace when he realized that there was someone sitting in a chair nearest the lamp. The figure saw him at the same time, stood up, and walked toward him. She was a small woman with jet-black hair and bronze-tinted skin, but she suddenly stopped, and with a look of astonishment gasped, "Mark?"

Not sure if he was hallucinating, Mark could only reply, "Rosa."

CHAPTER 54

Heartbreak

For what seemed to be an eternity, they both stood frozen in place as an avalanche of memories flowed through each of their minds. Mark took a step forward, holding out his hands. Rosa shook her head, "No, Mark. I'm not the Rosa you once knew."

Mark's knees were turning to jelly, and he had to sit down before he fell down. It had been years since he'd had to identify his only daughter's bruised and battered body that he'd felt such a rush of intense emotion. He was only a step away from the hearth in front of the fireplace, and he sat down on one of the pillows covering it. Rosa slowly walked over and sat next to him. She was shaking as she said, "Mark, there is so much you don't know."

"How? Why?" He felt so disoriented, and his head was spinning so fast that he hardly heard what Rosa was saying.

"Mark, please listen. When Lou was killed, I was about to help Marcus drag his body back to the truck. I looked up and I was looking directly at my brother, Andre. He had recognized me as well. I was sure that Marcus would kill him, so I ran toward my brother to protect him. At that moment, another charge detonated, and I lost consciousness. Andre's personal guard was a man named Diego Cano. He picked me up and carried me down the set of stairs used by the priest. It went down under the first floor to a service tunnel that ran all the way to the beach pavilion. Andre told me later that the largest and final charges went off just as we reached the tunnel. Andre was able to get me to a hospital, and I was in a coma for weeks. Even as I started to recover, my memory was only returning in bits and pieces. One thing is true: We each had believed that the other was dead. It's a long and complicated story. Please don't judge me until you've heard it all."

Mark started to ask a question, but before he could speak, Andre Mendez entered the room, walking rapidly toward where Mark and Rosa were seated. A large caliber revolver in his right hand was pointing toward Mark. Rosa and Mark stood up, and Mark realized that in his initial state of surprise, he'd laid his gun on the hearth and it was now well out of his reach. Andre was wearing only a robe with a sash tied tightly around his waist.

"So, Hermana, this man is one of the ones who slaughtered so many of my family and friends at the wedding?"

"This was settled a long time ago, Andre. That's ancient history. I don't think that has anything to do with why he's here at this moment."

"Your sister is right, Andre. I'm here because you were responsible for the deaths of my wife and daughter."

"What do you mean? I've never seen you before now."

"Think back real hard. Tampa, Florida. Remember a small restaurant across the street from your warehouse? You were having lunch with a man named Rick Sealy. You came to my table and called me a son of a whore, thinking that I couldn't speak Spanish."

Andre took a step closer toward Mark and looked intently at his face. "Yes, I do remember. You're the one who killed Sealy? Then you're probably also responsible for wrecking our business in Florida."

Mark smiled down at the shorter Andre and said, "I also killed your girlfriend, Charity. She died a gruesome and painful death for killing my daughter."

"You are a son of a whore," Andre said as his finger tightened on the trigger of the revolver he held.

It's strange how you sometimes focus on the oddest things at the most inappropriate times. Mark was staring at the gun Andre was holding and recognized it as a Smith & Wesson R8 357 Magnum from their custom shop. It was built on a lightweight alloy frame and the cylinder held eight rounds. It was a beautiful instrument and Mark thought it was going to be the last thing he'd see on this earth. What he heard was a scream, "Nooo!" as two shots were fired in quick succession.

Having known what her brother was going to do even before he knew himself, Rosa threw herself in front of Mark. Her body absorbed both Magnum rounds in the center of her chest.

There was a moment of silence following the deafening blasts before the reality of what he'd done registered on Andre's mind. With eyes blazing with hatred, he started to point the gun back toward Mark when another shot rang out from across the room. Samuel was standing with both shaking hands holding the Glock he'd fired toward Andre. The bullet had grazed Andre's ear and distracted him for a split-second, giving Mark enough time to lunge for the R8 in Andre's hand. As his hand clamped on Andre's wrist, he rolled to the floor, pulling Andre with him. Andre's hand hit the floor at such an angle that there was an audible snap as his wrist broke and the gun fell out of his grasp. Andre screamed in pain just as Mark hit him in the side of his head with a closed fist. Rolling Andre onto his stomach,

Mark pulled the sash from around his body and used it to tie his hands behind his body. Looking up at Samuel, he said, "Go in the kitchen and look for some kind of tape."

Knowing Andre wasn't going anywhere, he went over to where Rosa was lying on the floor. He sat down and cradled her head in his arms. Her eyes flickered open for a moment, and seeing Mark's face, she smiled and died.

While Mark remained frozen in place with Rosa's head cradled in his arms, several things happened around him. First Roe walked into the study with her arms around a trembling and confused Emelia. When Samuel saw them, he screamed Emelia's name and ran to her. As they tearfully embraced, Roe approached Mark, who was still on the floor holding Rosa. Because there was so much blood, Roe thought that Mark had been shot, but she soon realized that he was okay. But his reaction toward the strange woman was so out of character she wasn't quite sure what to say to him. Kneeling down next to him, she asked, "Mark, you knew her?"

"Once upon a time I thought I did. Now I'm not so sure."

While Roe was trying to talk to Mark, Alex the butler rushed into the room speaking rapidly. "Everybody stay in this room and keep quiet. Someone's coming to check on the gunshots." He headed toward the front entrance to meet them, and held up his hands to stop them. "You don't want to see Señor Mendez at the moment. He's pissed off at the meats that the grocer just brought. He just killed a ham in the fireplace and he's looking for something else to shoot. It might be better for you if you stay away until he's calmed down."

Knowing the capacity of Mendez's anger, they only smiled and were happy to walk away with no more questions.

By the time Alex returned to the study, Mark had lifted up Rosa's body and laid it on a sofa before covering her with a throw. Roe had found a roll of packaging tape in the adjacent office and bound Andre's legs so that he was totally immobilized.

Roe sensed that Mark was still not back to normal because he continued to stand next to where Rosa's body lay, and he still seemed to be unaware of anything else. Samuel and Emelia hadn't separated since their first embrace. Things had gone well so far, but Roe knew that their luck would not hold out. Looking at Alex, Roe asked, "Alex, where do they keep their laptops?"

"In the study."

"Is there a safe where they keep records?"

"Yes. Also, on the wall in the office. It's probably not locked. They usually don't lock it if they're both here."

Roe walked into the office next door and found two laptop computers on the expansive desk. The wall safe was behind a large painting on the wall behind the desk. Sure enough, it was unlocked. Picking up a cushion in the plush office, she unzipped the cover and pulled it off. Using it, she scooped everything out of the safe and into the case. She didn't even try to evaluate the contents, although she was aware of metal objects, bricks of cash, and a lot of paper records. Zipping up the cover, she carried it and the laptops back into the study.

Mark seemed to have recovered from whatever mental trauma had affected him, and he was standing next to Andre, who was still lying on his stomach on the floor. Mark looked at Roe and nodded. He rolled Andre over onto his back, ignoring his cry of pain as he lay on his broken wrist. Without the sash to hold his robe closed, when Andre was rolled onto his back, his robe was open, exposing his body. Mark picked up Andre's revolver from the floor nearby.

Andre's pleas for mercy fell on unsympathetic ears as Mark raised the R8 and aimed point-blank aim at Andre's head. Before Mark could pull the trigger, a voice said, "No."

Looking up, Mark realized that Emelia and Samuel had approached and were standing with them, looking down at the hapless Mendez. Emelia was holding a knife in her hands, and the expression of malevolence on her face sent chills down Mark's spine.

CHAPTER 55

Retributon

As Emelia knelt down next to Andre, Mark moved to the side and watched what Emelia did next. Mark experienced a sudden flashback to a time in his past. When he was in high school, he'd had a summer job working on a cattle ranch owned by the family of a young boy on his football team. The boy was small and frail with no athletic ability, but his dad had pushed him to play football. He'd been given the nickname Moonbeam by others on the team. The kid did try to compete, but he should have been on the debate team and not trying to play football.

One day after practice, Mark had stayed on the field throwing passes to the wide receivers. When he entered the locker room, a group of players were crowding around a locker laughing at something. When Mark approached, he realized what was happening. The most unpopular player on the team was a huge fat lineman everyone called Tank. His size alone made him a good high school player, but his stupidity and laziness would keep him from ever playing at a higher level. Tank had taken a locker that was not attached to a wall and had it turned upside down. Someone was inside the locker and was desperately trying to get out. Tank was leaning down speaking into the louvers built into the locker for ventilation and mocking the person inside. "Moonbeam, can you hear me now?" he was saying.

Without hesitation, Mark pushed through the group and kicked Tank across his ample rear end as hard as he could. Tank crashed headfirst into the metal locker, putting a huge dent in the side. He fell to the concrete floor holding his head and moaning. Mark opened the locker and helped the grateful Moonbeam back onto his feet. Embarrassed, the other players moved away.

Moonbeam and his family appreciated the fact that Mark had helped him, and Mark was guaranteed a good paying summer job while he was in high school.

It was the summer job that had caused Mark's mind to flashback. The job included branding and cutting the cattle. After the cattle had been round up from the swamps and forest, they were separated into pens and any cattle found to be unbranded were forthwith seared with the branding iron. All three- to four-month-old males were herded into a separate pen. Although Mark had killed more deer and hogs than he could remember, he never had a problem skinning and gutting the animals he'd killed. Cutting the young bulls was something that he never became comfortable with doing. It always amazed him how Moonbeam, who was helpless in football pads, was in his element when it came time to brand and cut the cattle.

Cutting the young males was a well-choreographed process. It could be done by two well-trained cowhands, but it was always easier with three. It reduced the possibility of a hoof against a head. The young animal was unceremoniously thrown to the ground with its rear legs held apart and the weight of two men's knees pinning it to the ground. The cutter, using a well-sharpened pocketknife, would slice out piece of the animal's scrotum and the testicles would be pulled out as far as possible, bringing out as much length of the vas deferens as possible. These would be severed close to the animal's body. The young animal would be released to rise up, no longer a bull but a steer, wondering what the hell had just happened.

Although Moonbeam had offered to let Mark do the cutting, Mark always demurred. All of these memories flashed through Mark's mind in an instant as he watched Emelia grab Andre Mendez's scrotum with her left hand and with the knife in her right hand severed it across the base. Andre realized what was happening and screamed as Emelia held her bloody hand over his stomach and dropped his testicles onto his belly. Meanwhile, Samuel reached out toward Mark and gestured toward the revolver Mark was holding. Mark handed the gun to Samuel, who took it and put it against Andre's head and pulled the trigger. It literally exploded his head, leaving spots of blood on Samuel's face.

Roe looked at Mark before speaking, "Mark, I don't think there's any doubt this time. Andre Mendez is dead."

"Yes, and we need to go now. Let me have that gun, Samuel. It still has five rounds left. Alex, be sure all the doors to the house are locked when we leave."

As Alex checked the doors, everyone hurried for the back entrance and the truck. Only Mark stayed alone in the study for a minute more. Reaching down, he uncovered Rosa's face. Leaning down, he kissed Rosa's lifeless body on the cheek, and choking back tears, recovered her with the throw and left her lying there.

Within three minutes the food truck was leaving the house and driving toward the main gate. The gate was just starting to open as they approached, and the guard was walking up toward the driver's window with a quizzical expression on his face. "What the hell happened back there? I heard that the boss was pissed. What did you do?"

Mark had rolled the window down and started to reply at the same moment that the guard realized that

Mark was covered in blood. As he started to raise his rifle, Mark was a second faster with the revolver he was holding in his lap. He fired one shot and the 357 hollow point round from the R8 entered his forehead, causing his head to jerk backward. He was dead before his body reached the ground. Mark had already pushed the accelerator to the floor, causing the truck to leap forward, barely missing the still opening gate.

When they reached the courtyard of the motel, they quickly moved from the truck and into the 4Runner, making sure they kept the laptops and material from the safe. Roe had insisted that Alex return to the US with them. He would be a dead man if he stayed, and he could be a valuable source of information for the DEA in the US.

The drive north to the US border was uneventful. Samuel and Emelia held on tightly to each other for the entire drive. Alex sat with them in the rear seat and remembered his son. It had taken him a long time, but he smiled with satisfaction knowing that at last he'd avenged him. Roe and Mark were silent and unable to openly talk about what they'd done and whether or not it had brought the closure they were seeking. For Roe, the circle was complete. All of the people who'd caused her so much pain were now accounted for.

Mark was the one who was undergoing the most inner turmoil. Killing Andre Mendez had not only brought back images of his wife and daughter, but it had also reawakened a part of his past that he'd buried many years before. What troubled him most was that instead of bringing any form of closure, it had only created questions that he'd never be able to answer. He was grateful that he had Roe as a surrogate daughter, and he was glad she had finally found peace considering what she'd endured. Peace of mind for himself was still an elusive dream.

CHAPTER 56

The Last Crossing

Roe had alerted Angel Ruiz. He was waiting at the border when they reached Brownsville. He facilitated entry for the group into the US without any holdup. Part of the arrangement with Angel was that Samuel, Emelia, and Alex would all agree to be questioned by authorities. They all had information that would be helpful in their pursuit of illegal activities. Mark was a little bit uncomfortable when he learned that one of the agents involved in the debriefings was Ron Lassiter, but he never heard anything further from Ron, so he dismissed it.

Roe made sure that Samuel and Emelia would never be questioned at the same time. How much of her ordeal Emelia would want to share with Samuel should be left up to her to determine. Alex proved to be an invaluable source of information and it seemed to provide him with a lot of satisfaction to pour out details that few people had access to. The computers were turned over to Angel as well. Mark remained under the radar. When Angel tried to get background information on Mark's past, he hit a brick wall. Actually, the response he got from Washington scared the hell out of him. A terse response came directly from the pentagon, simply stating that if he wanted to keep his job, he was to not question Mark Price under any circumstances. Furthermore, he should forget that such a person even existed.

Roe had become a legend among the DEA and Border Patrol. Although the details of her mission to Tampico were not disclosed, enough of the story was soon known. Angel jokingly told Roe a few days after they'd returned that she'd probably soon be his boss. She didn't become his boss, but she was soon hired by the DEA for a high-level position.

Several days after returning, all the depositions had been completed and Roe and Mark took Samuel and Emelia to dinner. It was the first time the four had been together since coming back to the US. Roe and Mark had talked at length about how Samuel and Emelia's relationship would survive after what they had endured. Emelia seemed to a different person after reuniting with Samuel. Neither Mark nor Roe were going to make any references to what might have happened to either of them. Whatever information the couple shared between themselves, they seemed to be at peace and were only anticipating a future together. It was a testament to the strength and maturity they both possessed. After some initial conversation, Samuel spoke.

"You'll never know how grateful Emelia and I are for the help and support you both have given us. Knowing there are good people like you helps blunt the bad stuff we've been through. We have had time to think about our future, and we've made a big decision. We're going back home to Chile. Emelia has been able to talk to her parents, and they want us to come home. Sometimes you learn the hard way that the grass is not always greener someplace else."

Roe and Mark listened to what Samuel was saying without interrupting before Mark replied, "I'm really not surprised. You both are going to find success wherever you choose to live. Samuel, we know you've helped us because it was your only way to find Emelia. But you've also had our backs as well. As you know, we turned over the laptops as well as the records we found in the safe to Angel and the DEA. What we didn't turn over or even disclose were the rest of the contents from the safe. Along with jewelry there was a lot of cash. I've converted some of the cash into cashier's checks that we planned to give to you as a wedding gift. You can take them with you and cash them in Chile. I'm sure Angel Ruiz will make sure you get home safely."

The rest of the evening was bittersweet for them all. Mark had developed a lot of respect for Samuel and Roe had bonded to Emelia by virtue of shared experiences. When they returned to their hotel and said good night, it was also farewell, because Emelia and Samuel would be leaving early the next day for their trip home to Chile. They both promised to stay in touch with Roe and Mark.

Her work required Roe to remain in Texas for a few more days, but Mark was missing his familiar surroundings in Jacksonville and was ready to leave so he booked a flight home. When he reached his home on the river, he immediately started a brutal workout routine. It was the only way he could prevent his mind from constantly dwelling on Rosa. At one point, as he walked down to his dock, he seriously thought about diving in the wide river and swimming across. If he made it, then he'd try to swim back. He shook his head at his stupidity. Being upset was one thing, but suicide was not a part of his plan. Roe had called earlier and said that she would be coming home in a couple of days. She told Mark that she needed to sit by the river for a few days and let her mind and body rest.

The next day, he'd returned from a five-mile run along the river and had collapsed into a lounge chair on his patio with a big glass of V8 juice. His rest was interrupted when a bell rang, indicating someone was at his front gate. Walking out to the gate, he saw a FedEx delivery truck parked by the curb and a middle-aged lady waiting for him at the gate. She was holding a small package in one hand and a pad and pen in her other.

"Mark Price?"

"That's me."

"I'm sorry, but I'm required to see a picture ID to deliver this."

Curious, Mark opened the gate for the lady and said, "Follow me. I'll need to go inside to get my wallet."

When they reached the back door that led into the house, Mark said, "Give me one minute," and disappeared inside. He came out holding his driver's license out for the lady to see.

"I'm sorry to trouble you with this, but they're pretty anal about this stuff."

"You're just doing your job," Mark replied as she handed him the package.

Mark walked her back to the gate and closed it before going back into his house with the package. It was about the size of a textbook, and it was well wrapped with plain brown paper. There was a wax seal and it was tied tightly with a heavy twine. Whoever had wrapped it wanted to ensure no one could possibly look at the contents and reseal it again without it being obvious. He carried the package to a small table in the kitchen area after getting a pair of scissors from a kitchen drawer. Other than his name and address, the only other thing he could tell was that it had been mailed from Mexico City, Mexico. He hesitated for a moment before he used the scissors to cut the twine around the package. His instinct told him that this was not something potentially dangerous. After he'd removed the wrapping paper, he was looking at a small standard shipping box. Opening the box, he found a brown envelope rolled up and held together with a heavy rubber band. Inside the envelope were two thumb drives. One of the drives was wrapped with a piece of tape with writing. The words *Play first* were easy to see. There was another envelope containing a single photograph.

By now Mark's curiosity was growing by the moment. Taking the thumb drive that had been marked into his study, he inserted it into the monitor and opened it up on the screen. He was suddenly looking at Rosa who smiled as she said, "Hello, Mark" before she began to speak.

CHAPTER 57

Revelation

It was late afternoon when a taxi dropped Roe off at the house. She put her suitcase down next to the stairs leading up to her garage apartment and entered the house.

"Hello, anybody home?"

"Out here, Roe."

When Roe walked out onto the patio, Mark stood up and greeted her with a hug and kiss on her cheek.

"Mark, it's always so good to come home. We've had quite an adventure."

Mark had a strange look on his face when he replied, "The adventure is just beginning for me."

"I've known that there was a lot about you that I didn't know. It became obvious the moment you drove up to those old ruins and especially after what happened at the ranch. Also, Angel told me what happened when he tried to look up your Army record. I haven't asked you any questions. I've known you'd tell me what you wanted me to know when you were ready. I'm not even asking you to now. I only want to know what you want me to know."

"I got a package this morning. I've been sitting out here thinking since I opened it. Roe, you're the only person alive who I can trust without any reservation. After learning the contents of the package I received, I have to share some things with you. It's a long story. Before I start, let me open a bottle of wine for you and pour myself a Tanqueray and lime. I think before I'm through, we'll both need it."

After he'd opened a bottle of wine and poured himself a very heavy drink, they settled into the comfortable deck chairs. Mark said, "I remember when we sat here, and I listened to you tell your story. Our positions are reversed now and I'm the one confessing."

Mark started from the time he'd enrolled in the Army after college. He left nothing out. He'd kept so much bottled up for so many years. It was like relieving a pressure that had been bottled up inside. Roe was a good listener. She understood because she'd been in the same position at one time, and she understood what it meant to bare your soul to another person.

When Mark reached the end of the story and after now understanding why he was so emotional with Rosa's death at the ranch, Roe was speechless. All she could do was reach over to him and take his hand, as he continued, "Roe, the story isn't over. There's more."

Standing up, he said, "Wait just a minute," and went inside the house. He came back with a laptop computer that he handed to Roe along with the thumb drive.

"While you watch this, I'm going to make myself another drink and walk down to the dock. I've watched this so many times I could recite every word of it."

Mark poured himself another drink and started walking down toward the river. Roe inserted the thumb drive and watched it boot up on the screen.

CHAPTER 58

Full Disclosure

As dumfounded as she had been listening to Mark relive his past, she was even more astonished as she tried to absorb the enormity of what she was watching. She was staring at the face of the sister of Andre Mendez, the woman who'd been killed at the ranch in Tampico. As she began to speak, Roe could hardly breathe as she listened to Rosa's words.

"Dear Mark, if you're watching this, it is because I am already dead. I have made arrangements with my attorneys in Mexico City to ensure that this package is delivered to you upon my death. Before I talk about us, I need to tell you one thing you need to do immediately. The thumb drive you're watching now is about you and me. The second one is your insurance policy. You need to make multiple copies and be sure they are in trusted places. There is an address and phone number of an office in Miami. After securing the copies of the drive you'll need to contact this office and let them know you have the information in a safe place, and that it will remain sealed as long as nothing unusual should happen to you or anyone closely connected to you. There is enough information on the drive to set the Colombian family business back for many years.

"Now, I know you will have so many questions you'll want to ask. I'm going to try and answer as many as I can. First, I want to tell you that what we had was real. You were the love of my life. There has been no other man in my life since we were together. For many years I assumed you were dead just as you've assumed the same of me. Several years ago, I finally made the decision to search the names of the people on our team. I almost went into shock when I found you. I wanted so badly to make contact with you, but after a lot of soul searching, I made a decision to leave things as they were. I was afraid of what it might do to your life if I suddenly resurfaced. I was also afraid that you would never be able to understand my decision to remain in Mexico. If I'd just been one step quicker and left the building in Tampico a little sooner, who knows how different our lives might have been? But I didn't.

"I had started to help Marcus drag Rich's body toward the elevators when I was suddenly staring at my dead twin brother who was coming toward us. I saw Marcus start to raise his gun toward him, and without thinking I ran toward my brother and pushed him back into the thick smoke. My brother recognized me at the same time that another charge detonated, and everything went blank. When I did begin to wake up in a strange hospital bed, I had no memory of what had happened. What I did recognize was my twin brother who was with me, and it was as if we'd never been separated. I remembered him as Ricardo. It took me a long time to call him Andre, the name he'd been given after our parent's death. He'd been told that I had died in the same fire with my parents. As I learned in time, our parents were not so pure as we'd thought. They had been planted in Mexico by the Colombian Cartel and it was a Mexican cartel that was responsible for their deaths. The Colombians were able to protect Ricardo and bring him back to Colombia while at the same time the Gomez family brought me back to the US and gave me a life there. So, for many years Ricardo and I lived separate lives unaware of the existence of the other.

"Fortunately for me, Andre had risen to a major leadership position in the Colombian Cartel. Only because of his influence was I allowed to live. They knew I was partly responsible for the slaughter, and they wanted my head.

"Now what I'm going to tell you next is the hardest part. During the weeks I spent in the hospital I discovered I was pregnant. Fortunately, the baby was healthy in spite of the trauma I'd received. Andre wanted me to name him Ricardo, but I named him Mark. The child became part of the deal Andre made with the Colombian family. The cartel agreed that if I stayed in Mexico, I could raise the child. I would also have to use my knowledge of the US authorities to facilitate the family operations out of Mexico. In time, Andre considered Mark to be the heir to the family's business, but although I never expressed it openly, I planned to make sure that never happened.

"By the time the baby was born, my memory had been restored for the most part. There were some voids, but by then I had been integrated into the family. Over time, I took control of the business while letting Andre think he was in charge. But my overriding goal was to protect my son. I was still under the eyes of the family in Colombia. I played my part well and in time my son—or I should say our son—attended a private school in Mexico City. As he grew older, I had more options as my influence in the family had increased. By the time he was college age, I convinced Andre that he should be attending school in the US if he were to ever be able to assume a leadership role in the business. Fortunately, Andre agreed, and I was able to send him to the US.

"Soon after arriving in the States, without anyone knowing it, Mark started applying for US citizenship. By the time he had finished law school, he had become a US citizen and had no intention of returning to Mexico to live. Andre and other family members from Colombia still believe he will become a family asset living in the US. That will never happen. At this point in time, Mark has limited knowledge of the family business, but he knows enough to be sure he wants no part of it. Up until now he has walked a fine line in his relationship with Andre and the family. His consideration for my safety has prevented him from making an outright denunciation of the business, just as my concerns for his safety has held me hostage for so many years. Knowing that I am dead will release him of any concerns for my safety. The information you now hold on the thumb drive will be his insurance as well as yours. That's why it's so important that you take immediate steps to safeguard it.

"Mark will be receiving a package at the same time you're seeing this. He has always believed that his father was killed in the raid in Tampico. He will be learning everything about you and I and what happened in Tampico. It's time for you both to know the truth. How you choose to go forward is a decision you will both have to make. The envelope contains his name, address, and phone number. He is working in a law firm in Atlanta, Georgia. I'm enclosing a recent picture of him. He has grown up to be a fine person much like his father. He could pass for your twin. I only hope that you will understand and forgive me. I will always love you."

Roe sat, unable to move for several minutes before she poured herself more wine and walked down the steps to the dock where Mark stood staring out at the river.

"I don't know what to say, Mark," Roe said as she put her arms around him.

"It does provide some degree of closure. At least now I can accept why Rosa chose to stay in Mexico. It also explains why no one from the cartel ever came after me . . . although that may be changing. Most important though, I have a son that I've never met."

CHAPTER 59

Insurance

Mark was up early the next morning driving into the rising sun toward downtown Jacksonville. The night before he'd called his longtime friend and attorney Moshe Gersten and said he needed to see him asap. Moshe offered for Mark to come to his home immediately, but Mark assured him that if he would make time for him first thing in the morning it would be okay.

As Mark drove toward Moshe's office, he realized how lucky he he'd been to have Moshe for a friend. Years before after Mark's mother had died, Moshe had saved Mark from accepting the first offer that he'd received for his mother's property. As it turned out, the property was literally a gold mine since it was sitting on two sides of a new interstate highway. Mark went from being a poor history professor to a very rich one in a short period of time. The monthly residual income from the properties alone were more than a year's salary as a professor. It had given Mark a lot of options. Both Moshe and his wife had been there for Mark during the time he lost his wife and daughter. Mark had entrusted Moshe with all of his finances with the exception of the illicit money Mark and Roe had kept when they successfully ambushed a drug deal on the Gulf Coast. Moshe knew nothing about the illegal things that he and Roe had done, and that applied to the stolen cash as well.

Mark parked in an underground garage and took the private elevator to Moshe's office, which commanded an entire floor of the building. The view across the river was spectacular, and he was met by Moshe as soon as he entered. Moshe had come a long way from his humble two-room office in an old building on University Avenue. But Moshe the man had not changed other than a few more gray hairs. He still reminded Mark of a hawk about to descend on its prey. Mark followed him into his corner office where Mark could smell the wonderful odor of coffee.

"You're always full of surprises, Mark. This must be something important, because I don't remember you ever using the term 'needing to meet asap.'"

"Moshe, it may just be the most important thing I've ever asked of you. Let me tell you what I need." Mark continued to explain what he wanted him to do. "I want to be certain that this drive is hidden in a safe place that is inaccessible to anyone. I want it to have a trigger that will initiate certain actions if it is ever pulled."

"You don't need to say any more. I've set up similar safeguards for other people. Usually, it has involved whistleblowers who feared for their safety. I don't need to know any more. I'll only need to know what or who you want your triggers to be and what should happen after."

After Mark and Moshe had settled on the details of the potential triggers and what to have happen if they were pulled, Moshe made Mark a copy of the thumb drive, which Mark put in his pocket. As he was leaving, Mark said to Moshe, "Thank you. I feel better already."

"Carol and I would like for you to come over for dinner one night."

"Give me a little time to iron out a few things and I'll take you up on it."

When Mark returned home, Roe was waiting with coffee and the smell of cooking bacon. After a quick breakfast, they went into Mark's study and made the call to the number in Miami that Rosa had sent. Mark turned on the speaker phone so Roe could listen to the call.

After several rings, a deep voice answered in Spanish, "Yes, who is this?"

Answering, Mark replied, "I have something that was passed to me by Rosa Gomez. I think it's something that will be of great interest to you."

"I'm not sure what you mean."

"It's a thumb drive containing a lot of data."

"Tell me who you are and where you are located, and I'll come and pick it up."

"No. I'll come to your office." Mark then read the Miami address out to the voice on the phone. "I'll be at your office tomorrow afternoon by 2:00 PM." He immediately hung up.

"Roe, it's too late to drive down today. It will be at least a six-hour drive. I want to go during business hours and not when things are shut down. The busier it is, the safer it will be. I'd also like to do some research on the address and see if any names are associated with the office."

The address was easy to locate. It was located in the downtown Miami financial district. The building was one of the many glass and steel high rises that made up the district. It listed suite number 1409 as belonging to Commodity Imports Limited, but Mark couldn't find any information on the company. He did feel better knowing that the office was in a safe and prestigious location. Although he didn't feel as if there were any imminent threat,

Roe and Mark both thought it best to play it safe and stay home until they left for Miami in the morning.

CHAPTER 60
Betrayal

Mark took two large ribeye steaks out of the freezer to thaw while he heated up coals on the grill. They enjoyed a leisure dinner on the patio before Roe left Mark sitting on the patio and went back up to her apartment. Soon after, Mark decided that the mosquitoes were going to win, and he went inside as well. He turned out most of the lights in the house, leaving only a couple of night lights on. He dressed for bed in his usual sleeping attire, consisting of a pair of running shorts and a loose cotton T-shirt.

He was just lying down when he suddenly sat back up. It wasn't just the noise of the outboard motor that got his attention. It was not unusual for people to fish for catfish on the river at night. It was that people rarely fished on this part of the river, especially at night. But most unusual was that the sound of the motor had stopped just before reaching his dock. The master bedroom had double doors that opened onto the patio, and he quickly looked out and down toward his dock. It was close to a full moon, and he could easily see a small boat drifting toward the dock. When three dark figures moved from the boat and onto the dock, he knew he had to move quickly. His phone was on a bedside table, and he punched in Roe's number on speed dial.

She answered in a sleepy voice, "Yes?"

"Roe, wake up quick. Three people are coming up to the house from the dock. Be ready."

Roe had hung up before he finished and was moving quickly. She threw on a robe and checked her service Beretta before rushing down the stairs from her apartment over the garage.

Mark's first thought was to pick up a revolver that he kept in his nightstand next to the bed. If he could avoid noise that might be heard by neighbors, it would be better. Running into the connecting study, he took something that had been hanging there for years. He had attended a banquet that was raising money for wildlife preservation. He'd bought several raffle tickets and had won a hunting crossbow. He'd only tried it out once at a range and had been surprised at how deadly it was, but he had no intention of ever hunting with it. He had stopped hunting deer years ago because he thought it was too easy and also unfair. The deer had no chance against a skilled hunter. He wasn't opposed to others hunting. He just no longer found any satisfaction in it. But it was a neat conversation piece and he had hung it on his study wall. There were four bolts attached to it.

After cocking the bow and loading a bolt, he went back through his bedroom and slipped out through the doors and onto the patio. The bedroom was at the end of his house and cloaked in shadows so that he was able to slip out over the patio's stone wall and into the shrubbery below. He continued to move down the hillside sloping toward the river until he could see the three figures moving up the steps leading to the patio. Patiently letting them pass and then following them up to the patio, he watched them pause before trying the door immediately in front of them. Mark knew it was unlocked and led into the sitting area. Mark waited until the first two had slipped inside the door before he fired the bolt at the trailing figure. A modern crossbow shoots a bolt of 400-plus grains at 350 to 400 fps. At this close range, accuracy was not a concern. The only question was what body part the shooter wanted to hit.

Mark aimed for the center of the man's back, just below the neckline. He could hear a large grunt as the figure staggered backwards clutching at his back. As Mark quickly loaded another bolt into the crossbow, he heard a muffled gunshot from inside the house. The third and last figure rushed out of the door in full retreat before suddenly stopping in his tracks, his eyes opening wide in astonishment before he pitched forward and landed face down. He shuddered for a moment before all movement ceased. The bolt Mark had fired had pierced his heart, killing him almost instantly. As he fell onto the deck, Roe came out of the door holding her Beretta in one hand and a small pillow in the other.

"Mark?"

"I'm here, Roe," he answered as he walked up the steps onto the patio. Looking at the first man he'd shot, he could see that he was making his last dying gasps as a red frothy foam poured from his mouth. He went inside and dragged the one Roe had killed out onto the patio and lay the body next to the other two. All three were dressed in black and wore black balaclavas. Two of them were short brown men with strongly Hispanic appearing faces. The third man was much larger, and when Mark tore off his mask, he was dumbfounded.

Roe asked, "Do you recognize him?"

"This is Ron Lassiter," Mark replied, suddenly realizing how they were targeted so quickly.

Roe turned and collapsed into a patio chair; "How could he do this? He was one of the agents who questioned Samuel and Emelia."

"They either paid him well or, most likely, they had a way to threaten him. I'm really sorry, but right now let's keep moving and get this mess cleaned up. Will you go into the garage workshop and bring me a pair of pruning clippers? Try to keep moving. We'll try to make sense of all this later."

One by one Mark dragged the three bodies down to the dock where he searched their pockets for ID but found nothing. It took a lot of effort, but he pulled the bolts out of both men he'd killed with the crossbow. He used the pruning shears on each one before he pushed them into the river. The current was swift enough, and he knew the bodies would be carried out into the river and toward the ocean if they weren't eaten by catfish and crabs first. Whether or not one or all of the bodies would be found was anyone's guess. Finding nothing in the boat, after throwing the men's guns in, he punched a hole in the bottom and pushed it out into the river as well. He thought it might go a mile or so before it sank.

Fortunately, there was no blood inside the house. Roe had shot the first man to enter the house in the head by shooting through a pillow at point-blank range. The noise from the subsonic round was muffled even more by the pillow. The round scrambled his brain but didn't exit his head, and the small entry wound bled very little. Mark used a water hose and washed all of the blood off the patio.

After he was sure all evidence of the men's presence had been removed, he and Roe sat down in his study and he tried to calm her down. The thought that one of the agents had been turned by the cartels had left her confused and shaken.

"Mark, it's not that I look at everyone as being perfect. I can accept that. No problem. But what would those men have done to us if you hadn't seen them coming?"

"We may never know. It certainly wouldn't have been good. We certainly can't ask anyone any questions. Maybe we'll find out something in Miami tomorrow. Like so many other things we've done, we'll have to keep it to ourselves. But now we need to get a little sleep. We need to be sharp tomorrow. Let me get you a blanket and you can sleep on the sofa here in the study. I'll be right next door."

"Thanks, Mark. But remember what you told me. I'm a big girl now. I'll be okay, and I'll sleep better in my own bed. Tomorrow's another day."

CHAPTER 61

Checkmate

Roe and Mark left Jacksonville before eight. Roe seemed to have recovered from the initial shock of the previous evening. They stopped at a Waffle House outside St. Augustine and ate cheese grits, scrambled eggs, and raisin toast, washed down with lot of black coffee. That was enough fuel to get them to Miami, staying on I-95 all the way to downtown Miami. Mark exited I-95 on SW 13th Street and then turned up South Miami Avenue in heavy traffic.

Mark commented, "Roe driving in Miami is worse than a root canal without Novocain. I actually think it's as bad as Bogotá, Colombia."

Roe couldn't help but laugh, "I told you, you should have let the little woman drive."

They entered a gated parking garage under the building. Mark found a parking spot near the elevators and got out of the car. Roe came around to the driver's seat.

"Watch the elevators, Roe. If I'm not alone and I'm being escorted out by anyone, start shooting, because it won't be voluntary." Mark then headed for the elevators.

Reaching the fourteenth floor, Mark found Suite 1409. There was no name on the door, only the suite number. There were only two other suites on the fourteenth floor. The hallway carpeting was deep and plush. It was definitely a high rent complex. Mark took a deep breath and opened the door. The room was small, with only two leather covered chairs. A single door was located in one side of the back wall. A mirror that was certainly one-way glass was set in the wall next to the door. When he entered the small room, he could hear a distant sound of chimes designed to alert the occupants of his presence. There were no bells to push, so Mark calmly sat down in one of the two chairs that faced the mirror. He had intentionally dressed for the meeting. He wore expensive khaki slacks, a blue button-down Oxford shirt open at the collar. He had on designer loafers and a black cashmere blazer. Mark didn't often dress this way, but he wanted to project an image for this meeting.

Within a couple of minutes, the door opened and two burly, well-dressed men came through the door. They were both holding wands, and one of them simply said, "Stand up." They were experienced and efficient as they scanned his entire body with the sensors. Mark was glad he'd not worn the tracking device as Roe had suggested.

They said, "Follow us," and Mark followed them into the connecting room, which was large enough to accommodate two desks and a sitting area. Several doors were connected to this room, all of which were closed. One of the men walked to one of the connecting doors and knocked respectfully. He opened it and motioned for Mark to go in.

It was a luxurious office with large windows that provided a view of Biscayne Bay. The man behind the expansive desk didn't bother to stand up but instead simply said, "Sit." A small placard on his desk had the name *Martin Armstrong, Esq.* Even though he was partially hidden behind the desk, it was apparent that he was a big man who may have once been in good physical shape, but too many martinis and expensive wines had softened him. He was also pompous, arrogant, and wanted to bully Mark when he demanded, "Let me see what you've got before we go any farther."

Mark said nothing as he reached into a pocket inside his blazer and took out the thumb drive and slid it very deliberately across the surface of the desk. The man who still had made no attempt to introduce himself picked it up and looked at it as if it were a piece of poop. He shook his head and pressed a button on his desk phone. One of the two men who'd escorted Mark in entered the room, and the man behind the desk handed it to him, saying, "Check this out." He closed the door as he left with the disk, leaving Mark and the man behind the desk staring at each other.

Mark was the first to speak, "Let me guess. You're a lawyer representing the organization."

"I represent a lot of people."

"I'm sure you do."

"You have a lot of nerve to come here. Let's hope for your sake it's worthwhile."

"I guess we'll find out pretty soon," Mark replied with a smile.

It didn't take long. The man who'd taken the drive came back into the room. This time he didn't knock but just said to the lawyer, "You'd better come with me."

Mark sat waiting patiently for at least twenty minutes, enjoying the view. When Armstrong returned, he was sweating profusely, and his face was noticeably redder. He dropped back into his chair and asked, "Where did you get this information?"

Smiling, Mark replied, "The question is not where I got it. The question is, how many copies did I make, where are they, and what do I intend to do with them?"

"So, okay, wise ass. How much money do you want for all of the copies?"

"You don't understand. It's not money I want. I want to be left alone. I want my friends to be left alone. You may not believe me when I tell you that I have not looked at the drive. I have no idea what it contains. I don't care what it contains, and I don't want to know what it contains. I realize that's a hard concept for you to accept considering what you do for a living. No one will ever know of the existence of this drive unless you pull a trigger. You just need to pray that I don't experience a mysterious accident or any kind of harm. This also applies to the two people I'm naming. Last night you came awfully close to pulling the trigger. You might think twice before you try it again. I'm not a very patient man."

As he finished speaking, Mark again reached into the inner pocket of his blazer and removed a Ziploc sandwich bag that he tossed across the desk towards the lawyer's lap.

Catching the bag before it settled into his lap, the startled man held it up so he could see it better. When he realized that it contained human thumbs, he dropped it like a hot potato and stood up gagging and almost throwing up. Mark remained calmly seated, smiling at the agitated man.

A door on one side of the office that had remained closed since Mark had first entered now suddenly opened. A tall stately man possibly in his early sixties entered the room. He was dressed in a light-colored linen suit with an off-white silk dress shirt but no tie. His full head of hair was white and was a marked contrast with his well-tanned skin that could only have come from spending a lot of leisure time in the sun. The only jewelry that he wore was a Patek Philippe watch that was worth more than most people's homes. Unlike Martin Armstrong, who tried to project a macho image, just his presence alone commanded attention and respect. When he spoke, it was with perfect English and a slight hint of Spanish. Very deliberately he walked over to the desk where Armstrong was trying to stand up.

Speaking in a low but commanding voice he said, "Martin, why don't you bring coffee for Mr. Price and myself?" Armstrong seemed to be happy to leave the room as he hurried out the door. Reaching across the desk, the man picked up the Ziploc bag and held it up so he could use the light coming through the large windows to examine it.

"Three thumbs. I am assuming the three men sent to your home last night are sleeping with the fish, as your Mafiosi would say." Smiling, he turned and looked down at Mark, who hadn't moved. "It is obvious that we have underestimated you, Mr. Price. My name is Carlos. Come sit with me. I think you and I have a lot to talk about."

Mark stood up and followed him over to one side of the large office where two comfortable chairs were separated by a small coffee table. The view from this point was even more spectacular. As they sat, one of the men who'd first ushered him in brought a silver service tray and placed it on the table between them. Carlos poured coffee from the server into white bone china cups. As Mark picked his cup up, Carlos said, "There is cream and sugar if you need it."

Smiling, Mark replied, "If it is good coffee, I would never ruin it with cream or sugar."

Carlos smiled back. "Mr. Price, my people have tried to trace your past and you have proven to be an enigma. Part of your past is a blank, but we have made the connection between you and Andre Mendez. We now understand how the death of your daughter brought you in contact with our organization in Florida several years ago. That was a mistake made by some low-level people. I am truly sorry. You are not a man to be taken lightly."

"Carlos, your people knew enough about me to come to my home with ill intentions. You certainly know something about me. I suspect that an agent named Ron Lassiter is responsible for my being targeted. You must have paid him well."

"You are half-correct, Mr. Price. It was Lassiter who provided the information we needed, but he was not paid with money. When he was just starting to work for the DEA, he led a drug bust, and during the operation, he lined three of our people up against a wall and executed them. He didn't realize he was being taped. Instead of seeking revenge, we realized that if we held this information over his head, he would occasionally provide us with useful information. And he has. It appears that you want to hold something over our head. I listened to your conversation with Martin, and I heard what you are offering. Who are the people who want to protect?"

"After myself, I want to ensure the safety of my close friend, Roe Estes. You may be concerned because she works for the DEA now. You will have to accept my word that she, like me, has not seen anything on the drive. And I can assure you that because it is in an untouchable place, she never will. The other person to fall under the umbrella is Rosa's son, Mark Gomez. I'm not sure what connection he might have to your business. His future relationship with his family is something for him to decide. I have never met him, and I have no idea what his intentions may be except that he also has not seen the thumb drive and does not even know that it exists."

"You have just confirmed what the family has suspected. The information on that drive could only have come from Mark's mother Rosa. There was obviously a strong connection between you and Rosa sometime in your past. Rosa was a brilliant woman. After she was rescued from the assault on the wedding in Tampico, she was assured that her parents had been killed by the Mexican cartels. Knowing that, as well as wanting to protect her son, helped us convince her to remain in Mexico and work with us. Five years ago, I now suspect that she discovered the real truth from a family member who had far too much liquor to drink while visiting her home. She discovered that her parents were not killed by Mexicans but by our own Colombian family. Her parents were stealing from the very people they were working for. No one had any idea how much this affected Rosa. She must have put together all of the information on the drive with the intention of punishing the family. We learned how she and her brother died from Agent Lassiter. Someone loyal to us learned that Rosa's attorney in Mexico City sent something out the minute he became aware of her death. With the proper motivation, the attorney revealed where the package had been sent. It appears, Mr. Price, that you have been one step ahead of our people."

"I would like for this to all end right here. My word is good when I say the thumb drive has been safely buried. I am acutely aware of the consequences if I'm not truthful. I know your family is a very resourceful one, and I know that you can find me any time you wish. I don't want to have to look over my shoulder for the rest of my life."

"We have a deal, Mr. Price. We will shake hands and never see or hear of each other ever again."

CHAPTER 62

First Contact

Mark wanted to stop in Boynton Beach and spend the night in his beachfront condo. He needed to check on his boat, which was moored at a marina just inside the Boynton Beach inlet, but Roe had to leave the next day for a conference in Dallas, so they drove straight through, stopping only to eat and change seats. They reached the house in Jacksonville just before midnight.

The message light on his answering machine in his study was blinking. Mark pushed the button to play the message without realizing that it would change his life forever. A firm voice said, "Mr. Price, my name is Mark Gomez. I recently received a message from my mother and in it she gave me your name. If you would like to meet and talk, I would be willing to do so. If you'd rather not reach into the past, I understand. You can reach me at this number if you want to contact me."

Mark sat down and felt as if the wind had been knocked out of him. He played the message two more times just to hear the voice. He found the envelope that had been in the package Rosa had sent. The photograph inside showed a smiling Rosa standing next to a tall boy wearing a graduation gown. He stared at the picture for a long time. He wanted Roe to hear the message, but she'd gone straight up to her apartment, and he was sure she was asleep by now. But he was wired up after listening to the message. Pouring himself a heavy dose of Tanqueray over ice with lime juice, he went out on his patio.

After his wife and daughter's death, he had finally been able to reach a level of mental stability and a reasonable degree of tranquility. The reemergence of Andre Mendez and Rosa had thrown his life back into a state of unrest. His mind played a continuous reel that never stopped or ended. He knew he was going to try and meet his son. It was the fear that it might not end well that caused him the greatest amount of apprehension.

Mark was up before Roe the next morning and had coffee brewing when she came down from her apartment.

"Roe, pour yourself some coffee and come listen to this message."

She followed him into his study and listed quietly as he replayed the message.

Looking at Mark, she said, "You are going to meet him, aren't you?"

"I am going to meet him, and I want to be sure you'll be there when I do. Whether it goes well or it doesn't, I'll want your support."

"Why don't you call him before I leave for Dallas? I'll try to make my schedule work so I can be there whenever you meet him."

After drinking more coffee and procrastinating for as long as he could, Mark took a deep breath and made the call.

The call was answered almost immediately. A firm voice said, "Hello."

"Mark Gomez?"

"Yes."

"This is Mark Price. I'm returning your call. I would like to take you up on your offer to meet."

"I feel the same, Mr. Price. I have a lot of questions. I'm scheduled to be in Tampa next week to take a deposition. Would it be possible to meet there?"

"Tell me when and where and I'll be there."

"I'll be staying at the airport Marriott. I'm arriving late on Thursday, but I'll be free on Friday morning. Maybe we could have an early breakfast. That would leave us time to talk. Will 7:30 be okay?"

"I'll be there."

The call was ended, and Mark realized that even though he'd faced life threatening situations, he couldn't remember ever shaking like he had been the moment he'd heard the voice on the phone. Roe was watching and smiling.

"Well done, Mark. I'll make arrangements to be in Tampa."

CHAPTER 63

A New Beginning

Mark drove to Tampa the day before he was scheduled to meet Mark Gomez. Roe had driven over from Orlando in a rented car. They had dinner and Roe offered Mark encouragement and assurance that all would go okay when he met his son.

"I've met Angel twice since I left Jacksonville," she told him. "It's hard to not ask any questions about Ron Lassiter. He hasn't mentioned him and I'm not about to ask any questions."

"I know that must be hard to not be able to say anything. Has Angel forgiven you for going to Tampico?"

"Yes. Apparently he has. He invited me to come with him to his mother's home in Miami for Rosh Hashanah. He said he's anxious for me to meet her. Somehow he thinks I'll have a lot in common with her. Actually, just thinking about it scares the hell out of me."

"That's fantastic. I know it will go well."

"Just as tomorrow will go well with you."

Mark was waiting in the lobby of the hotel by seven a.m. When the elevator doors opened at exactly seven thirty and several people came out, there was never a doubt which one was Mark Gomez. A tall, lean, broad-shouldered man with black hair and slightly tan skin color stepped out of the elevator. He was dressed in a business suit but without a tie. He took one look around the lobby and without a moment's hesitation walked straight toward where Mark was standing. When he reached Mark, he stopped, and they stared at each other eye to eye, both caught up in their own emotions and neither not quite sure what to do next.

It was Mark Gomez who spoke first. "My mother always smiled when she talked about you."

"Your mother was a beautiful person. She was obviously a good mother. I'm sorry it's taken us so long to meet."

"Mr. Price, we have a lot to talk about."

"Yes, we do. But please drop the 'Mr. Price.' Call me Mark." He reached his hand out, which was gladly accepted by the younger Mark.

Breakfast was forgotten. They sat in a quiet spot in the large lobby, and within a short time, they each poured out emotions that had been ignored or forgotten for so many years. They only separated when Mark, Jr. realized that he only had a few minutes before he had to meet his fellow attorneys for the deposition. He was flying back to Atlanta immediately after. They both stood up awkwardly trying to say goodbye but not quite sure how to do it. They both had tears in their eyes, and suddenly each reached out and they embraced with an emotional hug. Wiping away tears but smiling all the time, Mark walked away.

Roe met Mark in the hotel restaurant. He had a huge smile on his face as he met her. He looked as if a huge weight had been taken off his shoulders.

"It must have gone well," she said.

"Yes, it did. Mark is going to visit me at my condo for a fishing weekend."

"That's wonderful, Mark. I hope you realize what this means. You now have two people you're responsible for."

"Yes, I do, Roe. And what a wonderful thing it is."

Acknowledgements

I want to thank my wife Ruth for her patience. When she accuses me of only wanting to write and play tennis at the expense of everything else around me I will have to begrudgingly agree. There is something about writing that is addictive. The worlds that can live in the mind are so much more exciting than day to day reality. It is easy to loose yourself in those worlds. Secondly I want to thank the people who validated my efforts after reading my first novel, Mark's Way. David, Sue, Jon, Al and Lou are only the tip of the ice-berg of the people who were supportive. I have been truly humbled by all of your support. It was because of the incredibly positive feedback for Mark's Way that I continued to follow up with this second novel. My main characters have gained a life of their own and they continue to live on in this story. I am well into the third novel which continues to feature Mark Price and Roe Estes. My goal in writing is not to deliver a message or how to improve anything. I want my books to be the ones that you read while traveling, at the beach or late at night to forget the stress of everyday life. Happy reading,

Thomas Willis

About the Author

Thomas Willis was an Army officer during the Vietnam war, a practicing dentist and a university professor. He is retired and lives with his wife in South Florida. Last Night In Tampico follows his first novel Mark's Way. He is working on a third novel which will continue to feature Mark Price and Roe Estes. Look for its release in the spring of 2024.

Made in the USA
Columbia, SC
14 March 2024

33047814R00209